TUNNEL VISION

Also by Wendy Church

The Jessie O'Hara novels

MURDER ON THE SPANISH SEAS *
MURDER BEYOND THE PALE *

The Shadows of Chicago mysteries

KNIFE SKILLS *
TUNNEL VISION *

* available from Severn House

TUNNEL VISION

Wendy Church

SEVERN
HOUSE

First world edition published in Great Britain and the USA in 2025
by Severn House, an imprint of Canongate Books Ltd,
14 High Street, Edinburgh EH1 1TE.

severnhouse.com

Copyright © Wendy Church, 2025

Cover and jacket design by Piers Tilbury

All rights reserved including the right of reproduction in whole or in part in any form. The right of Wendy Church to be identified as the author of this work has been asserted in accordance with the Copyright, Designs & Patents Act 1988.

British Library Cataloguing-in-Publication Data
A CIP catalogue record for this title is available from the British Library.

ISBN-13: 978-1-4483-1322-8 (cased)
ISBN-13: 978-1-4483-1609-0 (e-book)

This is a work of fiction. Names, characters, places and incidents are either the product of the author's imagination or are used fictitiously. Except where actual historical events and characters are being described for the storyline of this novel, all situations in this publication are fictitious and any resemblance to actual persons, living or dead, business establishments, events or locales is purely coincidental.

All Severn House titles are printed on acid-free paper.

Typeset by Palimpsest Book Production Ltd., Falkirk,
Stirlingshire, Scotland.
Printed and bound in Great Britain by TJ Books,
Padstow, Cornwall.

Praise for Wendy Church

"Dizzying . . . Audiences who wished the TV series *The Bear* had made room for Russian mobsters are in for a treat" *Kirkus Reviews* Starred Review of *Knife Skills*

"With brisk pacing and dynamic characters, Church keeps readers enthralled" *Publishers Weekly* on *Knife Skills*

"A riveting, entertaining read that will appeal to fans of Janet Evanovich" *Booklist* on *Knife Skills*

"Fans of Janet Evanovich will enjoy meeting the freewheeling Jesse, and this debut gives an enticing hint of more adventures to come" *Booklist* Starred Review of *Murder on the Spanish Seas*

"Clever, transportive, and laugh-out-loud funny . . . the perfect book to read poolside – just not on the deck of a luxury ocean liner. I can't wait to read more from this wickedly entertaining new voice" Andrea Bartz, *New York Times* bestselling author of *We Were Never Here*, on *Murder on the Spanish Seas*

"Church has penned a whip-smart, sarcastic, amateur sleuth and a tightly plotted story that's perfect for fans of Ruth Ware, Catriona McPherson, and Darynda Jones. Readers will want to see Jesse again" *Library Journal* on *Murder on the Spanish Seas*

About the author

Wendy Church, PhD, is the author of the Shadows of Chicago Mysteries. *Knife Skills*, the first in the series, received a Starred Review from *Kirkus Reviews*. Her debut novel, and the first in the Jesse O'Hara series, *Murder on the Spanish Seas*, was named by Booklist as a Top 10 Debut Mystery & Thriller of 2023. Wendy's also authored a variety of nonfiction works, including a PhD dissertation in bioresource engineering, a few textbooks and book chapters on global issues, and a number of inappropriately long Facebook posts about navigating gluten-free pizza, and the relationship between yoga and Lord of the Rings. She lives in Seattle, Washington with her partner and several animals.

www.wendyschurch.com/

READER SPOILER ALERT!

Tunnel Vision is the second novel in the Shadows of Chicago series. And while it can be read as a stand-alone story, it reveals a rather significant twist that happens in the first book in the series, *Knife Skills*.

Knife Skills also stands alone, and would be fine to read second, but the series has more surprises and twists if you read them in order. However you decide to do it, thanks for taking the time to read.

For Michael

ONE

Crime scene tape was wound around the broken light poles that ringed the dark parking lot. A man's body, or, more accurately, the components of it, lay on the ground, illuminated by police car headlights. His arms and legs were separated from his torso like a disjointed doll.

I walked to the edge of the taped cordon and flashed my ID at the uniformed officer holding a clipboard.

'Hey Kaminski,' he said, looking up briefly. 'What're you doing here?'

As an analyst I didn't normally go to crime scenes, but this one was three blocks from my parents' house. I'd just been leaving when I heard the sirens. Not a common sound in Avondale, and way too close for comfort.

'My folks live down the street. Who is it?'

'Not sure. Maybe a local drug dealer.' He pointed to the limbless torso a few feet from the edge of the tape. On it lay several small glassine envelopes. Street drugs.

I looked around. 'Any suspects?'

'What do you think?'

'Do me a favor, Steve. Keep me in the loop on this, OK? If something's happening in this neighborhood I want to know about it.'

He nodded and turned back to the body.

I pulled out my phone. 'Mom, yeah, it's me . . . everything's fine. Listen, lock your doors tonight, OK? No, no, it's nothing to worry about. Just me being paranoid. I love you too. Bye.'

At six forty-five a.m. Deputy Chief Marcus Jefferson, head of the Chicago PD's Criminal Networks Group, walked into his office. I watched through the glass windows until he sat down, and then knocked on his door.

'Come.'

'Sir.'

'Ms Kaminski. Up early today,' he said, looking up from the stack of papers he was already signing.

'Sir, about the shooting in Avondale last night.'

'A local drug dealer.'

It didn't surprise me that he already knew about it. He seemed to know about everything almost before it happened.

'Yes, uh, I'd like to work on that case.'

'We still need you on the SK task force. I don't want you dividing your time,' he said, looking back down.

I'd been spending most of my time on the Stone Nation and Latin Kings task force, currently the longest running gang-focused task force the city had going. We were close to wrapping things up, but it was still a high priority given the size and influence of the gangs involved.

When I didn't leave the room he looked back up again.

'The shooting happened not far from my parents' house, sir. I know the area, I grew up there. If this is gang-related, which it looks like it is, you'll want my expertise.'

He stared at me in a way I knew made everyone else here uncomfortable.

'Do you know something I don't, Ms Kaminski?'

I frowned. 'I'm not sure what you mean, sir.'

He glanced up at the clock on the wall, then put down his pen and stood up.

'Come with me.'

He walked out of his office and down the hallway, turning into the main conference room where the morning briefing was just about to get underway.

Uniformed officers and detectives in suits were milling and talking casually, some gulping coffee, others stuffing breakfast sandwiches into their mouths.

'What are you doing here, goth geek?' asked Renfro as I sat down in the chair next to him, unfortunately the last one available.

He wasn't the only guy at the station to make fun of my looks, but most of the others had let it go by now. As a contractor I didn't come in to the station on a regular basis, and as such wasn't required to adhere to Chicago PD sartorial standards. I was in my usual ensemble of Carhartt pants, black combat boots, and a button-down shirt over a tank top, accessorized with dark eye makeup and my earrings, all twenty of them.

I started to respond when a hush came over the room as the deputy chief strode to the front. He never ran the briefing, and

Tunnel Vision

rarely attended. Commander Bowles who usually led these stood back from the podium as Jefferson stepped up to it.

'Good morning.' Jefferson gestured to a woman standing off to the side. 'This is Supervisory Special Agent Jacobs from the FBI.'

That she was FBI was no surprise. She was wearing a dark gray suit and white shirt open at the collar, with simple but highly polished black Oxfords. Her neatly combed, shoulder-length hair and tastefully minimal makeup all screamed 'buttoned-up federal law enforcement woman'.

'You will give her your undivided attention,' Jefferson said, turning away and walking out of the room. He winked at me on the way out.

SSA Jacobs walked to the front and brought the wall monitor to life.

Nothing like starting things off with a bang. The slide was photos of three corpses. All disembodied, with limbs ringing the torsos, each resting in its own pool of shiny blood. I sat up straight in my chair: one of the bodies was the one I'd seen the night before.

'Cartel work?' one of the uniforms asked.

These kinds of killings were a trademark of the cartel that had been flooding the city with drugs for decades. Most of the drugs that made their way to Chicago came from the Sinaloa and the Jalisco cartels, both out of Mexico. They not only provided the city with drugs, they also used Chicago as a hub to distribute elsewhere around the country. Public murders like this by them were rare in the US, but distinctive.

Jacobs nodded. 'We think so.' She changed the picture on the monitor to a close-up of one of the men's torsos. Laying on top of it were a number of glassine envelopes filled with white powder.

'Last night was the third of these murders in the city in as many weeks. All drug dealers. Each time we've seen this.' She used her laser pointer to circle the drugs on top of the torso. She clicked again, and zoomed in on the image to highlight the one on top of the stack.

'We're analyzing the contents of the envelopes. Preliminary indication is that it's fentanyl.'

No shock there. Cheap and strong, fentanyl had outstripped heroin and other opioids as the drug of choice on the street.

'Why would the cartel kill dealers distributing their own drugs?' asked Renfro.

'We don't think these are cartel drugs.'

4 Wendy Church

Jacobs stepped aside, and Bowles stepped in, his six-foot-plus frame dwarfing her. 'We're forming a task force—'

Groans erupted from around the room. Task forces sounded cool, but what they amounted to was a lot of extra work on top of everyone's existing workload.

'—to deal with this. McCullom, Nowak, Renfro and Kaminski, you've got the honor. Everyone else, BOLO for any other murders that resemble these. When, where, and who.'

He finished the briefing then dismissed everyone but me, Renfro, a red-haired guy I hadn't seen before, and a woman I assumed was Valerie Nowak. I'd never met her, but I'd heard about her. She had short blond hair like me, but was taller, which wasn't saying much. And while she was young, close to my age in her mid-twenties, she'd already made a name for herself as a skilled undercover officer.

'Every task force needs their nerd,' said Renfro out of the corner of his mouth.

'Every task force needs a meathead,' I shot back. He was marginally effective but I hated working with the guy. Somehow we always seemed to end up on the same teams.

'Shut it, Kaminski. Let's get started,' said Bowles, ignoring the fact that it was Renfro that started it.

Bowles wasn't a fan of me, or my work. He was a holdout from the old days. He valued old-school policing, and was suspicious, if not outright hostile, to new techniques, or anything that smelled of technology.

'This task force is a joint operation with the FBI. SSA Jacobs will be taking the lead.'

This wasn't surprising. While in the eighties and nineties the relationships between the FBI and local police jurisdictions were often tense, the agency had worked hard to learn how to best marry their virtually unlimited access to all kinds of toys and tools with the community-specific knowledge and resources of local law enforcement. The FBI's relationship with the Chicago PD was solid, and the city was so overloaded with gang problems that they were always happy for the help.

'Good morning everyone.' Jacobs was sitting down now in front of a computer, and with a few clicks put up the same image she'd started with earlier.

'Latin Kings?' I asked, recognizing the black and gold clothing on one of the bodies.

Tunnel Vision 5

She nodded and pointed to the image in the middle. 'Yes. In Wicker Park. Two weeks ago.'

'That's Maniacs territory,' I said. The Maniacs were the rival gang to the Kings in that area. If they committed the murder, it would be the start of another gang war. 'I thought you said this was cartel work?'

'I did, and it is.' She put up another picture on the monitor. A mugshot, of a bald and pockmarked middle-aged white man, superimposed over a map of Brooklyn, and surrounded with some familiar icons representing various crimes.

'This is Brajen Krol. He's the leader of the Polish Mafia in Brooklyn.'

Polish mafia? Chicago had over seventy gangs, crews, and cliques. I'd been working with the Criminal Networks Group for three years and had never heard of a Polish gang, despite Chicago's sizable Polish population. And why was she showing us a picture of a New York gangster?

She registered the confused look on everyone's faces. 'The Polish mafia has operated in this country for decades, in Brooklyn and Philadelphia. Brajen Krol runs the Greenpoint Crew in Brooklyn. They've made their money primarily in gunrunning and drug trafficking, alongside growing endeavors in extortion, car theft, armed robbery, and credit card fraud. They're extremely violent, even by gang standards.'

She used the laser pointer she took out of her pocket to point to the mugshot. 'Last year, Brajen Krol murdered a rival with a golf club. It was his tenth *personal* murder in the last two years, at least that we know of. His men are no less brutal.'

'Law enforcement has been able to crack down on the Greenpoint Crew in Brooklyn. They've set out a number of indictments, and the gang's close to being disbanded. But they've been unable to get to Brajen Krol, and there are strong signs that he and the few unindicted higher-level members have chosen your lovely city as a new site for their operations. Specifically, their drug operations. This task force is charged with keeping that from happening.'

'Ma'am, why do you think it's this Polish gang distributing the drugs?' Nowak spoke for the first time.

Jacobs changed the image to a close-up of one of the stacks of glassine envelopes that lay on the torsos. Each one had been stamped. She looked at me. 'Ms Kaminski, does this look familiar to you?'

6 Wendy Church

She used the laser pointer to highlight one of the stamps. A bird, outlined in red.

I nodded, ignoring the fact that she'd assumed that because I had a Polish name I was an expert on Polish culture. Mostly because I was. 'It's the national symbol of Poland, the bielik, eagle.' The bielik was typically a white-tailed eagle, often accompanied by a coat of arms, and sometimes by the red and white flag of Poland.

SSA Jacobs nodded. 'This eagle is one of the Greenpoint Crew's tags.'

'Sir,' interjected Renfro, looking at Bowles. No surprise that he was addressing his question to the man in the front. 'We're already stretched thin as it is, with other task forces, that are focused on the larger gangs. Does it make sense to divert resources to this?' He waved his hand dismissively at the monitor.

Bowles looked at Jacobs, who said, 'There are two reasons why this is a priority. The first is that we believe the Greenpoint Crew is trying to break into Chicago's fentanyl trade, which as you know is run by the cartels. They aren't about to let another player into their territory.' She switched the image back to the puppet bodies. 'As you can see.'

'Second: as you all know, every gang in Chicago is vying for a piece of the drug distribution business. Some of them will want to sell the Greenpoint Crew's drugs. The cartel isn't about to let that happen. They'll make an example out of anyone who tries to do that.

'To put it bluntly, adding a player to the mix will destabilize the city. That's why this task force is a priority.'

'*Destabilize*?' Renfro couldn't keep the disbelief out of his voice. 'You mean, more than the turf wars and retaliation strikes we're dealing with now?'

'Yes,' she said firmly. 'On a scale you can't believe. As I said, the Greenpoint Crew is known for being violent, excessively so, unlike the other gangs and the cartel, who try to keep a low profile with law enforcement. Usually, that is,' she said, looking back at the monitor. 'Two of these three murders were committed in relatively public places.

'The cartel is sending a message. They'll do whatever it takes to maintain and safeguard their income stream, no matter the consequence. Put those things together and we can expect an explosion in violence.' She emphasized her point by circling the bodies with

Tunnel Vision 7

her laser pointer. 'Now is *precisely* the time to go after them: we believe it will be easier to nip it in the bud, than deal with them once they're established.'

'Are we sure it's the Greenpoint Crew supplying the drugs?' I asked. 'The red eagle could be a coincidence. Or maybe it's the other gang, the one from Philly?'

She nodded. 'This task force is an extension of an operation we've been running in Brooklyn. We've had confidential informants, and an undercover agent, collecting information on the Greenpoint Crew for us for over a year, and the indictments are largely a result of that operation, during the course of which we developed strong intelligence that their intention is to start up again in Chicago.'

I'd done enough work with various law enforcement agencies to know that 'strong intelligence' could be anything from recorded, highly incriminating conversations, to a wild hunch from an over-eager CI. She saw the look on my face, and switched the image on the monitor to a map of Chicago.

'We've seen signs of them from here –' she pointed northwest of the now inaptly named 'Polish Triangle', the intersection of Ashland, Milwaukee and Division which at one time had been the center of Chicago's Polish population – 'up to here.' She moved the pointer north along Milwaukee Avenue to the Avondale neighborhood, where my parents lived, then to Jefferson Park and Portage Park. My neighborhood.

'Are we sure the murders are the work of the cartel?' asked Renfro, still trying to downplay the ominous situation that Jacobs was laying out. 'Maybe it's someone who wants to pin it on them?'

'None of the street gangs have claimed responsibility for these murders, which by itself tells us it's something new.'

That was compelling. One of the ways the cartel avoided the attention of law enforcement was to farm out any hands-on activities to the street gangs, who were more than willing to take the risk to get a bigger piece of the lucrative drug business. The fact that none of the gangs had claimed responsibility meant that these murders weren't the run-of-the-mill, targeted assassinations, but something more directly under the control of the cartel.

That, and the dismemberment, one of the cartel's calling cards.

'Sir,' said Renfro, looking at Bowles, 'the SK Network task force is close to—'

'This is not up for discussion, Detective Renfro.'

8 Wendy Church

I had a little more leeway than the officers and other employees in terms of how much I could push back on the chain of command. But I was getting my paycheck from the city, too, and had learned when to pick my battles. Renfro might be right, for once, but I could tell this was a done deal.

Jacobs shut down the computer, and nodded to Bowles, who handed each of us a thick binder from a stack on the floor against the wall.

'This is the background on the Greenpoint Crew and what we know about their operations to date, in New York, and what we've seen so far in Chicago,' said Jacobs. 'Get through these by the time the task force meets tomorrow. Detective Renfro, start working with your confidential informants in Avondale and the Polish Triangle. We want eyes on the ground as soon as possible. In particular, I want to know how much product they're moving. We need to get a handle on how big their operation is for when we start tracking the money.'

'In our spare time,' I heard Renfro mutter under his breath.

'Ms Kaminski. You're doing the network analysis?' asked Jacobs. I nodded.

'You'll be working with Intelligence Analyst McCullom –' she nodded to the red-haired man – 'to put together the network map of the group. Let him know what you require in terms of data. We're being supported by the OFC on this one, so don't be afraid to ask for what you need. A priority for us is to get an understanding of who's working directly with Brajen Krol, and who they're recruiting here to grow their operation.'

I'd long ago given up trying to keep track of the FBI's acronyms, but knew about the OFC. It was short for OCDETF Fusion Center, a platform for inter-agency information and intelligence sharing. That Jacobs had given me carte blanche to work with them meant that the powers-that-be were committed to this task force.

McCullom smiled at me and I nodded back. This would be interesting, and I was excited to be working with the FBI. They had more resources than we did, and were able to call on support staff and the latest technology, both in short supply in the Chicago PD.

'Officer Nowak, you'll be liaising with SSA Jacobs on the under-cover piece to this operation,' said Bowles, addressing the blond. 'In case you haven't figured it out,' he said to all of us, 'this task force is a high priority. Until further notice your regularly scheduled days off are canceled. You would be wise to cancel your weekend plans, and don't schedule vacation any time soon. Those of you in the PD have a blanket authorization for overtime. We'll all be spending a large chunk of that time in conference room three ten, our designated situation room.' He handed out the last binder to Nowak. 'You're dismissed. We'll see you all tomorrow morning at ten.'

Everyone stood up. McCullom walked over to me and put out his hand.

'Gavin McCullom. Excited for the chance to work with you.'

I shook his hand and he smiled, dark blue eyes under a healthy head of banged red hair that came down to just above his shoulders.

Built, too, I thought, noticing his biceps straining at the white button-down shirt he was wearing.

If his work was as tight as his body, this would be a good relationship. And I could get used to his Scottish brogue.

'Want to go for a wee coffee?' he asked.

'Sure.'

As we walked out of the room we were met by the deputy chief's assistant. 'Ms Kaminski? He wants to see you.'

'When?'

'Right now.'

'Rain check?' I said to McCullom as I followed the chief's assistant down the hall.

TWO

'Maude.'

Freezing cold water filled my nose and mouth. I tried to take a deep breath but ended up swallowing water instead. How had I ended up in the lake? I coughed as water ran down my throat.

'*MAUDE.*'

I came to, leaning against the tile wall underneath the shower. Sagarine was holding me up.

'What the hell?' I said, bleary.

'Thank fucking god,' she said, turning the water off.

She handed me a towel and walked out of the bathroom, stepping over the pile of my clothes on the floor.

I wrapped the towel around me and shuffled into our living room.

'Jesus,' she said, 'I thought you had alcohol poisoning.' She looked down at the coffee table, covered in empty beer cans and a half empty bottle of Sobieski vodka.

She pointed to the bottle. 'This is new. What's going on?'

I sat down unsteadily next to her. 'It's my brother,' I said, my head down.

'Mark? What happened?'

'Not Mark,' I mumbled. 'Michael.'

'*Michael?*'

I reached for the bottle, getting it close to my mouth before she grabbed it out of my hand and set it back on the table.

'Talk to me.'

After the task force meeting, Jefferson's assistant had escorted me back to the big man's office. I walked in and he shut the door behind me.

Jefferson was at his desk. I was surprised to see SSA Jeb Smith leaning against the wall, his FBI-issue black suit and white shirt spotless and wrinkle-free, as always.

Deputy Chief Marcus Jefferson was progressive, as far as the Chicago PD went, and had been one of the first to see the value in using analytics to deal with Chicago's gang problem. I'd interned

Tunnel Vision 11

for him during the summer when I was in college and he was a lieutenant; by the time I'd gotten my master's degree, he'd made it to the head of the Chicago PD's Criminal Networks Group. He'd hired me right after graduation to do network analysis on Chicago's gangs.

We had a great relationship, but I could count on one hand the number of times he'd called me into his office.

'Take a seat,' he said, gesturing to the chair on the other side of his desk.

'We're getting close on the SK network, sir,' I'd said, assuming he was bringing me in to reinforce the idea that I wasn't to let that work slip, by being on another task force. 'I'm—'

'This isn't about any of that. Please, sit down, Maude.'

Maude? He never called me that. And what was Jeb doing here? I sat down on the edge of the seat.

'One of our officers brought this in.' He'd pointed to a plastic-wrapped item on his desk.

I stood up and leaned over the desk to get a closer look.

A child's backpack.

I picked it up, not recognizing it at first. It was dirty, the original red color obscured by layers of grime. Not quite enough to cover up the large, oval eyes of Spiderman, or the swath of blue paint splashed on one side of it. The same color that Dad had used to repaint the house twenty years ago.

And, I realized, it was out of context. I'd never seen it when it wasn't in the grasp of the boy with blond curls.

I tore at the plastic and pulled it free.

'You can't—' started Jeb.

Jefferson put his hand up.

I widened the opening of the backpack, the zipper having long ago given up, and felt for the patch on the inside near the top.

A small piece of fabric, lovingly added by my mother. I ran my fingers over the sturdy sewing.

Michael Kaminski. 3519 Ridgeway Ave, Chicago.

I sat down, my legs no longer able to hold me up. 'Where?' I said quietly.

'What?'

'Where did they find it?'

'The tent city, on Taylor. It was among the things of a woman who lived there.'

'What woman?' I stared at the backpack numbly.

'Sheila Johnson, ostensibly.'

'Where is she? I want to talk to her.'

'You can't,' said Jefferson.

'Wanna bet?' I said, lifting my eyes to meet his. 'I don't care what—'

'She's dead, Maude,' interrupted Jeb softly. 'Suspected drug overdose. There was no sign of him,' he added, answering the next question he knew I would ask.

'When did they find this?'

Jefferson shifted in his chair.

I stared at him, then at Jeb. Neither of them would look me in the eye.

'When?'

'You have to understand, there was no mystery to her death, and no one showed up to claim her belongings,' said Jefferson.

'*When?*'

'Two months ago.'

'Two *months*?'

'I just got this today, Maude. And we, uh, wanted to show it to you, to confirm that it was your brother's, before we notify your parents,' said Jefferson.

'No.'

'I'm sorry, Maude, we're obligated to—'

'I'll do it,' I said, standing up and walking out of the room with the backpack.

Jeb followed me out. 'Maude, are you OK?' he said, reaching for me with his hand, and then stopping short. Our touching days were over.

'I'm fine,' I snapped.

I'd grabbed my bag and left the station, intending to go to my parents' house to give them the news. Somehow I ended up at the liquor store instead, and then back home to sit on the couch and drink myself into oblivion.

Pretty successfully, from the looks of things.

'They found his backpack,' I said to Sagarine.

'His backpack? What are you talking about?'

'He was carrying it when he disappeared. He always had it with him. They found it, with a dead woman, in a homeless camp.'

Sagarine's eyes went wide. 'Was he with her?'

Tunnel Vision 13

'If he was do you think I'd be sitting here?' I said more sharply than I needed to. I just wanted to be alone. Not answer questions, not think about it.

She leaned back as if slapped. We'd been roommates for over two years, and best friends for most of that time. We'd never had a fight, or anything close to it. Like me, Sagarine was drama-free, and laser-focused on her career. She was the new head chef and owner of Saga, a high-end restaurant in the neighborhood. She was good, and the restaurant was doing very well, quite an achievement in a city with over 150 restaurants boasting Michelin stars. She'd gotten her chance to run the restaurant when the previous head chef had been killed.

We'd also bonded over sibling trauma. Sagarine's sister Gigi was a drug addict. Occasionally she'd turn up at our apartment to crash or get money. She was a mess, but at least she was still around, in a way.

'I've never seen you like this.'

'Yeah, well, that's what all the therapy's been for.' I picked up the bottle again and took a drink, a fair amount of it landing on the towel.

'C'mon, is that really what you want to do?' she said, gently pulling the bottle out of my hand again and putting it on the table.

'What should I be doing?'

'What you always do. Figure it out. Who found the backpack?'

'I don't know, probably one of the officers who was called to the scene where the woman died.'

'Have you talked to the officer?'

I shook my head.

'That would be a good start, wouldn't it?'

She was right. And normally I'd have already laid out a plan to get more information. But this was different.

With the help of therapy I'd been able to manage my despair over Michael's disappearance, and eventually figured out how to put together something resembling a normal life. This was the first sign of him in over twenty years, and it was like all of the work I'd done to get myself right never happened.

I was eight when he disappeared. *Stay with your brother*, my mother had said. *I just need to try on this dress.* She'd stepped into the changing room. I hadn't noticed his hand slipping out of mine.

Then she was out, looking around. *Where is your brother?*

I didn't know. And the next thing I knew the entire place was in an uproar. My mother, calling for him. The store security huddled with us, announcements over the speakers about a missing boy.

We'd been in the Pedway, the underground pedestrian complex that connected the major stores under Chicago's downtown. She'd dragged me out of the store and into the yellow tiled walkway, holding my hand in a vise grip, walking back and forth in front of the store, calling his name.

Then the police, and our drive home, and a largely silent, tense vigil near the phone, my mother occasionally breaking into sobs. Hugging the rest of us, keeping us close.

No one ever said it was my fault. But I was the one that had lost him.

I tried to do all I could to make it better. I worked hard to be the perfect child, obedient at home, diligent at school. After a few years I realized that the guilt and pain weren't going away. But then I discovered drugs and alcohol, and for a little while every day I could enjoy not feeling miserable.

By the time I was in high school I was skipping classes, drinking heavily, staying out all night, and putting myself into increasingly dangerous situations, well on my way to an early life exit. I managed to make it to college, but with even less supervision, my attempts to accidentally kill myself were getting nearer to success. One night in a drunken pit of shame and guilt I tried to do it on purpose.

My dorm mate had found me, and they'd rushed me to the hospital. They pumped a bottle of aspirin out of my stomach and brought in a therapist.

She was the first person I'd talked to about it since it happened. *It's not your fault,* she told me. *You were only eight years old. Do you know how young that is? And no one in your family blames you, do they?*

No, I'd said. And with the help of regular counseling I'd gotten on with my life. I'd finished my information science degree at U of I, then went to Northwestern for my master's. I interned for Jefferson in the summer of graduate school, and when I graduated he'd brought me in as a regular contractor.

All together I'd created a pretty functional existence, supported by the therapist I still saw every week, a bulwark against the fetid ball of guilt that lived inside of me.

Guilt that was breaking out now with a vengeance.

The backpack was the first clue we'd ever had about what happened to my little brother. But I doubted investigating his disappearance would be a high priority for the Chicago PD, not based on the belongings of a dead homeless woman, and definitely not twenty years after he'd disappeared.

Maybe I could do something. I didn't just have skills, I had resources. And I owed it to Michael, and to my family, to use them, and see if I could find him. Or, at least, find out what happened to him.

I took a deep breath. 'You're right,' I said. 'But first I need to tell my parents.'

'Need' was the operative word. I had no desire to talk to them about this, and be confronted with their emotions on top of my own. Mom would be wrecked, likely in even worse shape than me. My dad would go silent, as always. They weren't the therapy type, and as far as I knew had never spoken to anyone about it.

'Is there anything I can do?' asked Sags.

'Yeah, there is. Come with me to their house.'

She stood up. 'No problem.'

'Not now,' I said. 'I need to sober up. And it's the middle of the night. Can you meet me at their place after work tomorrow, around six?'

'Sure. Zoe can handle a Wednesday dinner by herself at this point.'

'Thanks.'

I picked up my phone from the table and scrolled through my messages. Several from Jeb, checking in on me. We'd dated for a few months last year, and even though I'd been the one to end it, it hadn't stopped him from being a decent human being. At the moment I couldn't recall why I'd broken things off with him.

A message from my mom, asking me to dinner. I definitely wasn't going to answer that one.

Two more calls from the station.

They could all wait. I went into my bedroom, stuffed my feelings back to where they belonged, and went to sleep.

THREE

'd set my alarm early so I could go through the task force binder. I was massively hungover but didn't mind; I'd always found that physical discomfort was a good distraction from emotional pain. I'd trade a headache and nausea for crippling guilt and sadness any time.

I managed to skim through the information in time to take a long cold shower, grab a piece of toast, run out the door and hop in my car.

My usual mode of transportation was the L, an efficient and inexpensive way to get around the city. More importantly, it was almost entirely above ground. Ever since we'd lost Michael in the Pedway I couldn't bear to be underground. I hadn't realized it until years after he'd disappeared.

I'd been on the L's Blue Line, going to a friend's birthday party downtown. On the way the train descended into the Logan Square station, one of the underground stops. As the train moved downward my heart began racing. By the time it stopped I was having trouble breathing. As soon as the doors opened I'd rushed to get out and up the stairs, gulping huge breaths once I reached the surface.

Years later my therapist said it was because Michael had been taken in the Pedway, and I had PTSD about being underground.

No shit, Sherlock. From then on I avoided the underground stations at all costs. These days it was a little bit of a hassle, since the most direct way to police headquarters from my apartment was to take the Blue Line and switch to the Green Line at Clark and Lake. But that involved going underground.

Fortunately I could do most of my work from home, and didn't need to go into the office very often, once every couple of weeks or so unless there was task force business. But when I did, I'd drive. It took me an extra thirty minutes, and I had to pay for parking, but it was worth avoiding a panic attack.

I took the freeway to the 35th Street exit and went east towards the lake. I kept the AC on high, the cool air helpful for my pounding head and queasy stomach.

The police station was south of the fancy Magnificent Mile part of Michigan Avenue, and I found parking on the street. It was hot and humid outside of my car, typical for late August, and the building lobby was uncomfortably warm. By the time I made it through the metal detector and up the elevator to the third floor it was stifling, and I was regretting eating that piece of toast.

Just before ten I walked into the situation room. Room 310 was a medium-sized conference room, with whiteboards on either side of a long table, and a large screen in the front. One side of the room was a set of large windows that overlooked the front of the station. Everyone was there except for Jacobs and Bowles. Renfro looked at me and did a double take. The shower had woken me up, but didn't do anything for my bloodshot eyes and pallid skin.

'What happened to you, Kaminski? You look like twenty miles of bad road,' he said gleefully.

'Not as bad as you.' I usually had better comebacks than that, but today I wasn't firing on all cylinders.

McCullom was sitting on the far side of the table. *Dammit.* I'd completely forgotten about meeting with him for coffee yesterday. I made my way over and sat next to him.

'Gavin, I'm really sorry. The meeting with the deputy chief rearranged my day. Can I make it up to you, buy you a coffee after the meeting?' It was the last thing I wanted to do, but if we were going to be working together I needed to not burn any bridges. As the technical guy he'd be the one I'd be relying on most.

'Sure,' he said, smiling. 'Rough night?'

'You could say that.'

At ten on the dot SSA Jacobs and Bowles walked in. She jumped right into things without preamble.

'I assume everyone's had a chance to go through the binder. Any questions?' She looked at us for a half second. 'Good. Because our first action is this weekend.'

Jesus. This woman didn't mess around.

'We're setting up an information gathering event at the Taste of Polonia festival.'

Chicago was famous for its festivals. Greek festival in Greektown, where you could eat gyros and drink all the ouzo it took to vomit. Meatballs and cannoli at Little Italy's Festa, Humboldt Park's Puerto Rican Fest, with pastilillos, pasteles and plantains. There were also Thai, Korean, and countless other food festivals, along with scores related to music and art.

The Taste of Polonia was one of the largest, which wasn't a surprise; Chicago until recently held the second largest Polish population in the world, after Warsaw.

'Here's the background. As I shared yesterday, we believe that Brajen Krol and possibly two or three of his lieutenants are operating in Chicago, and are recruiting locally to expand. We want to start building a database of who's in the gang, who they're recruiting, and how the gang is structured. Our goal is to build an organizational chart of the gang.' She pointed to the back wall, where she'd pinned up Brajen Krol's picture near the top, along with a few others below him that they'd already identified.

She handed out a stack of folders to Renfro who was sitting next to her. 'Take one and pass it down. These folders contain pictures of every Chicago street kid and crew member that is in our system and likely to be a possible recruit.'

I grabbed a folder and opened it up. The first image was of a teenager. I looked at the summary. Filip Palka. He'd done some work for the Latin Kings, who occasionally brought in white kids to work on their crews. I flipped through the rest of the photos.

'These kids are all white,' I said.

Jacobs nodded. 'The Greenpoint Crew only allows whites into their gang. Preferably Poles. That's why we're focused on Avondale and the Triangle. Our early intelligence indicates this is where they're doing the bulk of their recruiting.'

'What's the play?' asked Renfro.

'The Taste of Polonia festival lasts four days, over Labor Day weekend. We're going to operate a surveillance operation to capture cell phone data, and link it to images of Krol and his top men, existing gang members, and the likely recruits. We'll use that data to build the gang org chart, and to focus the takedown portion of the operation.'

'That festival is huge,' I said. I'd been going to the Taste of Polonia since I was a kid. It was held at the Copernicus Center in Jefferson Park, and one of the largest Polish festival in the country, each year attracting over 40,000 people. The festival schedule included bands that played on four indoor and outdoor stages, numerous food vendors, and a variety of games, arts and crafts, even a casino.

'How do we know he's going to be there, and even if he is, how are we going to find him?'

Tunnel Vision

'He never missed the Polish festival in Philly, and we don't think he'll miss this one. The headliner band is Warsaw Station, it's one of his favorites. We've arranged it so Warsaw Station is playing on one of the outdoor stages that we've designated. We'll be setting up surveillance and cell phone capture in that area.

'Also, one of the food vendors is working with us. She'll be serving what we know to be Krol's favorite foods. We'll have cameras and microphones at her tent, in addition to several of our people in the area working surveillance. Once Krol and his close associates show up to either the stage or the food vendor, he'll be tailed and discretely photographed, along with everyone he comes into contact with.'

I was skeptical; depending on the weather the festival would be a crush of humanity. But field work wasn't in my wheelhouse, so I kept silent.

'Is the festival free?' asked Renfro.

I shook my head. 'Twenty dollars to get in.'

He looked at Jacobs, shaking his head. 'These guys –' he held up the folder with the people in it that we expected might be recruits – 'aren't going to be able to afford that.'

She nodded. 'I know. We've enlisted the help of local community organizations to gin up interest and attendance with a certain demographic.'

'A "certain demographic"?'

She nodded. 'Entrance into the festival will be free to people with tickets. They're being distributed to white men and women in the target neighborhoods who are out of work, those with records, and who we know to be working on the street in some capacity, including all of the ones in your folders.'

In some capacity. A nice euphemism for boys and girls selling themselves on the street, I thought.

She brought up a map of the Copernicus Center and surrounding streets on the monitor, and used her laser pointer to point to one of the stages.

'Warsaw Station is playing on this stage Friday and Saturday at eight thirty. This –' she pointed to a spot around the corner from the stage – 'is where our food vendor will be set up. We'll be using a StingRay to capture cell phone use, and cameras to link phones with faces.'

'StingRay?' asked Renfro. Most of his field work had been of the luddite variety, busting doors and working CIs, rather than anything technological.

'It's for IMSI capture. It stands for "international mobile subscriber identity-catcher". Basically an eavesdropping device used for intercepting cell phone traffic and location data. Commander Bowles and I will be running comms in a van in this alley –' she pointed to a spot on the map – 'Ms Kaminski, Officer Nowak and Mr McCullom, you'll attend the event as locals. Mr McCullom will have the portable KingFish unit. As you're instructed by the comms van you will be notified to discretely pick up specific conversations, messages and images. The KingFish has a radius of about twenty-five meters, so it should cover the operational area.'

'I'm an analyst,' I said. 'I don't do field work.' There was a reason I was an analyst. I had no desire to be in the field. Even the simplest operations often resulted in undercover cops getting injured, or worse.

'You do now, Ms Kaminski. And it's hardly real undercover work. We just need a female to sit with Mr McCullom; a couple is less suspicious than a single man. You won't be interacting with anyone other than Mr McCullom. And you speak Polish, don't you?' she said.

I hesitated, then nodded.

'There's a chance you might be able to pick up things we don't get. Don't worry, we'll be using your technical skills soon enough. Once we get the cell data, you'll be putting together the network map of the gang.

'You'll be fine. No one's going to even notice you. You don't look at all like a cop.'

'That's for sure,' Renfro snorted. 'What am I going to be doing?'

'You'll be working in the food tent, with our chef.'

'The *food* tent? Seriously?'

Jacobs ignored him. 'Officer Nowak will be specifically assigned to tail Brajen Krol. Once she or anyone else has identified him, she'll surveil him, taking pictures of him and who he meets to add to the cell phone captures. The goal will be to get pictures of anyone he talks to, and acquire their associated cell numbers. This is how we build up our org chart of the gang.' She turned off the monitor and looked around. 'The details of the event are in your folders, when and where, including more information on your roles. It's a fairly simple operation, we're just gathering data at this point. No contact with the targets. Any questions?'

Tunnel Vision 21

I had a million of them, but would hold off until I read through the material again.

'Dismissed.'

'So, what about that coffee?' asked McCullom, smiling.

'Sure. I'll meet you in the lobby in ten.' I had one stop to make. I left the conference room and headed for the office cubicles. Officer Martinez had been the one who'd brought Sheila Johnson's belongings into the station. I found him at his desk in front of his computer.

'Martinez?'

'Yeah?' he said, staring at his screen.

'You brought Sheila Johnson's belongings into the station?'

'Who?' he said, looking up. When he saw me he smiled, revealing perfect white teeth.

'What can I do for you, uh . . .?'

'Maude Kaminski, Analyst.' I flashed my contractor ID.

'What can I do for you, Maude Kaminski, Analyst?' he said, his smile deepening.

'You were the one on the call about the dead woman, about two months ago. You brought her things back to the station?'

'Two months ago? A dead woman?' He shook his head and raised his eyebrows. 'You're going to need to narrow it down a little more than that.'

'From the tent city on Taylor. Sheila Johnson? She OD'd. There was a kid's backpack. Spiderman?'

'Oh, yeah, that was me. She was DOA.'

'Was there any investigation?'

He shook his head. 'Not that I'm aware. We don't have the resources to investigate every time a homeless junkie dies. You might want to check with the medical examiner.'

No shock there. They probably hadn't even done an autopsy. 'What can you tell me about her?'

He shrugged. 'She looked about fifty but was probably younger. Dirty, living on the street for a while, I think. We found a few envelopes with her stuff, probably fentanyl.'

'How did you ID her?'

'Fingerprints.'

'Was she on file?' If she had a criminal record that would take things in a whole different direction.

'No, the Indigent Disposition Program ID'd her.'

22 Wendy Church

'Was she with anyone else?'

'What do you mean?'

'I mean, was there anyone else nearby, anyone who looked like they might be with her? Maybe, uh, someone younger? A bo– I mean, a young man? Late teens, early twenties?'

'Not that I recall. Just the normal homeless group. Hard to say who's with who.'

'You brought her things back. Was there anything else besides the backpack?'

'No. Just the stuff that was in the backpack, it's all down with the property clerk.'

'Can you give me the number?'

'Sure,' he said, turning back to his computer. 'What's this about?'

'It's a long story. I'm looking for someone, someone she may have known.' I pulled a city map out of my bag.

'Can you show me exactly where you found her?' I said, laying the map on his desk.

He peered at the map. 'There, underneath the Dan Ryan, near Taylor,' he said, pointing. He looked back at his monitor. 'Here it is. Sheila Johnson.' He turned the monitor to show me the number.

'Thanks,' I said, writing it down. 'Is there a picture of her?'

He scrolled further down the screen revealing a photo of her, clearly taken where she'd died.

'Can you send that to me?' I left him my card.

'No problem. Anything else I can help you with, Analyst Kaminski, maybe over a beer?'

'Some other time.'

I headed downstairs to the property clerk's dungeon and waited in line behind a loud and very unhappy Sergeant Richard Slivey.

'Whaddya mean, you can't get it now?' he barked at the uniformed woman behind the counter.

'I mean, it's going to take some time. Come back after lunch,' she said, her voice even but raised to meet his.

'What's the problem? It's a damn box.'

He pointed to the locked gate behind her, beyond which were wall-to-wall shelves holding stacks of property and evidence. 'I can see it, right there,' he said, pointing to a shelf directly behind the fence.

'You know, now that I think about it, *Dick*, I'm not sure I'll have time to get to it by this afternoon. Try tomorrow,' she said, daring

Tunnel Vision

him to continue berating her and increase the wait time. She stared at him without blinking until he turned and walked away, muttering. Couldn't happen to a nicer guy. Dick Slivey, aka 'Slimey', was a complete jerk. There was a reason he'd been in the force for over twenty years and had never risen above the level of sergeant. He was infamous for being lazy, calling in sick and leaving his crew short-handed when he wanted a day off, and finding others to blame for his own screwups, which were numerous.

'Hi Linda.'

Her face transformed instantly, and she gave me a warm smile. 'Hey Kaminski. Good to see you. How are things?' She looked me up and down. 'Not so good it looks like. What's going on?'

'Just a little hungover. You?'

'You know, hanging in there. They're moving me to computer crimes next week.'

'Yikes.' Computer crimes was one of the worst jobs in the precinct, primarily consisting of hours of mind-numbing tedium on cases that would never get solved, given the department's minuscule budget for non-violent crimes.

'Yeah. But you know me. They can move me to hell and I'm not leaving.'

Officer – at the time – Linda Cohen, had caught a bullet in the hip early on in her career, effectively ending her street days. It was a shame, as she'd been a rising star before that, working undercover in vice and narcotics, demonstrating a singular ability to get results. She had the skill and intelligence that would have moved her quickly into the detective ranks. But she'd never fully recovered from being shot, her limp still noticeable, even though she worked hard to hide it.

The brass wanted her to retire but she'd refused, so they'd given her increasingly punitive desk duties. Prior to working the property desk she'd been assigned to communications, school resource officer, and citizen's complaints, the trifecta of shitty police jobs. At this point in her mid-forties she'd worked in almost every department in the building.

A lesser human being would have quit long ago. She'd managed to keep her chin up, and not only taken what they gave her, but took and passed the sergeant's exam. 'What brings you into the dungeon?'

'I'm looking for something that came in a couple of months ago.

Sheila Johnson. Has anyone come in for it?' I asked, giving her the case number.

She turned to her monitor and entered in the number. 'Doesn't look like it. It should still be here.'

'Can I take a look?'

'No problem, hon. Give me a second.'

She opened the gate and disappeared among the shelves, a few moments later returning with a box. She set it on the counter in front of me, then pushed the register over for me to sign.

'Thanks a bunch, Linda,' I said, signing my name and picking up the box.

'Anything for you, doll.' She leaned across the desk and lowered her voice. 'You, uh, finished anything lately?'

'I sure did. Here you go.' I pulled two thin books out of my bag and handed them to her.

She took them, reading the titles. '*Saving Ryan's Privates* and *G-spot Jane*.' She giggled, then flipped through, opening to the pages I'd signed for her. She tucked them under the counter. 'Bill and I read them together. Very spicy.' She giggled again. 'He loves Betty Phang. And he really wants to meet you. Any chance of that happening?'

Betty Phang was my pen name. I'd started writing years ago, on the suggestion of my therapist, who thought journaling would help me deal with the trauma over my brother's disappearance. She hadn't given me much instruction, just to 'write what you're thinking about'. So my journaling had taken the form of what I liked to think of as 'female-centered pleasure books'. Other people called it porn. Whatever it was, I'm not sure it's what my therapist envisioned when she suggested journaling. But I found it relaxing. And along with my job, it kept me busy for the bulk of my waking hours.

I'd written fifteen books by now, and had a small but faithful group of readers who were always interested in the latest from Betty Phang.

'Sorry Linda. You know the deal. Nobody knows. Thanks again.'

'Sure thing.' She pulled one of the books back out as I walked away.

I took the stairs two at a time and parked myself at my desk, then opened the box.

FOUR

Someone once told me that people who had lived on the street for a short time carried things with them that were about the future. Hopeful things, things that would help them work their way out of their situation, and possibly keep, or get, a job. Things like soap, and nail clippers, extra socks, maybe a phone.

People who had been there for a long time carried things about the past, items with sentimental value.

From the looks of it, Sheila Johnson had been on the street for a while, and wasn't expecting much from the future.

A dank smell wafted out of the box as I opened it up. Laying on top was a single shoe and a set of clothes, including a woman's blouse, socks that might have once been white, and stained light blue polyester pants. Presumably the clothes she died in. I pulled them out and set them on the desk.

There were no blankets. She must have had some; no one could survive the winter here outside without them. I guessed those were taken by the others when she died.

Underneath the clothes was a book. *The Hobbit*. As I pulled it out a photo slipped out from between the pages.

An old Polaroid. I compared it with the picture of Sheila from the file that Martinez emailed me. It was definitely her, but younger, and less dead. She was standing on the beach, smiling, Lake Michigan in the background.

No drugs. Martinez would have gone through the pack when he picked it up, and taken out any drugs or food before turning it over to property.

At the bottom of the box were some pieces of paper. One was a ticket from the Lincoln Park Zoo. That made sense, it was one of the only free zoos in the country. The ticket was dated July 7, 2002.

Underneath the ticket was a half sheet of paper, dirty and torn almost in half. In the corner was a faded seal, something official.

The only other thing in the box was a rumpled business card, so dirty I could barely read the name on it. Some kind of community shelter.

That was it. The entirety of Sheila Johnson's life. And nothing that led to Michael.

I didn't know what I'd been expecting. A picture of the two of them? His address? As far as I knew she'd just found his backpack, and had never met him.

Still, it was worth a trip to the shelter. They might have a record of her. And there'd been no real investigation at the homeless camp. Someone might remember something there, too.

I needed to start talking to people before any more time had passed. I wished they hadn't waited two months to tell me about the backpack. Memories fade, especially in drug addicts.

I pocketed the Polaroid, the business card, and the half sheet, and returned the box to Linda, then left the station via the back door to the parking lot.

I drove to the expressway and got off at Taylor, then parked in the Halsted parking structure. Consulting my map I walked to the underpass where Martinez said he'd found Sheila Johnson's body.

I went to the intersection and started to walk through the camp, carrying the backpack and the two photos of Sheila Johnson.

There were people for as far down as I could see underneath the expressway. Some alone, some couples, some in small groups, leaning against walls, sitting on cardboard, under tarps, or next to ratty tents. The ground was littered with needles, glassine envelopes, and small baggies. There were lots of bikes and a few shopping carts. And, heartbreakingly, toys.

Rotting garbage was everywhere. I'd need to change my shoes when I got home. And throw this pair out.

The smell was overpoweringly thick, a physical force. A combination of garbage and every secretion a human body could make. I wish I'd worn a mask, and made an effort to breathe through my mouth.

'Hi,' I said, as I approached the first person. A woman, who, like Sheila, could have been fifty, or thirty. She was standing up, leaning against a stone pillar. She looked at me without saying anything. 'Did you, uh, know this woman? Sheila Johnson?' I asked, showing her the photos.

She turned her face away and said nothing. I moved on, to a couple sitting on the ground in front of a faded orange camping tent. 'Did either of you know Sheila Johnson?' I asked, showing the photos to both of them. 'Do you recognize this?' I held up the backpack.

They both shook their heads.

Tunnel Vision

I walked through the camp, asking everyone there if they knew Sheila, or recognized the backpack, and showing them her pictures. A few of the addicts were already too high to interact, one man shuffling slowly back and forth next to the camp with his head bobbing, open sores visible on his arms that were hanging limply at his sides. Those that weren't already high looked at the pictures. One by one they shook their heads.

I was nearing the end of one side of the camp, on the far side of the underpass. A brown-bearded man was sitting on the ground in front of a shopping cart, regarding me with suspicion.

'Excuse me, do you know this woman?' I asked, showing him the photos.

'That's not yours,' he said, pointing to the backpack.

'Did you know the woman who owned this?' I asked excitedly.

'She's not here anymore,' he said. 'She died. Did you take her backpack?'

'No, I borrowed it from the police,' I said, kneeling down next to him. 'Did you know her?'

'Like I know everyone here.'

'Did she, uh, was there a young man with her?'

He frowned. 'A young man?'

'Yes, possibly with blond hair.' Now that I had found someone who knew her, I didn't know what I wanted to ask.

He stared off into the distance. 'She wasn't from here.'

'What do you mean?'

'She didn't live here, with us.' He waved his hand at the other people in the encampment. 'She showed up one morning. She was dead.'

He abruptly stood up and walked away, muttering.

I went back up the other side of the camp, making an effort to talk to every one of the forty or so people living there. No one seemed to know anything about Sheila.

That seemed strange; I thought that at homeless camps people tended to know each other. Maybe the muttering guy was right, that she'd ambled in from somewhere else and died there.

I left and drove west on Harrison to the medical examiner's building. I wondered when they built it if they knew it would be fortuitous to put it five hundred feet from Chicago's infamous Heroin Highway.

The building was an imposing, relatively modern-looking, three-storied structure. I parked and walked into the lobby. I showed my ID and made my way to the clerk's office.

28 Wendy Church

I showed my ID again, to a woman at the counter sitting in front of a computer. 'I'm looking for information on a dead woman, Sheila Johnson. She would have come in about two months ago. Here's the case number,' I said, handing her the number.

She typed it in and peered at her screen. 'Here it is. Sheila Johnson. What is it you want to know?'

'Was there an autopsy?'

'No. But it says here she died of a drug overdose.'

'Who made the determination?'

'Dr Alvarez.'

'Thanks. Where's his office?'

'Second floor. But he's probably downstairs.'

'Thanks.'

I took the elevator down, where it opened to a long hallway with viewable examination rooms on either side followed by a set of closed doors. No one was working at any of the tables, although I could see cloth-covered bodies laying on several of them. I started down the hallway to knock on doors when one of them opened. A woman walked out, unrolling her sleeves.

'Excuse me, is Dr Alvarez down here?'

'He's in the change room.' She pointed to the door she'd just come out of.

I cracked open the door to the room. A man was standing in front of a locker, taking off scrubs and throwing them into a bin.

'Dr Alvarez?'

'Yes?' he said, not looking up.

'I'm Maude Kaminski, I'm a crime analyst with the Criminal Network Group. I'm here about a woman who came in about two months ago. Sheila Johnson.'

He turned and walked briskly out of the changing room, waving his hand at me to follow him into the elevator.

'Do you have the case number?'

'Yes.' I started to read it and he waved me off. He got out on the second floor and I followed him into his office.

'Case number,' he said, standing near a filing cabinet.

I gave him the number and he opened up a file cabinet, pulling out a folder and opening it.

'Sheila Johnson. Drug overdose,' he said, flipping through the pages.

'There was no autopsy?'

'No,' he said, going through the rest of the pages. 'We only autopsy

Tunnel Vision 29

a few percent of the people who die on the street. There was no mystery about the cause of death, and we don't have the resources to autopsy every overdose.' He looked through the remaining pages in the file. 'I did a cursory examination of her body.'

'Can I see the report?'

'Knock yourself out.' He handed me the folder and sat down behind his desk, opening the laptop computer and starting to type.

There wasn't much in the notes. She'd had bruising to her face, and some old scarring. 'What's this: "Lividity not consistent with body position"?'

He looked up and reached for the folder, then scanned the notes. 'She'd been moved.'

'From where?'

'I don't know. But where she died is not where they found her,' he said, handing the folder back to me.

This matched what the muttering man at the encampment had said.

'Doesn't that make it suspicious? Wouldn't there normally be an investigation for something like that?'

'It's not my call, Ms Kaminski. We have thousands of cases each year, and barely the resources to keep up with the high priority ones. Yes, she'd been moved, but her cause of death was a suspected drug overdose. As a long-term addict this is not suspicious in itself. Tragic, but not suspicious. A dead body being moved isn't a priority for us or the police, not when we have hundreds of homicides every year.'

'*Suspected* drug overdose?'

'We did do a blood test. She had high levels of fentanyl in her system, and xylazine.'

I looked back down at the notes. 'Vitamin D deficiency?'

'Not fatal, and common in populations without access to sun or high quality food.'

'She'd been living on the street. It seems like she'd have more sun than most people.'

He shrugged, and I put the folder down on his desk. 'Thanks for your time. Here's my card,' I said, laying one on his desk, 'if you, uh, find anything else about her.'

He nodded, not looking up from his monitor.

There was no reason for me to go back to the office, so I drove home to spend the rest of the afternoon going through the task force material.

I walked into my apartment and sat on the couch, looking longingly at the vodka on the coffee table.

Nope. I put it away, and threw out the beer cans. I picked up the thick binder and opened it up to the first page.

'Task Force: Meatless.'

Very funny. A nod to the Kielbasa gang, the other Polish gang that operated out of Philly.

The operation this weekend was surveillance and cell phone capture, ideally to gain enough information to understand the structure and members of the gang. It was fairly simple, at least my part of it. My job was primarily to provide cover for McCullom, while he used the KingFish to capture cell numbers and contacts from suspected gang members. The only operational duty I had was to take photos as instructed of whoever he was targeting for capture.

That, and pick up any conversations in Polish I happened to hear from the targets, all of whom would be identified and communicated to us from the comms team in the van. They'd be getting the head's up from Nowak who'd be wandering around the festival, looking for known members, and particularly Brajen Krol.

There was to be no contact, by anyone on the team, with our targets. This was probably the only reason I was allowed to participate. Normally they'd never put an analyst in the field, but I had strict instructions not to leave our seats or interact with anyone.

I went through the material until quarter to six, making it through the binder and re-reading several parts that related to my role in the weekend operation, which amounted to little more than pretending to be McCullom's girlfriend, and taking a few photos when prompted, any time I could do it discretely, through pretend couple shots and selfies.

Nowak would be doing the bulk of the photography, and we'd get shots from the food tent, but they wanted us all to contribute. There was no such thing as too many photos.

It didn't seem all that complicated, but I wasn't comfortable with field work. My skills were with a computer. I did social network analysis, SNA, using data to map relationships among gangs and gang members, that helped the police target their work with the gangs.

While the department as a whole appreciated the work of crime analysts, and there were never enough of them, everyone other than Deputy Chief Jefferson had been skeptical of SNA when I'd started.

Tunnel Vision 31

That changed quickly when my work helped solve two high-profile cases.

In one case my analysis had revealed an unusually strong connection between one of the gang leaders and his girlfriend. Unlike most of the other gang members, who bounced from woman to woman, he was devoted to her. They'd just had a child, and there were signs his enthusiasm for gang life was waning. The PD focused their resources on getting her to turn, and as a result she convinced her boyfriend to leave the gang.

In the other case, my analysis had shown that a large gang with a lot of sub-cliques was tied together by just one man. The PD put their efforts towards getting him off the street, and once that happened, the larger structure broke apart into smaller groups, that individually had far less impact.

Now almost everyone in the force was on board with my work. The Chicago PD was woefully understaffed in relation to the enormous gang problem in the city, and I helped them decide where to apply their limited resources. At this point the last holdout was Bowles, and even he must have not objected too much to having me on the Meatless task force. If he had I wouldn't be there.

At five fifty I closed the binder and put on my coat. I grabbed the Spiderman backpack, put it into a brown paper bag and left the apartment.

To say I was dreading telling my parents was an understatement of epic proportion.

Dad had never talked about Michael's disappearance, throwing himself into his work, and drinking more than he should, although he'd kept it together for the most part. Mom had devoted herself to caring for the rest of us, smothering me, my older brother Mark, Lidia and Sophie. Sophie had been born after Michael, so didn't remember him, or carry a sense of loss, although she must have felt the effects of the grief on the rest of us.

Despite the trauma my folks must have done something right. Mark had moved out and started his own family, with one kid already and one on the way. Lidia was close to graduating from USC with a degree in psychology, and Sophie was a star at school, and in the various extracurricular activities she was involved in. We'd all gotten on with our lives, more or less. That was all about to change.

FIVE

My parents' place in Avondale was ten minutes away from my apartment in Portage Park, both neighborhoods located in the northwest of the city.

Bounded on the east by the Chicago River, and partially on the west by the Kennedy Expressway, Avondale is home to Chicago's Polish Village, historically one of the largest concentrations of Poles in the US.

Polish immigration to Chicago surged after the American Civil War, and continued unabated for years, finally slowing a few decades ago when conditions changed in Poland, offering better opportunities than had been available before. Gone were the days of hearing almost exclusively Polish spoken on Milwaukee Avenue, as Polish immigration was replaced by an influx of people from the former Soviet States and Latin America. Still, Avondale retained a vibrant Polish community, with cultural and arts offerings, as well as being home to the famous Polish cathedral, St Hyacinth Basilica. For reasons I'd never uncovered, Avondale had gained the moniker as 'the neighborhood that built Chicago'. It may have had something to do with the largely working class that now and before made up the community.

When I got to my folks' house Sagarine was already there, standing on the stoop in front of the door. To my surprise Jeb was standing next to her.

'Jeb? What are you doing here?'

'I called in reinforcements,' she said.

I felt my throat constrict, and my eyes start to tear. For Sags to call Jeb for help was a big deal.

It was an understatement to say their relationship was strained. Last year she'd gotten a job as the personal chef for the head of a Russian gang, and Jeb had strong-armed her to collect information on them. It turned out to be way more dangerous than he'd thought it would be, and she'd almost gotten killed.

With her help the FBI had managed to put the gang out of commission, but in the process of working together Jeb had suspected

Tunnel Vision 33

that she'd killed some men herself, going back over ten years. Every one of them had been a violent rapist or drug dealer. One had been serially abusing her sister, and Sags' boss, head chef Louie Ferrar, had tried to rape Sags in his restaurant.

Jeb had taken all of that into account, likely in addition to his own guilt for putting Sags in harm's way. They'd made a deal, in exchange for continuing to be available to him for undercover projects, he wouldn't investigate her for it. Somewhere in that calculus was a realization on Jeb's part that it would have been difficult to prosecute her, anyway.

Jeb gave me a hug, which I returned gratefully. We'd dated but he'd never met my parents. I'd learned long ago not to bring anyone I was dating to see them. Mom would immediately start in with the 'when are you two going to tie the knot' and 'does this mean I'm finally going to get some grandchildren out of you?' business. Unless and until I was committed to someone, and had an actual wedding date, there was no point in sharing it with her. And those things were a long ways off, if ever. Jeb and I had lasted three months, a relationship record for me.

I was glad they were both here. This wasn't going to be easy.

I reached for the door handle and then paused, turning back to them.

'Look, you guys, no one in my family knows about Betty Phang, so keep that quiet. And, uh, it goes without saying, Sags, don't mention that Jeb thinks you're a serial killer. My parents don't care that you're gay, but murdering people crosses the line.'

'I'm not a serial killer,' she said. 'And whoever killed those guys – a pedophile, some rapists and a drug dealer – is a vigilante, not a serial killer.'

'Technically, Maude's right,' offered Jeb. 'After three it's considered a serial killer. But in this case, it's also a vigilante, so you're both right.'

She shot him a venomous look.

'Serial killer, vigilante, I don't care. Just don't bring it up.'

'Wouldn't think of it,' said Sags. Jeb nodded.

I knocked and opened the door to the house, and we stepped into the living room.

As always the first thing to hit me was the aroma of Mom's cooking. Baking something, from the smell of it. I'd told them we were coming, and of course she'd been in the kitchen, likely since the phone call.

34   Wendy Church

She came out from the kitchen and met us at the door, wiping her hands on a towel, and gave me a big hug.

'Who's this?' she said, smiling as she turned to Jeb.

'Hello, ma'am, I'm Jeb Smith,' he said, putting out his hand. Nice of him to not scare her by bringing out the FBI stuff right away. He'd taken off his tie and looked more or less normal.

She shook his hand, then moved to hug Sags.

The second thing to hit me, and anyone who lived within a mile of the house, was the cacophony from the back room. I walked over and opened the sliding door to the den.

Nana was in her chair, laughing at the television. I guess you haven't really experienced *The Golden Girls* until you've watched it at 140 decibels.

'*Hej, Nana*,' I yelled over Rue McClanahan bemoaning her lack of dating prospects.

'*Kochanie*,' she said, putting her arms out. I leaned down and gave her a careful hug, her ongoing weight loss evident in her diminishing shoulders and back that at this point were little more than skin and bone.

'*Jak się masz?*' (How are you?)

'*Dobre dla starszej kobiety.*' (Good for an old woman)

'*Czy jesz wystarczająco dużo?*' (Are you eating enough?)

'*Dlaczego muszę jeść?*' (Why do I have to eat?)

I kissed her on the cheek and left the room, closing the door behind me, only slightly muting Betty White's confused ramblings.

'Where's Dad?' I said, walking back into the living room and looking around.

'Right here,' he said, coming down the stairs with a beer in his hand. Mocny Full, a really shitty Polish beer. 'To what do we owe this pleasure?' he said.

'I have some, uh, news. Why don't we all sit down?' Everyone sat down but my mom.

'You know better than that,' she said, shaking her head. She disappeared into the kitchen, and came back shortly with a tray loaded with a teapot and cups, and a plate of kolaczki. Still warm.

I wasn't hungry, but took a cup of tea while Mom poured. I didn't think Jeb or Sags were tea drinkers, but to their credit they let Mom serve them. Jeb grabbed two of the redolent cookies.

Finally she sat down next to my dad on the couch. They were both looking at the brown paper bag in my hands.

Tunnel Vision 35

'Where's Sophie?' I asked, stalling.

'She's at her band practice. She's so committed,' said my mom, smiling at Jeb and Sags.

Time to get it over with. I took a deep breath. 'I don't know how to say this, so I'm just going to say it.' I pulled the backpack out of the bag. 'The police found this.'

It wasn't out for a second before my mother gave a gasp, and then a low moan.

'Is that . . .?' my dad started.

'Yes. It's Michael's.'

Mom reached for it and I handed it to her. She widened the opening and looked inside at the patch she'd sewn, then hugged it to her chest.

'Have they found him?' my dad asked quietly.

I shook my head. Mom was leaning over, her head almost touching her knees, her body quietly heaving in silent sobs.

My eyes moved to the mantel, crowded with family photos. My parents' wedding photo, one of Nana, mostly pictures of me and my siblings. Everyone grown up: Mark in his thirties, me in my twenties, Lidia in her late teens, Sophie in her early teens. All except for one. Placed liberally along the mantel were pictures of a smiling two-year-old boy, with blond curls and blue eyes.

'Where did you get this?' Dad asked.

'A homeless woman died, it was among her belongings.'

My mother inhaled sharply and let out something between a gasp and a scream. Dad leaned over and put his arm around her. 'A homeless woman?' he asked.

I nodded. 'Her name was Sheila Johnson. She died of a drug overdose. She'd been living in one of the tent cities.'

'Tent city? The one down the street?' he said, referring to the homeless camp underneath the freeway a few blocks from their house.

'No, south of the Loop. Underneath the Dan Ryan, near Taylor.'

He nodded numbly. 'Do they think Michael is, is he . . .?' He couldn't finish the sentence.

'I don't know, Dad. She could have known him, or she could have gotten his backpack some other way.'

'What other way?' he asked.

I didn't want to say all of the other ways that she could have gotten it. It would have been all speculation, and none of that kind of speculating would be positive.

Jeb jumped in. 'It's common, Mr Kaminski, for people to share their belongings in an encampment. It's possible that Michael was there,' he said noncommittedly.

Mom lifted her head and spoke for the first time. 'You mean he could still be alive?'

Uh-oh. Chances were that Sheila Johnson had ended up with his backpack the same way everyone else there picked up things. After he died. Getting Mom's hopes up and then dashing them again would be beyond cruel.

She didn't wait for him to answer. She stood up. 'What are the police doing about it? Are they looking for him?'

Shit. 'I don't think so, Mom,' I said weakly.

'Don't you work for the police?' Her voice was shrill. 'You need to get them to do something. He could be out there.'

This was a mistake. I should have let Jefferson do the notification. He'd handled situations like this millions of times.

'Mrs Kaminski, I don't know if Maude told you,' said Jeb, reaching for her hand, and guiding her back down, 'but I work for the FBI. We're not currently working on the case, but we will be sure to update Michael's missing person status.'

I knew updating his status wouldn't amount to much, other than checking a different box on the original paperwork, and I wondered whether or not it made sense to imply that anything would actually come of it. But at the moment all I wanted to do was get out of there.

I'd carefully managed my own grief until now, and could feel that effort coming apart in the presence of my parents' anguish. I looked longingly at the front door. But Mom's reaction to Michael's disappearance had always been to gather her kids and pull them close, and when she held her hand out to me, I dutifully joined her and my dad on the couch. She leaned into me, and the three of us sat there, holding each other, for what seemed like hours.

The silence was broken by the front door banging open.

'Hey,' said Sophie as she stomped in. 'What's happened?'

Mom put out a hand and gestured to her. Sophie walked to the couch and let herself be engulfed in the family hug.

Now that there were reinforcements I could make a guilt-free exit, and I used the opportunity to extricate myself.

Sags knew me well. Looking at her phone, she said gently, 'Uh, Mr and Mrs Kaminski, I'm sorry, but we've got a thing at the restaurant.'

I felt like a jerk, leaving them to tell Nana, but I looked at her gratefully and nodded. My dad got up and hugged me again, then Sags, then shook hands with Jeb. Mom stayed on the couch, silently holding Sophie close to her. Tight enough to constrict breathing, I knew. But Sophie would be fine; like the rest of us, she'd learned to take a huge breath before one of Mom's hugs.

I resisted the urge to run out the door. 'Wanna get a drink?' I said, as soon as the door was closed.

'Sure,' said Sags. 'Let's go to the restaurant. I actually really do have a thing.' She looked down at her phone. 'Gigi's showed up at the restaurant again.'

One of the downsides of having an addict as a sister was that occasionally she'd show up at Sags' workplace. Prior to getting her own restaurant, it had often resulted in Sags losing her job; restaurants had a hard enough time without having an out-of-control addict show up during dinner service. Now that Sags was in charge of her own place, there was no danger of her getting canned. But she didn't like her staff to have to deal with it.

'You wanna come?' I asked Jeb.

'No,' he said, looking at his watch. 'I've got something else I have to do.'

'Thanks,' I said, giving him a hug. I lingered on his scent, trying and failing again to remember why I'd broken things off with him.

'I'm guessing our "inside chef" at the Taste of Polonia is you?' I asked Sags as we got into my car.

She nodded.

'You could have told me.'

'I just found out this week,' she said irritably. 'You think they'd give me a little more notice. It's not like I don't have a restaurant to run or anything.'

'I don't think they knew until this week they'd be doing it. Jacobs is moving this task force at lightning speed. And they're putting *me* undercover.'

'You're kidding.'

I shook my head. 'No. They need me and one of the guys to be a fake couple while he captures cell phone numbers. Apparently it's less suspicious than a man sitting by himself.'

'That doesn't sound too dangerous.'

'I don't think it is. But you know I'm not a field person. I'm perfectly happy behind my computer.'

'I know. This whole thing is a little strange. I'm surprised Smith is lending my time out to someone else.'

'I'm not. He and Jacobs go back, apparently. And the FBI tends to help each other out.'

'Maybe he owes her. Or he's into her?' she said.

I scoffed. 'Not likely.' I couldn't picture the two of them together.

'Well, it's not like I have a choice.'

She was right there. As a condition of not putting her in prison when he found out she'd been vigilante-ing her way around Chicago for the last ten years, Jeb had her on the hook for helping him when he needed it.

'But I can't really complain. It gives me a chance to make food I wouldn't try at the restaurant.'

'Polish food? It's not exactly haute cuisine,' I said.

'Just because it's rustic doesn't mean it can't be elevated. They gave me a menu based on the bad guy you're trying to attract, so I don't have a lot of leeway. But I do have a couple of surprises up my sleeve.'

'Of course you do.' I knew whatever she made would be great.

We pulled into Saga's small parking lot in the rear of the restaurant. She'd been working there when it was called Louie's; now that Louie was gone and she'd taken over the place, the quality of the food was elevated several levels. She'd brought creativity and innovation to the menu, along with some elements of molecular gastronomy, transforming food into a tasty and adventurous experience. The uninspired Italian fare and 'big dumb salads' that were Louie's go-to offerings had been replaced by a chef's tasting menu that always included several perfect courses of meat, fish and vegetables, whatever was in season, and one highly experimental course. They were now fully booking the restaurant four and five weeks out.

'You know they've assigned Renfro to work with you in the food tent, yeah?' I said, getting out of the car. She'd heard me talk about him over the last couple of years and knew what a dick he was.

She nodded. 'He won't have to do much. Take tickets, change money, follow my orders. And I'm not letting him touch the food.'

'That's good. I think his idea of a fancy meal is one he has to get out of his car to eat.'

We went into the restaurant through the employee entrance in the back, then walked through the busy kitchen and swinging double

Tunnel Vision

doors to the main space. We turned right to the front desk and the dining room, away from the bar area, the two sections partially separated by long planters with fake trees.

Gigi was near the front door, trying and failing to get past Stephen, the host, to join one of the guest tables. Sags walked to the front and put her arms around her, turning her back towards the door.

'I'll be back in a minute,' she said over her shoulder as she escorted Gigi quickly outside. Not fast enough for me to miss the black and blue bruises covering one side of Gigi's face.

I walked through the dining area and took a seat at the bar. Courtney must have seen us come in as she had a dirty vodka martini ready for me when I sat down. I nodded gratefully and took a drink.

'Long day?' she asked.

'You have no idea,' I said.

My phone buzzed. *Taking her home, back soon.*

Gigi spent the night on our couch every six or eight weeks. Whenever she turned up high Sags would convince her to stay at our place to sleep it off in relative safety. I knew Sags was holding out hope that Gigi would go back to rehab. I didn't think it was likely, but I didn't blame her. What wouldn't I give to have my brother in my life, in any state?

Our place was only a few blocks from the restaurant, and Sags was back in fifteen minutes. She poked her head into the kitchen to make sure everything was running smoothly, and then sat down next to me at the bar.

She asked Courtney to bring her a beer. 'That sonofabitch Rando beat her up again,' Sags said, furious.

Rando was Gigi's current drug dealer. When she was out of money he'd give her drugs, in exchange for her turning tricks for him. Any reticence on her part would result in a beating.

'I hate that fucking guy,' she said, putting most of the beer away in one long sip.

'Want another?' asked Courtney.

'No,' she said, standing up. 'I don't want to leave Gigi alone too long. She might start helping herself to our stuff.'

'So what? She's cleaned us out before.' After the first time we'd left her alone in our place to sleep it off we'd noticed all of our cash and jewelry was gone. Since then we'd put our valuables away in a safe in my room, so as not to tempt her.

She shook her head. 'You coming?'

'Not yet.' I'd finished my drink and nodded at Courtney to make me another.

'I'm not going to be dragging you into the shower again tonight, am I?'

'No. If I wanted to do that I'd go home to drink. Thanks again for going with me to my folks' house.'

'Any time, roomie.'

I took my time on the martini and then headed home. Gigi was asleep on the couch and Sags' door was closed. I sat on the floor and pulled out my computer and started to write.

SIX

'd been writing since my therapist suggested it as a way to deal with my grief. It helped me relax, and took my mind off of things I didn't want to think about. It also felt like I was making a contribution to society with female-centered porn. Among other things, all of my books included a diagram of the female body in the back, complete with labels.

Panty Raiders of the Lost Ark was my first novel, and I'd been surprised when I'd been able to find a small publishing house for it. They didn't sell millions, and the royalties were almost nil, but they'd actually printed paperback copies of that one, and then of all of my subsequent books.

Raiders was followed by *Fuck, Actually*, and *She's Gotta Have it Again. Coming at Home* had been the most popular, *G-spot Jane* the most recent. I was halfway through the next one, tentatively entitled, *It Rhymes with Dolores*.

I used my own life to fuel the stories, although lately I'd had to call on historical liaisons, as my love life had slowed since Jeb and I broke up. Fortunately I had a wealth of experiences to draw from, good and bad, and as usual I stayed up writing until late, finally turning in after three.

As I was getting into bed I heard the front door open. It wasn't all that surprising that Sags had gone out. As a chef she was on a different schedule than everyone else, often staying up or out until dawn. Normally I'd stay up and talk to her, but I had a stop to make the next morning before going in to the station.

The business card that I'd taken from Sheila Johnson's things was for some kind of community services center. The logo was too faded to read, but a quick online search had revealed a shelter with the same blue and white logo: 'City Community Shelter, helping the homeless since 1995'.

The shelter was located on the north side of the Chicago River, several miles from where Sheila's body had been found, but fairly close to a homeless encampment on Lower Wacker Drive. I drove down to the shelter and parked on the street.

The single story building was old, and nestled between two tall, newer office buildings that probably wished it would go away. I walked through the glass front doors and into a crowded lobby. Next to the door was a resources desk, on top of which was a stack of cards. They were a match to the one I'd found in Sheila Johnson's things.

So far, so good.

I waited in a line, and after a few minutes was in front of a woman behind the counter.

'Can I help you?'

'Yes. I'm looking for information about a woman who might have used your shelter, some time ago.'

'We don't give out information about the people we help.'

'I'm with the police,' I said, pulling out my ID card.

'Doesn't matter,' she said, not looking at it. 'The homeless have a right to privacy too, you know.'

'Her name is Sheila Johnson. Did you know that she's dead?'

'No.' She frowned. 'When did it happen?'

'About two months ago. She died of a drug overdose.'

She nodded, but said, 'That doesn't change anything.'

'Look . . .' I peered at her name tag. 'Debra, they found something on her, something that belonged to my little brother. He disappeared over twenty years ago, and I'm trying to find out what happened to him. Anything you can tell me about Sheila could help.'

She looked at me skeptically.

'Please.' I pulled out my wallet, and opened it to show her. 'This is my brother, Michael, just before he disappeared. This is the first sign of him since we lost him,' I was almost on the verge of tears. Which in this case, seemed to help.

She sighed and turned to her monitor.

'Sheila Johnson, you said?'

I nodded.

She typed the name into her system and scanned through.

'I'm sorry, I don't have any record of a Sheila Johnson. Are you sure she came to this shelter?'

Dammit. 'No. I just have a business card.'

Sheila Johnson may not have used her real name. Or maybe she'd never even been here. 'Thanks,' I mumbled, turning away.

Tunnel Vision 43

'Of course, she could have visited our other location,' Debra said to my back.

'What other location?' I asked, turning around.

'We have another location on the north side, in Ravenswood.'

'Wouldn't you have the same records that they do?' I asked. No reason to drive up there if they were going to tell me the same thing.

'Not necessarily. That facility is just now in the process of moving their paper records to digital. It's possible they worked with her, but her information hasn't made it to the system yet. Particularly if it was some time ago. They digitize in order of recency.'

'OK, thank you.'

I left and drove back up north to the shelter in Ravenswood, where I parked on the street and entered another brick building, this one with a larger lobby, and no lines.

'Hi,' I said, stepping up to the counter. 'I'm looking for information about a woman you may have helped here. She died a short time ago,' I added quickly, before she could tell me they couldn't share information. 'We're trying to track down any members of her family, and I have reason to believe she may have come here at some point.' Based on the reaction of the woman at the first shelter, I thought this story would be more likely to overcome any hesitation to share information.

'What was her name?'

'Sheila Johnson.'

She looked through her screen. 'I'm sorry, we don't have any record of a woman with that name.'

'It could have been as much as twenty years ago. Perhaps there's a paper file?'

She rolled her eyes, but got up and went to the back room.

She was gone for over twenty minutes. As she came back through the door I saw she was carrying a thin folder. She sat back down at her terminal and opened it up.

'We did provide services to a Sheila Johnson, in 2004. It looks like . . . some vaccinations.'

'For what?'

'MMR.'

'MMR?'

'Measles, mumps, rubella.'

'Those sound like childhood vaccina—' *Oh my god . . .* I leaned towards her, gripping the counter tightly.

'Yes, they were for her son. Luke Roberts.'

Luke Roberts? 'Does it have his age?' I said, holding my breath.

'It says here he was five. The MMR booster is for children four through six years of age.' Michael would have only been three that year. I let out a long sigh. For some reason, Sheila Johnson had taken her son to be vaccinated at a homeless shelter.

This was a dead end, it had nothing to do with Michael.

'Is there any other information about her son?' I asked, perfunctorily.

'I thought you said you were interested in Sheila Johnson?' she asked, suspicious.

'He wasn't with her when she died, the police would probably like to let him know what happened.'

'Oh. Well, I don't think I can help you. We only have her coming in one time for this set of vaccinations. As far as I can tell they never stayed here, or took advantage of any other services.'

'Don't you provide shelter for parents with children?'

'Yes, of course. But it says here she was using drugs. One of the conditions of staying here is that people not do drugs on the premises.'

She continued to look through the file, then pulled out a half sheet of paper.

'I do have a copy of Luke Roberts' birth certificate.'

'His birth certificate? Can I see it?'

I reached over and she handed it to me. 'May I make a copy of this?'

'Sure.' She pointed to a machine against the wall.

I made a copy and thanked her and left. When I got to my car I pulled out the faded page I'd taken out of Sheila's box of things at the station.

It was hard to read, but I could make out the outline of a seal in the corner, the same one on the copy I'd just made of Luke Roberts' birth certificate. They looked like the same document, other than this one was legible. It confirmed that Sheila Johnson had been forty-five years old when she died, that Evan Roberts was Luke's father, and possibly Sheila's husband, and that he had lived in Oak Park.

He might know something more about Sheila, something that could lead to Michael.

It was a long shot. If Sheila had been homeless for twenty years, and in care of their son, it meant that Evan Roberts was out of the picture. But it wasn't like I had any other leads.

I looked at my watch. It was nine forty-five. I could be back at the station by ten fifteen, find Roberts' address in a few minutes, in an only slightly illegal use of the department's database, then be back out by quarter to eleven. There were probably more than one Evan Roberts, but I could . . .

Shit. The ten o'clock task force meeting.

SEVEN

I ran to my car and drove as fast as I could back to the station, then took the stairs up to the conference room, arriving ten minutes late.

When I got there the whole team was assembled. Jacobs was sitting in front of her computer. She made a point to look up at the clock but didn't say anything. Bowles scowled at me.

I took a seat next to McCullom. 'Sorry,' I said to the group. He didn't look at me.

Dammit. I'd stood him up again.

'Please continue,' Jacobs said to Renfro.

He was standing up in front of the monitor, his laser pointer focused on a slide with one of the glassine envelopes with the red eagle stamp. 'My CI tells me everyone's calling this new stuff "Red". It's been coming out in dribs and drabs starting about three months ago. Over the last few weeks there's been a lot more of it on the street.'

'This confirms what we believe, that they're ramping up their production,' said Jacobs.

Renfro nodded. 'Yeah, and junkies can't get enough of it. It packs more of a punch than what the cartel is producing. And my CI has seen an uptick in overdose deaths, which seems to correlate with higher usage of this stuff.'

'I think I know why,' said Jacobs. She held up a folder. 'I just got these results from the lab.' Damn, Bowles must have really leaned on them to get results this fast.

'The residue in the Red envelopes found on the dealers tested as fentanyl mixed with xylazine.'

Low whistles came from around the room.

'They're making Philly Dope,' said Renfro. 'Nasty.'

Nasty was right.

Fentanyl was bad enough. One hundred times stronger than heroin, the difference between a normal high and death could be less than two milligrams, basically ten to fifteen grains of table salt. It was also much cheaper than other opioids. Fentanyl is one hundred percent synthetic, meaning it isn't dependent on poppy production.

Tunnel Vision

Relatively simple to manufacture in a lab, fentanyl doesn't require a lot of exotic precursor components, and those it does require can be obtained easily. The precursor chemicals to make it are banned in the US, but not in China, where companies advertise the chemicals on the dark web, along with instructions, and often even an 'ask the scientist' feature that helps work out manufacturing problems. Just about anyone could set up a lab and produce it.

It was no surprise then that since fentanyl had outstripped other opioids in popularity, overdoses in Chicago and the rest of the country had skyrocketed, to the point that fentanyl overdose was now the leading cause of death among US citizens between the ages of eighteen and forty-five. In Chicago alone we had over a thousand fentanyl-related deaths a year.

The problem was huge and growing, with no signs of it leveling off. First responders were now carrying Narcan with them, the brand name for naloxone, a medicine that if administered to someone overdosing on opioids would rapidly reverse the overdose, with no side effects. An added benefit of naloxone was that if mistakenly given to someone not experiencing an opioid overdose, there were no negative consequences. Unfortunately it was still not approved as an OTC drug and required a prescription.

But fentanyl mixed with xylazine, aka Philly Dope, or Tranq Dope, was much worse. Xylazine was a veterinary tranquilizer. Mixed with fentanyl it provided a higher high than fentanyl, and it lasted longer. Unfortunately, unlike fentanyl, it didn't respond to naloxone. People OD'ing on Philly Dope died at a much higher rate than other fentanyl users.

There was something very creepy and horrible about a Philly Dope high. People tripping on it would resemble zombies from *The Walking Dead*. Aimless shuffling, arms straight at the sides, vacant stares, made worse by the fact that when snorted, smoked or injected over time, its use resulted in wounds that often turned necrotic. More than one Philly Dope addict was walking around with large open sores, sometimes exposing bone, or amputated limbs.

'Something else. The lab says the tests of the residue in the bags indicated that the formulations are consistent among the bags at each of the three murder sites. That indicates that whoever's making this is doing quality control, and using some kind of testing equipment.'

Another reason fentanyl was so cheap, and increasingly ubiquitous, is that it can be manufactured anywhere – it doesn't require

48   Wendy Church

elaborate manufacturing facilities. That the drugs in the different packets we'd found on the dead bodies was similar in formulation was interesting, though, and potentially useful. In general, the smaller, crude, more decentralized drug labs were known for variable quality, typically cutting their product with whatever was cheapest at the time, like laxatives, and other, cheaper drugs. But if they were using testing equipment we could use that to find them.

'So, why don't we just find it and shut down their manufacturing?' asked McCullom.

'We'd love to,' said Jacobs. 'But we don't know where it is. And obviously the cartel doesn't either.'

'Aren't there signs?' McCullom asked. 'Explosions? Fires?'

'That's meth. Fentanyl production doesn't carry those risk factors,' said Renfro.

I thought McCullom was on the right track. 'Still, they have to get precursor chemicals and equipment to make it, right?' The narcotics division had found one fentanyl lab in the city earlier in the year by tracking the purchase of pill machines.

Renfro shook his head. 'They're making powder, not pills, so we can't track pill machines. And it takes fifty to a hundred times more heroin to produce the same high as fentanyl, so we're talking tiny amounts. A small lab can produce hundreds of thousands of doses a week. The Narc guys are keeping their eye out for manufacturing sites, but so far they've found nothing.

'The good news is that we might be able to track the purchase and shipment of the equipment they're using to test it. Handheld infrared spectroscopy machines aren't all that common.'

'What about the dealers? Can't we find out from them where they're getting it?' asked McCullom.

'The dealers aren't talking,' Jacobs said, taking over the monitor from Renfro, and putting up a slide of a disjointed body. 'Another dealer was murdered last night.'

'Where?'

'Logan Square, near Armitage and Pulaski.'

'The cartel?' I said.

'Probably. Although this one wasn't in as high profile of an area as the others. They found him in an alley, behind a gas station. And they didn't find any Red on him,' she said, zooming in on the picture to show the glassine envelopes on his torso, all without the red eagle stamp. 'But that probably doesn't mean anything. He could have been selling from both organizations, and just didn't have any Red on him at the time.'

She shook her head. 'The cartel is going to continue to murder people until the dealers stop selling Red.'

'If it's so dangerous, why are the dealers still moving it?' asked Nowak.

Jacobs looked at Renfro, who said, 'Money. The Greenpoint Crew are the only ones making Philly Dope here in any quantity, and dealers can get almost twice as much per bag as the fentanyl the cartel is putting on the streets. At least for now. But even when the cartel ramps up their own production, it will still be cheaper from the Greenpoint Crew – they're not paying to ship it from Mexico, and there are fewer middlemen to pay, particularly if the Crew is doing the distribution to the dealers themselves.'

'So, can't we put some surveillance on the dealers, find out who they're getting it from, and track those guys to the source?' asked McCullom.

'That's our next move,' said Jacobs. 'Right after we build up our understanding of who's in the gang. This is our last meeting before the festival. If you have anything to ask about it, now is the time.'

She waited a whole second. 'Good. I'll expect you all tomorrow in your roles at the designated times in your folders.'

'Dismissed,' Bowles said. 'Everyone but Kaminski.'

When everyone but he and Jacobs had left the room, Bowles closed the door. Turning to me, he said, 'Are we interfering with your personal life, Kaminski?'

'No, I'm sorry, sir. And ma'am.' I turned to her. 'It won't happen again.'

'It better not. We need people who are committed to this task force. Do I need to find someone else?'

'No, sir.'

'Be on time. We meet at ten o'clock every day, unless we're in the field.'

'Yes, sir.' I walked out and made a beeline for McCullom's workstation.

He looked up at me and looked away, rolling his eyes.

'Gavin, I'm really sorry. I have a . . . uh, family thing going on. Can I buy you that coffee, right now? We can talk about our roles for this weekend.'

He smiled. 'Sure.' He stood up. 'We can flesh out our backstory.

I'm thinking that you and I are madly in love, and we can't keep our hands off of each other.'

I laughed. It felt strange, it had been a while since I'd had a reason to laugh. Despite my discomfort with doing field work, I realized I was looking forward to spending the day with him tomorrow.

We left the station to go for a coffee. On our way out we passed Jeb in the lobby, who looked away as we walked by.

My coffee with Gavin turned into an early lunch. He was smart, and funny, and I found myself feeling a little less worried about the surveillance work we'd be doing tomorrow. Afterwards he went back to the station, and I left for my weekly appointment with my therapist.

One of the first things I'd done when I moved back to Chicago was to find a therapist. I knew myself well enough to know that my successful, functional life was one crisis away from dissolving into the guilt-laden wreck I'd been as a kid.

My therapist, Abby, worked out of a small building behind her house in Portage Park, complete with a couch, two chairs, book-shelves, and boxes of Kleenex I never used.

'I found out yesterday that they found Michael's backpack,' I said. 'On a dead woman who was living on the street. There was no sign of him.'

'What did you do when you found out?' she said, after the long pause she always employed after I said anything.

'I got drunk.'

'That's not like you.'

'No.'

She wrote something in her notebook. 'What then?'

'I went back to work.'

She nodded. 'What are you doing on your downtime?'

'Downtime?' As usual, she was asking a question that didn't seem to relate to what I'd just told her. 'You know. Journaling. Like you told me.'

'*Journaling*. Right. You've been prolific,' she said, nodding to her bookshelf, on which I could see all of my titles. 'But when you're not working, or writing, what are you doing?'

'Sleeping, I guess.'

She sighed and put her pen down. 'Do you think there's a possibility that you're keeping busy to avoid your feelings?'

Tunnel Vision

'What do you mean? I feel lots of things.'

'We've talked about you distracting yourself with work, and writing. The journal exercise was intended for you to express yourself.'

'I am expressing myself.'

'Expressing how you *feel*.'

'Why? I'm not drinking, I mean, not to excess, except for that one night. But I'm OK now.'

'Really?' she asked, her eyebrows raised. 'When was your last relationship?' she asked, after another long silence.

'Last year.'

'With Jeb,' she said.

'Yeah.' I shifted in my seat.

'How long did you go out with him?'

'About three months.'

'Three months. And what ended it?'

I didn't know. 'You know, it just, ended.'

'How did it end?' She flipped through her notes. 'You were the one to break it off with him, weren't you?'

'Yeah.'

'Why?'

She waited. When I didn't add anything, she said, 'Tell me about Jeb.'

'We're still working together. He's a friend, I guess.'

After another minute of silence she prompted me. 'Did you like him?'

'Yes.'

'And there was chemistry between you, yes?'

'Yes, surprisingly,' I said, smiling. 'On the surface he was buttoned-up, professional, in control.'

But I'd seen him when he cut loose. And he was completely unlike I expected in bed, inspiring one of my better books, *Jurassic Cock*.

'How many relationships would you say you've had, as an adult?'

'You mean with men? Lots.'

'Relationships, not hook ups.'

'Oh. I don't know,' I said, looking down.

'How long do they usually last, your actual relationships?'

'I don't know,' I said again, starting to feel annoyed.

'So, it lasted three months with Jeb. And then you ended it. Why?'

I shrugged. 'I told you before. I don't know.'

'Would it be fair to say that it was the most time you've spent with one person?'

'Probably.' My longest relationship before him had been a three-day weekend.

'Try to think about why.' She waited, again giving me ample time to think.

I sat there, my mind a blank.

'OK, let's try this. How did you feel when you were with him?'

'I felt good.' Away from the office and his work he was funny, in a deadpan sort of way. And we'd had fun together.

'C'mon, Maude, you can do better than that.'

'I felt . . . it felt . . . real. Like a real thing. Like he really knew me. And wanted to know me.'

'Good. Now tell me what you felt when you broke up with him?'

'Like I had to do it.'

'What made you feel like you had to do it? Think back, to what was going on in your head at the time.'

I closed my eyes and went back to that Sunday morning at his place. He'd brought me coffee in bed, and kissed me on the cheek. And then he just sat there, looking at me, his eyes full and sparkling.

I remembered thinking I couldn't wait to get out of there.

'I felt . . . panicked. I called him the next day and broke up.'

'Did you tell him why?'

'Something about not being ready for a relationship.'

She nodded. 'What do you think it would take you to be ready?'

I was generally very articulate in therapy sessions, and not afraid to talk. I knew myself pretty well, and had no qualms discussing my emotions, and what might be behind them.

But right now my mind was a blank. It had happened a few times before, when something she'd asked or suggested sent my brain into a dark closet, where I had no insight, no thoughts.

After what felt like an hour I shook my head. 'I have no idea.'

'I'm going to give you some homework. Try to spend at least ten minutes a day not working, not writing, not sleeping, and definitely not drinking. By yourself.'

I couldn't imagine doing that. 'I can't do that.'

'Why not?'

'I don't have time.'

That sounded as lame and dishonest as it was.

Tunnel Vision 53

'Maude, if you want to move forward, at some point you're going to have to deal with your emotions surrounding your brother. Yes, you're highly functional. You keep busy. You do important work. But it's masking some real trauma that you haven't fully addressed. And it's going to come up more now, given what you've found out about Michael.'

'What does that mean? What am I supposed to do, to "address" it?'

'It means you need to let yourself feel it. *Really* feel it. Don't distract yourself with work, and writing, to the point where there's no room for your feelings to come out.'

'I did that, when they found his backpack. I ended up passed out in the shower.'

She shook her head. 'Numbing yourself with alcohol isn't feeling it. You need to let your feelings come out.'

'I don't want them to come out.' My strategy had been working perfectly up until they found his backpack.

'That's your choice. But I can tell you that you won't be able to have real relationships until you do.'

'I do have real relationships. Sags and I are best friends.'

'Yes, that's right. And it's good. But you're not emotionally intimate with her. She's not my patient, but from what you've described, you're both distancing yourselves from your childhood guilt by throwing yourselves into your careers. And I don't recall her having relationship success, either.'

That was true, unless we counted the Russian gangster she'd hooked up with last year.

'Why are you doing this? I'm doing fine. I'm fine,' I said, realizing with horror that I was choking up, and might need to use a Kleenex.

She leaned back in her chair. 'You have a big well of feelings in you, Maude. And you're covering it up with activity, hoping it will go away. It won't. You need to let it out. It doesn't have to be in here, but you need to do it. Because if you don't, it will make its own space.'

EIGHT

Gavin picked me up at my place the next morning at noon and drove us to the festival, parking in the designated lot. As we walked toward the entrance he grabbed my hand. 'Need to make it look real,' he said, winking.

We paid and went in, and found our seats in the designated area, a large section of picnic tables and four tops close to the food vendors, spitting distance from Sags' food tent.

She'd gotten there before me to set up her stall, which consisted of a tented space over tables where she prepped her food, and a counter for ordering, paying and serving. The menu was posted on a large chalkboard propped on the counter, in Polish and English, advertising a combo pierogi plate, bigos, borscht, and dessert.

Jacobs' comms team had worked on the promotion for the event, putting together messaging designed to attract the kinds of people that Krol would want to recruit into the gang. Posters had been put up in the key neighborhoods, and flyers had been placed in every business within a mile. Everyone knew about the festival, but they wanted to be sure that people knew if they couldn't afford to go that there would be tickets available.

I'd studied my folder of pictures the night before, including Brajen Krol and his likely lieutenants, some people known to be in the gang, and street toughs known for working this neighborhood. As important as recognizing faces, I knew, was what they'd set up to capture cell phone numbers. Jacobs and Bowles were in the comms vehicle, a beat-up white van parked along one of the side roads near the parking lot. They had already identified a few of the known gang members' phone numbers, that if used anywhere in the vicinity, the FBI's DCS-3000 system would track the numbers it called.

It was an innovative way to go about generating the network information, in addition to gathering evidence to keep them off the streets once we caught them.

Gavin bought us a couple of coffees, and for a while we sat at the table, talking, and surreptitiously watching. So far nothing had come over the mics we had in our ears. The portable KingFish unit

Tunnel Vision 55

that he'd be using once the comms van ID'd our targets fit in the backpack he had over his shoulder. Targets would be communicated to us from the van, sourced either from cell phones identified in the van by the StingRay system, or by Nowak's surveillance. Gavin would then wander close to the identified targets, and capture the cell phone usage with the KingFish.

When he gave me the signal, which was him mugging for the camera, I'd take a picture of him next to our target. The idea was to get the image of the target close to the same time he picked up the cell information. With that we'd be able then to match up faces with specific cell phone use.

It sounded complicated, but really was simple: we'd match cell phones to faces, identify them, and based on the calls among the members, build an organizational chart of the gang.

We were lucky in that the weather, which could change quickly as summer turned to fall, was dry and not too hot. The smell of cooking kielbasa lent an air of outdoor barbeque party to the ambiance, and I'd almost forgotten that we were on an operation, and not on a date, when Jacobs' voice crackled in my ear.

'The man at the Pierogi Pierogi food tent, standing in line. Tall, bald, red jacket. One of Krol's lieutenants.' Jacobs and Bowles were getting their information from Nowak, who was circulating around. She was good, I hadn't noticed her.

Gavin nodded at me and got up. He walked to a food line in front of one of the vendors adjacent to the line with the bald man. Gavin reached into his backpack and pulled out his wallet, at the same time I knew he activated the KingFish tracker. He turned to me and made a funny face and waved, which was my signal to take a picture of him, one that captured the bald man in the background.

He waited in line and then ordered food. Not too much, given that we'd have to pace ourselves, then brought the trays back to our seats.

'That wasn't so hard, was it?' he said, stuffing a pierogi in his mouth.

'No,' I said. There were worse things than sitting around in the sun all day and eating pierogis. I could get used to surveillance work.

I looked over at Sags' food tent. Long lines were forming at all of the food vendors except for hers. I wasn't all that surprised. The other vendors had been coming here for years, some with associated

56 Wendy Church

restaurants that were well known to the community. She was the newcomer.

Eventually the lines got too long at the other tents, and a few hungry and impatient people made their way to hers. I watched a group of the men who got their food from her walk back to their table. Their eyes lit up once they started to eat.

It didn't take long for word to get out, and soon the lines in front of Sags' tent were longer than the rest.

It was just her, Renfro and Declan working the tent. Declan was one of the city's best pastry chefs and had worked at Louie's for years. Sags had managed to keep her working at Saga by letting her use the restaurant's sizable kitchen to start her own side business.

As it got busier Sags started barking orders at Renfro, who was collecting money and tickets, occasionally reacting to her commands to fill up a chafing dish, or restock service items. I was a little surprised to see him following her instructions. To his credit he seemed to be getting into it, and doing what needed to happen to keep things moving.

Declan was putting the finishing touches on the dessert that accompanied each combo plate, and Sags was doing everything else. They were working like a well-oiled machine, and turning out the combination meals at a fast pace.

I envied how busy she was. Nowak's surveillance must not be picking up much, as Gavin and I had little to do for most of the afternoon. I didn't mind, though, we never seemed to run out of things to talk about. By this point it should have felt like the longest date from history, but I was enjoying his company, not to mention I wasn't getting tired of looking at him.

I was surprised again when the radio crackled on. 'Five men, in a group, walking towards you from the northeast. The man in front is wearing a red jacket and gray sweatpants.'

A group of men walking in a pack strode into the tabled area from the stages, cutting to the front of one of the food lines and ordering plates. Once they got their trays they moved like a dirty amoeba to one of the tables near us. They sat down, and when one of them pulled out his phone, Gavin reached into his backpack to turn on the KingFish. He smiled and made a face, my signal to take another picture of him, getting the men in the background.

The hours dragged on. Occasionally Gavin would leave briefly to get us snacks, or beer. I'd been given strict instructions not to

Tunnel Vision

leave the table, and I envied him the simple pleasure of getting up to walk somewhere. I now understood what cops meant when they said that policing is twenty-three hours of mind-numbing tedium, interrupted by a few minutes of absolute terror. Gavin wasn't mind-numbingly boring, but I was excited when dinner time came, and I'd finally get the chance to try some of Sags' food.

Based on Krol's predilections, Sags was offering a pierogi plate combo, and bigos, a traditional Polish hunter's stew. One of the most popular dishes in Polish cuisine, bigos had countless variations, the only two 'must have' ingredients sauerkraut and meat, preferably dark cuts of meat, and especially game.

Sags' version was over the top, while still presenting the traditional comfort element. She'd made it with smoked kielbasa, venison, porcini mushrooms, prunes and onions. Spicy, sweet, and sour, it smelled like she'd been cooking it for days.

Alongside the pierogis and stew was red and white borscht, and bread. In addition to making the dessert, Sags had asked Declan to bake authentic Polish bread. We had our choice of rye, or chleb pszenny, simple white bread. The meal was topped off by Declan's Kremówka dessert, basically custard cream sandwiched with thin puff pastry.

Sags was in her element. She loved cooking, and I'd seen her like this before. Eyes sparkling, pupils dilated almost to the point of blocking out her grey irises, cheeks flushed. She was having a blast.

Gavin brought our trays back to the table and we dug in. The half-moon-shaped pierogis were stuffed, each one scrimped along the edges and then boiled. She'd made four different fillings: minced venison, onion and mint; sauerkraut and mushrooms; potato and cheese; and roast duck with apples, mushrooms and minced pork. As an added bonus, for the roast duck pierogi she'd employed her molecular gastronomy magic.

One of the most famous and fantastical creations of early molecular gastronomy endeavors was 'disappearing raviolis', originally made famous at El Bulli in the Catalonia region of Spain. Instead of regular pasta folded around a filling, the shell in disappearing raviolis was a transparent, pasta-like edible disc made out of potato starch and soy lecithin. When eaten the shell instantly disappeared in your mouth, resulting in a unique sensation of having immediate and surprising access to the filling. Which had better be good.

Of course Sags' was fantastic. I heard delighted murmurs of

58   Wendy Church

surprise from the tables around us, as people with her trays were trying the 'Disappearing Pierogi'.

She'd also used her special techniques for the borscht, creating translucent noodles out of red beets that nestled in a white soup base, the notion that it reflected the red and white of the Polish flag. I grew up with authentic Polish food, and Sags' ability to match the flavor memory was uncanny. We hadn't seen Brajen Krol yet, but word would get around, and I'd be shocked if he didn't make a point to try it.

Gavin and I finished our food and continued our fake date. By seven thirty it was starting to get dark. The plan had been to stay and collect images and cell phone numbers until the start of Warsaw Station's performance. We had at least an hour and a half to go.

'I'll be right back,' I said to Gavin, standing up.

'What are you doing?' he asked, frowning. 'You're supposed to stay here.'

'I'll just be a second,' I said. 'Nature calls.'

I headed towards the women's bathrooms. By this time of day there was a sizable line. I'd waited too long, I realized. The coffees and beer had gone right through me.

The line moved at glacial speed. I was one person away from relief when my radio crackled.

It was Bowles. 'McCullom, Kaminski, the table next to you. Three men just brought food over. Get images and cell capture, Kaminski see what you can pick up from the conversation.'

Shit. I looked behind me. The line was growing longer, and there was just one more person in front of me. And there was no way I could wait another thirty minutes.

Finally the last stall was free and I went as fast as I could, getting frowns as I left the bathroom without washing my hands.

When I got back to our table Gavin was shaking his head. 'That was a big mistake.'

'I couldn't help it. By the way, how have you managed to sit here all day and not need the bathroom?'

'First rule of stakeouts: don't drink anything.' He moved his eyes quickly downward, and I could see small puddles of coffee and beer on the ground next to him.

That would've been nice to know beforehand.

'They wanted you to pick up a conversation happening over there,' he said, nodding his head slightly at the table next to us that

Tunnel Vision 59

Bowles had designated. The men had finished their food and were getting up. I recognized one of them from a picture in our folders.

'Can we do it now?'

He shook his head. 'Too late,' he said.

Jacobs wasn't going to be happy about this.

'Maude?'

I heard a familiar voice and turned around. *Oh, no.*

'Mom?' She was standing next to my dad near the entrance to the food area.

She broke into a huge smile and waved, then walked over to our table, taking a seat next to me. Gavin looked at me in barely disguised horror.

'*Mom*,' I whispered under my breath. 'You can't be here.'

'What are you talking about? Isn't that your friend, cooking?' She pointed to Sags' tent, and waved. Sags looked at me and gave her a quick wave back. 'Look,' she said, reaching into her purse. 'I have tickets, from Father Pavel.'

'Mom,' I said, looking around. 'Please, you have to leave.' I grabbed her arm and started to stand up. She pulled away from me. 'I'm not going anywhere until I try the food.'

I looked at Gavin, who shrugged. I let go of her and she and my dad went up to Sagarine's tent.

'I think it's better to just let them eat, then leave. It will be worse if you create a scene,' he said.

They came back to the table with food trays, and chatted and ate, like it was a party. My mom pronounced Sags' food 'almost authentic'.

They took forever to finish. When they finally left I heard the radio crackle.

'Kaminski, what the hell?' Bowles yelled in my ear.

Nice of Nowak to rat me out. 'I'm sorry, sir, I didn't know they were coming.'

He clicked off without answering.

'How bad is it?' I asked.

Gavin shook his head. 'I guess we'll find out tomorrow.'

By nine thirty I was dragging. The event was winding down, and we'd only been instructed to capture and photograph people three times the entire day, including the one I'd missed. I hoped Nowak had better luck.

At ten Jacobs called it. We walked back to Gavin's car and he drove me to my apartment. To my surprise he didn't get out.

'Thanks for the date,' he joked. 'I'd love to stay and chat, but I've got to get all of this information entered in.'

'Seriously? You're going back to work?'

'Yeah. I've worked with Jacobs before. She's a ball buster, that one. And buster of lady parts, too,' he added. 'Wants everything yesterday. Climbing the ladder, it looks.' He leaned over and kissed me on the cheek.

'K. See you tomorrow.'

He drove off and I went into my apartment and pulled out my computer. I transcribed the few notes I'd taken into the task force's Google doc. Once I did that I cracked open a beer.

Sitting around all day made me more tired than I expected, and I fell asleep on the couch. I woke up to Sags' key in the door. It was three in the morning.

She looked tired but happy. It never ceased to amaze me how little sleep she needed.

'What'd you think?' she asked, settling on the couch after grabbing her own beer.

'I haven't talked with anyone else, but from our end it looked like a bust. We only saw a few of the people we were targeting. But your food was fantastic,' I said, leaving out the parts about my screw-up going to the bathroom, and my parents showing up.

'Yeah, I was pretty happy with it. Who knows? Maybe I'll open up a Polish restaurant,' she said, taking a sip.

'How many days are you going to cook there?'

'Smith said I was on the hook all four days of the festival. I don't mind, it worked out great for me. Normally, I'd need to do my own advertising, get the permits, all that shit. But the FBI took care of all of that, all I had to do was cook and serve. And they're reimbursing for the food.' Her idea of heaven.

We sat there for a while, her obviously elated, and me anxious about the dressing-down I was going get in the morning from Bowles. I finished my beer and stood up to go to bed when I heard sirens.

Loud, and getting louder.

I went to the window. As I pulled the curtain back my phone rang. It was Smith.

'Hey, what's up?'

'There's been another death,' he said.

'Yeah, we can hear the sirens.'

'It's in Portage Park, down the street from your apartment.'

NINE

I put on my shoes and went outside, walking towards flashing lights from the gathering police cars. They were setting up police tape around the entrance to an alley less than a hundred yards from my apartment.

I showed my ID and walked towards a ring of uniforms and two men in suits who were standing just outside of the taped cordon, looking at a body that lay in the center of it.

One of them looked at a uniform and barked, 'I thought I told you to keep the public— Oh, hi Kaminski.'

'Hey, Carter,' I said.

Detective John Carter was from our 16th Precinct. I'd worked with him and his partner, Sergeant Stan Nowicki, a few times over the years on gang-related operations.

'This looks familiar,' I said, looking over at the body. 'You mind?' I asked.

Carter shook his head and stepped aside to let me next to the tape so I could get a closer look at the body. Like the others, the limbs were separated from the torso, and several glassine envelopes were laying on the stomach. Unlike the previous ones, the bags weren't stamped with the red eagle.

'Were there any other drugs found with the body?' I asked.

Carter shook his head. 'Is that important?'

I'd worked with him before. He was smart, and curious, and didn't accept the easy answer if there was something else that made more sense.

'I don't know. Maybe.'

I stepped away from the tape and wandered back out of the alley.

When I got home I went to bed but had trouble getting to sleep. Why would the cartel kill one of their own dealers? Was the dealer moving different products, and all he had on him at the time was the cartel's drugs?

It felt like I'd been asleep all of five minutes when my alarm went off in the morning. I managed to take a shower and get out the door in time to make it to the task force conference room by

62 Wendy Church

ten, bleary-eyed again, but on time, just before Jacobs and Bowles walked in.

Jacobs wasted no time. 'Brajen Krol didn't show up,' she snapped. She turned to Gavin. 'Did you get anything?'

'Fifteen cell phones, just a few matches to our target list.'

She swore under her breath. It was an expensive operation to run, and after one day there was little to show for it.

'All right. Same deal today. We're going until it closes tonight. Officer Nowak, I want you to replace Ms Kaminski as Mr McCullom's date,' she said, not looking at me.

'Dismissed,' said Bowles. 'All except you, Kaminski.'

Everyone shuffled out, Gavin giving me a sympathetic look as he went out the door.

'What the hell, Kaminski?' said Bowles. 'I thought you wanted to work on this task force?'

I stayed silent. I knew from experience it wouldn't matter what I said. He needed to get it out of his system.

'You left your post in the middle of the operation,' he said, frowning. 'I thought we were clear, that you weren't supposed to leave your seat. Is that your idea of focus?' He was ramping up now, his voice louder. 'And in what universe did you think it was a good idea to invite your *mother* to an undercover operation?'

'I didn't invite her, sir, she just showed up. She goes every year,' I said, immediately regretting it.

He took a step towards me, looking down, using his heavily muscled, six-foot-something frame to intimidate. 'The reason you're on this team is because SSA Jacobs thinks we might need your network analysis bullshit. Don't think we haven't noticed you showing up late, hungover, and skipping out of the station during the day to do whatever.' He looked me up and down. 'You look like shit, by the way. Up all night, again?' He didn't wait for my answer. 'I don't know how the rest of the Chicago PD handles their contractors, but in my world, you're either on the team or you're off. The only reason we're not kicking you off the task force is because we literally have no one else who can do your technical shit. And because Deputy Chief Jefferson tells me you're a rock star.

'I don't see it. I need you to get your head in the game, Kaminski. And no more field work for you, even something as simple as this.' He said 'this' with as much disdain as he could stuff into it. 'Distracted people who don't follow orders put everyone in danger.'

Tunnel Vision 63

It wasn't like I'd begged them to go into the field, and I knew it was ultimately their responsibility for putting me into that situation with no training. But it wouldn't do any good to say anything. Jacobs was standing next to him, staring daggers at me. He stepped back, I thought to give her a chance to weigh in, but I was saved from further ass chewing when the chief's assistant opened the door and poked his head in.

'Ms Kaminski? The Deputy Chief wants to see you.'

Saved by the bell. Both of them glowered at me as I walked out.

'Close the door, Ms Kaminski,' said Jefferson when I entered his office.

Uh-oh. He didn't look happy.

'I've been talking with Commander Bowles. He tells me you're not pulling your weight on the task force.'

I started to say something but he put his hand up.

'I don't want to hear it. Commander Bowles is complaining to me that you're showing up hung over, coming in late. And he said you disappeared in the middle of a surveillance operation?'

'Disappeared' made it sound like I'd taken off for happy hour, instead of leaving for ten minutes one time to go to the bathroom.

'You're not a field agent, and I blame Commander Bowles for putting you into a position for which you weren't trained. But deviating in the slightest bit from your instructions is a safety issue. I also know you're going through a tough time with your family right now. But if you don't pull it together I'm going to have to remove you from the task force.'

'Yes sir, I know, it won't happen again.'

'Make sure that it doesn't. I know you're not an employee, but in this case it doesn't matter.'

'Got it. Thanks, sir,' I said, leaving his office.

I'd *told* them I didn't want to be in the field. And the fact that the team hadn't been successful on the first day wasn't my fault. This was Bowles and Jacobs needing to blame someone for their shitty results.

The positive side of being pulled off of the surveillance part of the operation was that I now had more time to track down Sheila Johnson's husband. I went to my desk and looked up the results of my database search on Evan Roberts.

There were several Evan Robertses living in Oak Park. Three were in their forties. Only one of those had an 872 area code.

64 Wendy Church

Hopefully he would be the Evan Roberts who'd had a child with Sheila. I looked up his address, then closed up my computer and left the station.

Approximately fifty suburbs ringed Chicago on the north, west and south sides, linked to the city by two-level Metra train cars. Oak Park was directly west, and getting there by car at this time of day and in this direction took me just over fifteen minutes.

I parked on a quiet, tree-lined street. 'No Parking between 8 a.m. and 10 a.m.' signs were posted at regular intervals on decorative light poles.

All of the houses had large yards between the street and their covered porches. Evan Roberts' house was no exception, and like a few others had a set of child-sized temporary soccer goal nets set up on the front lawn.

I walked to the porch and hit the doorbell. I heard footsteps and a woman answered the door.

She was in her forties, pretty, casually dressed but with earrings and a necklace that didn't look cheap. Behind her was a trail of toys and clothes.

'Yes?' she said, smiling.

'Hi, I'm looking for Evan Roberts.'

'Can I ask who's calling?'

'I'm Maude Kaminski, I work with the Chicago PD.' She frowned, and I pulled out my ID card, adding quickly, 'He's not in any trouble. It's about a missing person. We think he might have some information.'

'Oh. OK. He's in the back. Would you like to come in?'

'Sure, thanks.'

I stepped inside and waited in the foyer while she left to get him. Sounds of cartoons and something like a truck horn came from upstairs, accompanied by young voices, at least two of them.

A few moments later a man came down the hallway.

'Evan Roberts?' I asked.

He nodded.

'May I speak to you a moment?'

'What's this about, Miss—'

'Kaminski. Maude Kaminski.'

'My wife said you think I might have information about a missing person? Who is it?'

'It's, uh, a bit complicated. Did you know a Sheila Johnson?'

Tunnel Vision 65

At the mention of her name he said, 'Let's talk outside,' reaching around me to open the door and ushering me outside to the porch. He closed the door softly behind him.

'What is it you want?' he said, less friendly.

'So, you did know Sheila Johnson?'

'Yes.'

'I'm sorry to tell you this, but she was found dead.'

He didn't seem too surprised by that. 'When?'

'About two months ago. They found her in the tent city, on Taylor.'

'Drug overdose?'

'Yes.'

He nodded.

'Uh, I'm guessing your wife doesn't know about her?'

'She knows. We just don't talk about it. It was a previous life.' He stared at the ground. 'So, there is no missing person?'

'Actually, there is. It relates to your son, Luke.'

He looked up, his face instantly transformed into a grimace.

'My son died, twenty-two years ago, Miss Kaminski.'

'Would you mind telling me what happened?'

'Why? What's the point of dredging this up?' He stood up. 'I think you should leave.'

'Mr Roberts, there really is a missing person. It's my brother, Michael. He disappeared twenty years ago. There's some indication that he might have known Sheila. We never knew what happened to him.'

Roberts didn't say anything, but his hand that was reaching for the door dropped back down to his side.

'You know the pain of losing a child. Imagine losing a child, and never knowing what happened to him?'

'I don't see how this will help,' he said, a little less harsh.

'Please, this is the first sign of my brother we've had in twenty years. Anything we can uncover about Sheila Johnson might help us find out what happened to him. Is there anything you can tell me about her? What was she like?'

He sighed and sat back down. 'Sheila was one of the most amazing people I've ever known. She was very smart, you know, extremely capable, but also really warm.'

It didn't surprise me that she had once been very capable. She would have had to have something going for her, to last on the street for as long as she did.

'She was working as a brand manager for McDonald's. I met her at a fundraising event, and I fell in love with her at first sight. We were married in 1990. Three years later we had a son, Luke.' He reached into his back pocket and produced his wallet. From inside, behind a stack of other cards, he pulled out a picture.

He looked at it a moment, then showed it to me. It was Sheila, at the beach. In it she looked a lot like she did in the picture I'd found in the backpack, healthy and happy. But in this one she was with Evan, and she was holding hands with a toddler. Two or three years old, blond and blue-eyed.

'We were so happy. We'd been trying for years to have him. We'd almost given up.'

He went silent, remembering.

'What happened?' I asked gently.

'They were in a car accident. A bad one. They were rammed in the side by a drunk teenager. Sheila broke both of her legs.' He took a shallow breath. 'Luke's baby seat was on the side of the impact. He died.'

He put the picture back in his wallet.

'When was this?'

'October fifteenth, 1996,' he said, without hesitation.

'1996?' I said, frowning.

He looked at me sharply. 'You don't forget the day you lose your child.'

So who was the boy Sheila took in to be vaccinated? Had Roberts got the date wrong?

I doubted it. He was right. You didn't forget the day you lost someone.

'Did you and Sheila have any other children?'

'No. I loved her, and I wanted to try again . . .' He trailed off.

'But . . .?'

'She'd broken both of her femurs in the accident, and had structural damage to her face. She underwent five surgeries in five weeks. They gave her fentanyl for the pain.'

I could see where this was going.

'She became addicted. Between the physical pain and losing Luke, she never recovered. I didn't realize it at first, and neither did the doctor. When he stopped filling her prescriptions for it she went to other doctors. By the time we finally figured out what she was doing, she was hooked. When the doctors stopped writing her prescriptions she started buying it on the street.

Tunnel Vision   67

'After she OD'd the second time we got her in to rehab. She left before she completed it.'

'When was the last time you saw her?'

'March, 1998. She'd OD'd again, and almost died. At that point I always kept naloxone in the house. I took her straight back to rehab. They told me she just walked out one night. She never came home.'

This was horrible. I didn't know what to say.

'But I think I might have seen her again. Once, on the street. North of the river, getting a coffee before a meeting. I thought I saw her coming out of a building next door. Some kind of homeless services, I think.'

'When was this?'

He looked up, thinking. 'Later that year. It was cold, but not freezing. Fall, I think.'

'Did she have anyone with her? A little boy?' I held my breath.

'A little boy? No. As far as I could tell she was alone. But like I said, I'm not one hundred percent sure it was her.'

I had nothing more to ask him. And he looked wrecked. We sat in silence for a few moments. Then he seemed to snap out of it.

'Is there anything else?' he said, standing up again.

'I just have one more question. Was your son vaccinated?' I had to be sure.

'Vaccinated?'

'Yes, against the standard childhood diseases. Like measles.'

'Of course he was.'

'Do you remember when you took him for that, or where?'

'No. Sheila took care of all of that.'

My brain was going in several different directions.

'Is that all, Miss Kaminski?'

'Yes, thank you for your time. And, I'm sorry.'

He shook his head. 'I have a new life now. Please, don't come back.' He turned and walked into his house.

I went home, thinking so hard I barely noticed when I pulled in front of our apartment. I grabbed a beer out of the refrigerator and sat on the couch.

I was still up when Sags came home after midnight.

'Where were you today?' she asked.

'I got kicked off of the surveillance team. Fine with me. It's not my thing. How'd it go at the festival?'

'I don't know. I was busy, that's all I know. They don't share the details of what they're doing with me. What have you been up to?'

I blew out a big puff of air. 'Sheila Johnson, the junkie they found with Michael's backpack? Before she was living on the street she'd been married, living in Oak Park. I talked to her former husband today. They had a son, Luke, who was killed in a car accident.'

'And this is important, how?'

'Sheila Johnson had Luke vaccinated in 2004. Eight years after he died.'

TEN

I woke early the next morning, my mind going a hundred miles an hour. I'd sat up most of the night before, long after Sags went to bed, thinking about Sheila Johnson.

Michael had disappeared in the Pedway. Had Sheila Johnson been the one to take him?

I went into Sags' room and over to her bed.

'C'mon, let's go,' I said, pulling on one of her shoulders.

'Where are we going?' she mumbled, looking at the clock. '*Jesus*, Maude, do you see what time it is? I have to be back at the festival in three hours. Let me sleep,' she said, turning over.

I threw the covers back. 'You asked me what you could do to help. I need you to come with me.'

'Where are we going?'

'To the Pedway.'

'*Shopping*? Seriously?'

'No. C'mon,' I said, dragging the covers on to the floor.

'Do I at least have time to take a shower?'

'A quick one,' I said, walking out of her room.

Once we were in the car driving downtown I shared my idea with Sags. She was in a better mood now that I'd gotten her a cup of coffee.

'Let me see if I have this straight,' she said. 'Sheila Johnson, the woman who was living on the street and died of a fentanyl overdose, had a child, a boy. She'd lost him tragically when he was three. Until then, she was a healthy, happy person, living in the suburbs, working a demanding job and managing a household. After her son died she fell apart, started using, got addicted, and ended up on the streets. She sees a boy – your brother – that resembles her dead son, and kidnaps him? That's your theory?'

It had made sense in my mind. Now that she was saying it out loud I wasn't so sure.

'She took a child about Michael's age in for vaccinations. And we know it wasn't her own son.'

She looked at me, eyebrows up.

'Think about it. She's destroyed at the death of her son. So much so that it wrecks her entire life. We've seen what opioid addiction does to people. What if she wasn't in her right mind? What if she saw Michael, and thought, *That's my boy*? They both looked a lot alike when they were kids.'

'That's a stretch.'

'Do you have a better explanation?'

'Not at the moment. Maybe after I get more than two hours of sleep I will have. In any case, what's the point of the trip to the Pedway?'

'The point is I need to see for myself, is it even possible that a woman could have taken Michael in broad daylight, and gotten away without anyone seeing her?'

We drove the rest of the way in silence. I pulled into a self parking lot on Wells and we walked to one of the entrances.

I'd avoided the Pedway since the day that we lost Michael. But I felt like I had to see where he'd gone missing. Did it even make sense that someone could have kidnapped him here? Was it possible that a homeless addict could whisk him away with no one noticing, and then disappear?

As we walked down the first flight of stairs I felt my investigatory resolve draining away. The Pedway was a five-mile underground system that connected roughly forty blocks in Chicago's central business district. Access points from dozens of stores and hotels allow people to walk between them, and shop in the winter months unimpeded by the weather. The Pedway itself contained its own shops and restaurants, its multileveled corridors a labyrinthine structure of hallways, stairwells and escalators.

The atmosphere of each section of the system could be starkly different, as it was the responsibility of the adjacent businesses to decorate their portion of the hallways as they saw fit. Accordingly, some of the hallways were well lit, clean and glitzy, some even had stained glass windows built into the walls. Others were bleak, with peeling gray paint on the walls and exposed pipes. Wide, open, banistered stairs that led down half-levels were juxtaposed with narrow, closed-in stairwells that wound down several floors.

I gripped the handrail tightly as we made our way to the second level, little waves of nausea washing over me as we moved lower into the system. When we reached the next floor we walked down a yellow tiled walkway to where the clothing store had been.

Tunnel Vision 71

'This is where we lost him,' I said, looking up at the sign, choking back bile. The clothing store was gone, replaced by a gift shop.

We went into the shop and I walked the perimeter. The original store was gone, but from what I could remember they'd done little to alter the structure. There were no doors or exits, at least none open to the public. We walked back out and continued down the hallway.

'How many levels is this thing?' Sags asked, as we moved down yet another set of stairs.

'I don't remember,' I said through gritted teeth.

At the bottom of the stairs was another line of shops and restaurants, with a set of wide stairs in the center of them leading up.

I walked up the stairs, Sags trailing me. 'Jesus, I can see how you could lose someone in here,' she said, looking around.

The stairs stopped at a large opening, with numerous branches leading to several doors, an escalator going down, and three long hallways, two of which contained more stores and restaurants, and one with a flashing green 'Exit' sign on the wall.

She pointed to a sign at the top of the escalator. 'That one leads to the Metra train station.'

So there it was. A short walk from the store where Michael had been taken, someone could go down a short stairwell, up another set of stairs and then down an escalator to the train station, where she could be just about anywhere in the city within minutes.

I nodded. 'Let's go back. I'm done.'

I'd done what I came here to do; establish whether or not it was even possible that a drug addict could kidnap a child and escape easily. She definitely could have.

Evan Roberts had said Sheila had once been a resourceful, competent woman. If anything could bring that aspect of her back, it would be seeing a boy who she thought was her son.

'Do you want to go down to the tracks?' Sags said, heading to the escalator.

I shook my head and staggered to the wall. She rushed over and put her arm around my waist as I slid down to the floor.

The blood was pounding in my ears and I felt like I was going to vomit. Sags helped me up, letting me lean on her as we walked towards the exit hallway. As we made our way down the hallway I felt myself walking faster, and eventually I pulled away from her, fast-walking, and then running, slowing down at each intersection, frantically looking up and down the hallways for anything that resembled an exit that would get me to the surface.

After what seemed like hours there was another exit sign at the bottom of a set of stairs. I took the stairs two at a time. A few feet away from the top were glass double doors. I rammed myself through them and staggered out on to the cement sidewalk.

I leaned over, hands on my knees, hyperventilating. Sags put her hand on my shoulder and I shrugged it away. 'I'll be fine,' I said.

I should have known better than to go in there. I couldn't stand to be in an underground L station for one minute. What was I thinking, going into the Pedway?

Sags drove us home. I sat in the passenger side with my head out the window, still gulping fresh air. I was feeling better, and had satisfied myself that it was at least possible that Sheila Johnson could have taken Michael in the Pedway.

When we got back to the apartment she changed clothes and headed off to the festival. I went to bed.

By the time I woke up it was late afternoon. I spent the rest of the day writing. Abby had said I needed to stop distracting myself, but I found it immensely calming, and uplifting, to write. And it took my mind off Michael and the Pedway.

Monday was more of the same. I didn't bother going in to the station, Jacobs had cancelled the Monday meeting, and there was nothing for me to do until they had the cell phone data. I spent the day working on *It Rhymes with Delores*.

I was still up writing when Sags came in after two a.m.

'You're late. I thought the festival ended at ten?' I said.

'It did. I had to stop by the restaurant on the way home,' she said, dropping her bag in her room and joining me on the couch.

'How did it go?' I asked.

'Fine. Good, I sold lots of food,' she said.

'How was Renfro?'

'Not bad. For someone who's never worked in food service he was surprisingly helpful.'

I had a hard time imagining Renfro following directions, but who knows, maybe he'd found his true calling.

'There was some kind of incident at the festival.'

'What do you mean? What kind of incident?'

'Sirens, and police cars.'

'What? Where?' I said, pulling out my phone, dialing Gavin.
'On the street, not in the festival itself. Close by, I think, though.'
Gavin picked up on the first ring. 'Yeah,' he said, sounding sleepy.
'Did something happen at the festival?'
'Yeah. Nowak's been shot.'

ELEVEN

Everyone on the team was in the conference room early. Jacobs and Bowles came in together again right at ten.

'First, everyone, Officer Nowak just got out of surgery, and they've told us they believe she will be OK. They'll keep her at least one more night for observation, but she may come home as early as tomorrow.'

I heard sighs of relief from around the room.

'What happened?' I asked.

'She was following Brajen Krol. They shot her.'

'They shot her? Why? Did they know she was trailing them?'

'We don't know. It was at the end of the day, when they were leaving. As soon as she's out of surgery we'll get more details.'

'Was anyone else hurt?'

'No. It was outside of the festival grounds. They were a block away from the center.'

'What was she doing outside of the festival grounds?' I asked.

I'd been happy they'd taken me off the surveillance part of the operation, but it didn't seem fair that I'd left my post for ten minutes and got canned, and Nowak had left the whole place and gotten herself shot. Not to mention that she was supposed to be taking my place, sitting with Gavin.

'I don't—' started Jacobs.

'Officer Nowak is an experienced undercover officer, Kaminski,' interrupted Bowles. 'If she was out there she had a damn good reason. We'll be getting a full report from her when she wakes up.'

Jacobs seemed eager to change the subject. 'It goes without saying that them taking a shot at one of us ramps up the urgency. But I'm happy to share that we hit the jackpot these last few days. Brajen Krol was there, along with most of our recruit targets. Before she was shot, Officer Nowak was able to take a lot of photos, including many of the people in our potential recruit files. We also have some good images from others of you. Nice work, Mr McCullom, Detective Renfro.' She didn't mention me, but I was OK with that. My time to shine was coming up.

Tunnel Vision

'Ms Kaminski, how long before you have the network map of the gang? We know who is at the top, what we're looking for in particular is his command structure, who among Brajen Krol and his lieutenants are communicating directly with the rank and file, and who are the most active among those.'

This was pretty standard gang rollup procedure. Identify as many people as possible in the gang, determine who interacts with who, then bring in the lower level members, the ones actually doing the criminal activity. Get one or more of them to snitch, 'flip', on whoever they reported to, then bring that guy in and pressure him. Rinse and repeat, until one of them linked directly to Brajen Krol gave him up.

'Once I get the data, I can have something within a few hours, ma'am.'

'Oh.' She seemed surprised, and not displeased. She looked at Gavin.

'I've been putting in the data as we go. I'll need to get the rest of it from the van team from yesterday, but it should be ready to go by later this morning.'

Jacobs looked at me, raising her eyebrows. 'I assume you can get to work on it right away, Ms Kaminski? No pressing engagements this afternoon?' she asked sarcastically.

'No, ma'am. I'll have it by the end of the day.'

'Good. As soon as we have that we can get going on the next phase.' She pulled out a stack of folders, and handed them to Renfro to pass out.

'Here's what we're doing next.'

I flipped through the thick folder. It was the detailed operational plan for the next phase. Jacobs must never sleep.

'There are two parts to this phase. The first is tracking their money. Detective Renfro's CIs have given us an estimate of how much product they're moving, so we have a rough idea of how much money is involved. It's a lot, and they need a way to launder it. Mr McCullom will be digging into Krol's and the other leaders' finances.

'The other objective is to find the manufacturing site. Now that we have an idea of who's in the gang, we can start trailing them back to where they're making it. We're setting up an undercover operation at one of the encampments locations where they're known to be distributing Red.'

'Why don't we just put cars at the sites, and watch for them?' asked Gavin.

I saw nods of agreement. Surveillance cars seemed easier and safer than putting someone out on the street.

'Cars sitting around these sites are suspicious. There's not a lot going on at the camps, and not many people who aren't homeless, addicts or dealers. Not to mention that we don't have the manpower to do round-the-clock surveillance of multiple sites. These –' she pointed to a map on the monitor, with several red markers – 'are where Detective Renfro's CIs have told us they're moving the most Red. We'll insert just one person at the most favorable site, to blend in with the people that are living there. It was going to be Officer Nowak, but I'm in the process of looking for someone to replace her.'

'I'll do it,' said Renfro. He'd always wanted to work undercover. *Glamour boy.*

Jacobs shook her head. 'We need a female. Single men are suspicious. In the meantime, you all have your assignments. Familiarize yourself with the material in the folders by the time we meet tomorrow.'

She dismissed us and I went to my cubicle to wait for Gavin's data. Just before eleven his spreadsheet appeared in my inbox.

I'd given him very specific instructions for formatting the data file. Looking it over I saw that he'd followed them to the letter, the names, roles, and cell numbers of each recruit and gang member in appropriate columns and rows. I fired up my computer and inputted the data into the SNA software.

Social network analysis, originally, was an extensively time-consuming and difficult mathematical challenge. And while the development of user-friendly SNA software allowed people familiar with data science to create graphical depictions of social networks, it took a fair amount of skill and experience to know how to format the data, structure the graphics, and interpret results in meaningful ways. There were still only a few SNA graduate programs in the country, and I was one of a handful of people with experience in applying it to law enforcement.

Within an hour I had a draft of the gang's relational network, including a visual depiction of how people were connected to each other, the direction of the connections – who contacted who – and how strong the connections were; i.e., how many times calls were made between various people.

The data we had included hundreds of calls, and the initial diagram created by the software looked like a hairball. I spent the next hour removing spurious data points, adding names where we had them, and coding each person in the network by color: purple for leaders, blue for known members, green for potential recruits, and red for unknown. I reoriented the diagram so that the identified leaders were at the top, and the lowest level gang members and potential recruits at the bottom.

By the time I was done there was a clear picture of how the gang was structured, at least as far as we knew. At the top was Brajen Krol. There were many connections between him and four men, three of whom we'd already identified that he'd brought with him from Brooklyn. His lieutenants.

Already this was proving useful; he'd picked up an additional lieutenant that we didn't know about. Who, by the looks of things, was as important to him as the others.

Maybe more importantly, the analysis indicated that there were no connections directly between Krol or his lieutenants and the low-level gang members that were working the streets. Instead, the lower level members were connected to a set of middlemen. Unlike most of the rest of people on the map, there were no names associated with that layer of the gang.

This was surprising. Jacobs had assumed that the structure of the gang would be similar to what Krol had run in Brooklyn. There he'd communicated directly with his street operators, which was different from most of the gangs we looked at, where the leaders didn't get close to the actual criminal activity, or the people actively engaged in it.

But the analysis showed that neither Krol nor his lieutenants were communicating directly with the rank and file. Instead, the unidentified middlemen communicated upwards with Krol, and downwards with the lower level of gang members.

I wasn't sure what this meant, but I knew it was important. Jacobs had counted on Krol's hands-on approach to facilitate making a solid case against him. A buffer layer of people between him and the criminal activity would complicate our ability to take him down. She wouldn't be happy about that.

I went through my data, checking and rechecking, and was surprised when I looked at the time. Two o'clock.

I went down to the cafeteria to grab a sandwich. On the way back up I passed Gavin in the hallway.

'How's it going?' he asked.

'Good. Hey, listen, do you have a minute?'

'For you? Of course.'

We walked back to my cubicle and I showed him the network map.

'See, here?' I said, pointing to the cluster of middlemen in the gang map. 'It looks to me like there's an entire additional middle management layer between Brajen Krol and the guys doing the work.'

'And we don't know who they are?'

'No. It's odd, we have names for at least some people at every layer of his organization except for this one. But the important thing is that it looks like Krol's communication with the rank and file goes only through this layer of contacts.'

'So who are these guys?' he mused.

'No idea.'

'Jacobs isn't going to like this. It messes with her idea of how they're structured. It also means there's a whole other set of important people that we didn't know about. Are you sure this is right?'

I nodded. 'Identifying these guys in the middle should be a priority. They're the link between Krol and the on-the-ground operation. If we have any hope of getting to him we need to find out who these guys are.'

I turned back to my computer.

Gavin was still standing there. 'Are you, uh, going to the cruise tonight?'

Stan Nowicki was retiring, and they were throwing a party for him. I didn't normally go to those, unless I was close to someone, but he'd been with the force for forty years, and was something of an icon. On top of that, the event was being held on the *Enterprise*, an upscale Lake Michigan dinner cruise boat. Normally something like that would be out of the financial realm for the department, but Nowicki had a community benefactor who was footing the bill.

'Yes.'

'Would you like to go together?'

I didn't normally date men I worked with; Jeb had been an outlier. But Gavin and I were just going to be working together on this one project. And he wasn't based in Chicago, Jacobs had brought him here from Philly for this task force. So it wasn't *really* dating someone I worked with.

'Sure,' I said.

Just then Jeb poked his head into the cubicle with a smile. It faded when he saw Gavin.

Tunnel Vision

'So, pick you up at five thirty?' asked Gavin, a little too loudly.

'OK, I'll send you my address.'

'Howzit, mate,' he said to Jeb, walking out.

'Hey,' I said to Jeb.

'Hi, uh, I wanted to see if you needed a ride to the cruise tonight. I guess you don't.'

'Oh, no, thanks. See you there, though.'

The muscle on the side of his face twitched. He rarely verbalized it when he was angry or upset. But when something bothered him he would clench his jaw, causing that muscle to flex. It was usually the sole sign that anything was amiss.

'Oh. OK. Well, I guess I'll see you there,' he said, turning around and leaving abruptly.

What was that about? It wasn't like we were still dating.

Whatever. I wrapped up my report and left. I walked by Jefferson's office on the way out. The door was closed, and inside was Chief Wade Jennings, Jefferson's boss. He didn't look happy. He never came by unless something was really wrong.

On the way home I stopped by the Northwestern hospital to check in on Nowak. I hardly knew her, but we were on the same team, and our community was small enough that it was important to show support.

Any time someone was shot in the line of duty other officers would never leave them alone, and would volunteer their time to stay at the hospital. Valerie Nowak was young but well liked on the force, and the hallway leading to her room was crowded with members of the Chicago PD, many in street clothes, along with two uniformed officers that made up the formal rotation of guards at the door. This was standard procedure when gangs or cartels were involved.

Her door was open, and I knocked on it, leaning in. She was on the phone but hung up and gestured at me to come in.

'Hey Valerie, how're you doing?'

Her left arm was in a sling and bandaged at the top. 'Fine.' She smiled. 'I got lucky, it was a through and through.'

That was good, that meant the surgery would have been minor, with no bullet to remove, and no broken bones or organ damage to deal with.

'Are you in a lot of pain?' I asked, looking at the assortment of flowers, cards and balloons displayed around the room.

'Not right now,' she laughed, pointing to her IV. 'Good drugs.'

'What happened?'

'It's nothing,' she said. 'I got careless, followed too close. One of them took a shot.'

'Do you think they made you?'

'No,' she said quickly. 'We know they're a trigger-happy bunch. How's the network map going?' she asked.

I was surprised she wanted to change the subject. Most cops I knew liked to talk about how they survived physical altercations. It was a little bit of a badge of honor. But I guessed it wasn't exactly praiseworthy to get identified and then shot as a UC. And even though I'd never heard anything about Nowak being careless, no matter how good you were, you couldn't keep your edge all of the time. The fourth day of what had to be a tedious task following a bunch of guys and taking pictures would dull anyone's senses.

In any case, it matched with what we knew about the Greenpoint Crew. Just shooting someone on the street was consistent with their MO of not caring about collateral damage.

'Good, I think I made a breakthrough today.'

'Oh yeah?'

'Yeah, the gang structure, I don't think it's what Jacobs envisioned.'

'What do you mean?'

'I mean, it looks like there's a whole other set of players, between Brajen Krol and the rank and file.'

She frowned. 'That's not what Jacobs told us, and she's got a lot of experience with this group. Are you sure?'

'Yeah.'

'Would you mind,' she said, pointing to a glass of water on the table next to her bed.

I handed it to her. 'Jacobs told us you should be able to be back on in no time,' I said.

'That's what I'm hoping. A week or two to recover, they said. But I'm staying on the team, Jacobs is having me help out with other things until I can get back on the street.'

'That's great, Valerie.' I looked up at the clock. 'I gotta go.'

'Going to the retirement party?'

'Yeah. Hard to pass up the chance for a free dinner cruise.'

'Have fun. I hear it's on the *Enterprise*. I might try to come.'

'Seriously?'

'Yeah, I've heard about that boat, it's supposed to be fantastic. I'm not feeling that bad, and it doesn't take two arms to drink,' she said with a smile. 'Thanks for stopping by.'

TWELVE

I put the finishing touches on my makeup and met Sags in the living room.

'You ready?' I asked. She was wearing her standard issue for fancy events: black ankle boots, slim fit satin black pants, a button-down shirt and leather jacket with a mandarin collar.

'Yeah.' She looked me over. 'You look nice. Any particular reason you're tarting it up?'

I blushed. 'No. I don't go to these things very often.'

Minimal eye makeup had replaced my normal heavy goth black, and the gaggle of earrings I wore every day were substituted with single pearls.

'Let's go,' I said, grabbing my coat and walking out the door.

Sags had heard who the chef was going to be at the dinner and wanted to go as my 'plus one', so I'd let Gavin know we'd meet him at the boat. If he was disappointed he didn't indicate it; another check in the positive column for him. We took a Lyft to Navy Pier and joined the crowd of people making their way to the *Enterprise*, a six-hundred-person capacity 'mega yacht', our floating event space for the evening.

The Chicago PD didn't sponsor retirement parties, as it was considered a 'gifting of public funds'. The standard retirement offering from the department typically amounted to a card, a cake and a plaque. Any retirement events had to be sponsored by friends or family, and dinner cruises, particularly one like this, were well above most people's budget. But Nowicki was the beneficiary of a wealthy northsider, whose missing daughter had been tracked down and found by Nowicki a number of years back. The father had been beyond grateful, and was footing the bill for the evening.

I didn't get down to Navy Pier very often, and had forgotten how beautiful it was. Open to the public in 1915, and originally named 'Municipal Pier', the three-thousand-foot pier jutted out into Lake Michigan just north of downtown. Plants and flowers lined the wide walking areas between the center row of bars and restaurants and the railings. It was one of Chicago's most popular attractions, for both tourists and locals, offering amusement park rides, restaurants, parks, shopping, and gardens, the dominant feature the lighted 150-foot-tall ferris wheel that towered above the buildings. My favorite site on the pier was one that many people missed. On the far end from the shore, off to the side, was the bronze Bob Newhart statue, a metal couch where you could sit next to the great man himself.

We made our way to the *Enterprise* and waited in line to show our tickets. I was glad to see that security was tight. A boat filled with law enforcement would be a tempting target-rich environment for terrorists, or anyone with a grudge against law enforcement.

'Where to?' asked Sags, after we'd boarded, looking up at the several stories of gleaming white-and-glass trimmed observation decks.

'There's supposed to be multiple bars on this thing. Let's find one.'

We skipped the first door to the interior that was bottlenecked, and entered through one away from the entry and closer to the bow of the ship. Up a flight of stairs was a full, line-free bar with a white-liveried bartender.

'Hello, what can I get for you?' he said, placing gloved hands on the counter.

In honor of Nowicki's retirement they were offering a specialty drink for the evening, the 'Stan the Man', basically a boilermaker, honoring Nowicki's penchant for whiskey with an Old Style chaser.

Sags ordered a beer and I went with a dirty martini, as it was a little early in the evening for beer and shots. The drinks were free for the first two hours and we left a hefty tip. I'm sure Nowicki's benefactor would have been fine paying for an open bar all night, but the brass didn't think it was a good idea to have several hundred cops drinking their heads off on a boat all night, so had requested that the free booze period be capped at two hours.

We got our drinks and wandered back down to the main dining room, which was already filling up. Glass and chrome tables with white napkins were set up around the room, gently illuminated by pendant lights. Windows allowed an almost 360-degree view of the skyline and the water. Most people were standing, as couples or in small clusters, with the exception of one larger group surrounding Nowicki, the man of the hour.

'Let's go pay our respects.'

Tunnel Vision 83

We walked to the edge of the crowd and waited. Clearly already a few drinks in, Nowicki looked about the same as always, balding, stomach straining at his button-down shirt, and a red-veined nose that looked a little redder than usual.

I'd worked with him on a few cases when his precinct had needed some help identifying the form of the gangs in his precinct. We'd always gotten along, and when we got close I stuck out my hand. 'Congratulations, Stan.'

He surprised me by pulling me into a tight hug. It occurred to me that maybe he wasn't excited about retiring, perhaps wondering what he'd do all day.

'Thanks for coming, Maude,' he said, letting up on the hug but still holding on to my hand with both of his. 'It means a lot.'

'What are you going to do with all of your free time?'

He looked away. 'I don't know. Mary's gone, you know. So, I don't know . . .' He trailed off, and I was sorry I'd asked. His wife had passed away two years ago from breast cancer. It was possible the job was all he had.

Standing next to Nowicki was his partner Carter. 'Hey John,' I said.

'Hi, Maude,' he said, with a slight smile, which disappeared when he saw Sags.

'Carter,' she said, nodding to him.

There was no love lost between these two, and he stared daggers at her. Carter had been responsible for the investigation into Louie Ferrar's death last year, one that eventually resulted in the capture of a violent gang lord in Portage Park. Carter had originally suspected that she had something to do with his death, and despite the arrest, he still did.

Correctly, as it turned out, but with help from Jeb, who'd 'found' some evidence, he'd been forced to look elsewhere for his suspect. Jeb made sure that the innocent – at least for this murder, although not several others – man was eventually released on a technicality, but no one was ever held accountable for Louie's death.

I wasn't so sure why Carter was so hot on Sags. Louie had been a serial rapist and an overall dirtbag. Whatever the reason, he'd never given up his belief that she'd had something to do with it.

'Don't think you're out of the woods, Pfister. I'm watching you,' he growled.

'Don't you have something better to do? Like catch real criminals?'

84   Wendy Church

'I'm looking at one right now,' he said, his eyes narrowed into slits.

She waved a hand at him and turned away.

I gave Nowicki another hug and turned to join her. 'Let's find some seats,' I said, scanning the room. I was surprised to see Valerie Nowak sitting at a table by the window, her arm in a sling. She saw me and waved with the other one. I waved back.

'Nowak looks great,' I said to Sags.

'Isn't she the one who got shot?'

'Yeah. They weren't going to let her out until tomorrow.'

'Who's that she's with?'

'I don't know. Boyfriend, by the way he's all over her.'

Linda and her husband Bill were sitting in a booth by a window. 'Wanna join them?' I asked, pointing.

Sags nodded. As we made our way across the room I felt a hand on my elbow.

'Excuse me, I don't think we've met. Can I buy you a . . . oh.'

I turned to see Renfro standing next to me, open-mouthed.

'It's a free bar, meathead. I'll get my own drinks.'

He actually blushed. 'You clean up well, Kaminski,' he managed to get out before walking away abruptly.

Sags laughed out loud. 'That dude was actually hitting on you. Don't you work with him every day?'

'Yeah.' I wasn't all that surprised he hadn't recognized me. He never saw me in anything but Carhartts and T-shirts.

Jeb was standing on the other side of the room. He saw me and gave a small wave. I changed direction and walked towards him. We exchanged an awkward hug and a quick peck on the cheek.

'Hello, Sagarine,' he said to Sags.

'Smith.'

'How is the . . . uh, how are your parents?' He was never a master at small talk.

'OK, consider—'

'*Maude!*'

'Hey, Gavin.' He'd walked up and was giving me the once-over. 'You look wonderful,' he said, leaning over and kissing me on the cheek.

Gavin had gone all out for the event, wearing a green tartan kilt, black socks, and a loose, black satin, button-down shirt, tucked in and open at the collar, the open neck offering a fine view of his

Tunnel Vision 85

hefty pec muscles. Over his shoulder, bound by a silver brooch, was a large piece of cloth that matched the color of his kilt. A leather pouch hung from his belt in the front.

'And who is this smart lass?' he said, turning to Sags.

She stuck her hand out.

'This is Sagarine, my roommate.'

'Pleasure to meet you,' he said, shaking her hand.

He finally turned to Jeb. 'Smith,' he said, sticking his hand out. Jeb put his hand out and gave an even more desultory greeting than he'd given to Sags, his jaw muscle flexing.

'I'm not interrupting anything, am I?' Gavin said, looking at me and Jeb.

'No,' Jeb said sourly.

'Up for a walk on the deck?' he said to me. 'Uh, both of you?' he said to Sags.

'Sure,' I said.

'No, thanks,' said Sags, looking towards the front of the room. 'I'm going to check out the kitchen.'

Gavin looked at my empty drink. 'Let's fill up first.'

'Sure.' I looked back at Jeb, who'd already turned his back on us.

Gavin reached down for my hand and we went to the main bar, getting our drinks and heading outside.

The sun was down and it was starting to get a little chilly. Gavin took off the cloth over his shoulder, a 'fly plaid', he said, and drew it around me. We walked to the railing and looked toward the city. From here we could see the Chicago skyline in all its splendor.

The skyline was punctuated by the double-spired Willis Tower, which many people still referred to as the Sears Tower, even though it had been renamed in 2009. Anchoring the view on the other side were the iconic, slanted, diamond-shaped top of the Crain Communications Building, and the Aon Center.

The lake was calm, and the effect of the buildings' reflections on the water was that we were looking at two cities.

I leaned on the railing. 'It's beautiful.'

'Aye,' he said.

He was looking at me, and when I turned to him he leaned over and gently kissed me on the lips. It was a little Titanic-esque for me, but it had been a while since I'd been on a date, and I put my arms around his neck. His hands were on my waist and he pulled me towards him.

The soft chimes of the dinner bell rang too soon, no doubt a directive from the powers-that-be to not wait too long between the open bar and food service. Nevertheless I was flushed and worked up. It had been a while since I'd been with anyone, and right now I was looking forward to a quick dinner and Gavin's company at my place, feeling a little irritated that we were on a boat and couldn't just get up and leave.

Sags was sitting at one of the smaller tables next to a window and had saved seats for us. We sat down and shortly thereafter were served the first course.

Menu cards at each place setting informed us that we would be treated to a chef's tasting menu. 'A Celebration of Midwestern Food Groups: Potatoes, Mayonnaise, Corn, Hot Dogs, Jello, and Meat.'

'Yikes,' I said.

'I wouldn't worry,' said Sags, smiling.

I didn't believe her, and was digging around in my purse for a power bar when the first course arrived. The waiter placed the small plates in front of us.

'Your potato course: potatoes with caviar,' he announced.

Oh.

I took a bite and realized that this course was worth the price of admission by itself. Thinly sliced layers of crisp but tender potatoes, layered with cream and cut into small cylinders served as the foundation for a generous dollop of Ossetra caviar.

'Told you,' said Sags, smiling as she popped it into her mouth.

The plates were cleared quickly and replaced with the second course, a generous portion of homemade tartar sauce that accompanied nuggets of smoked and then deep-fried Lake Michigan chub, a small white fish, alongside fresh coleslaw.

'This is amazing,' I said, tasting the tartar sauce. It had a luxurious depth I'd never experienced.

'It's the duck eggs,' she said. 'And it's fresh. Homemade mayonnaise is a completely different animal than what you get from a jar.'

Next to each plate was a small ramekin of corn soup. And not just any corn soup. Unlike the cloying chunky soups I was used to, this tasted like the perfect essence of fresh corn.

'What's in this?' I asked, scraping the sides of the bowl with my spoon for the last bit.

'Nothing, other than corn, and butter, and a little salt.'

'Seriously?'

Tunnel Vision

'Yeah. Some of her food is complicated, but really good chefs know how to respect ingredients. In this case, the corn doesn't need to be elevated, it's a perfect flavor by itself.'

Next was the salad course, consisting of sliced heirloom beefsteak tomatoes and something the waiter called '*Casserole de haricots verts déconstruite*', a small stack of fresh steamed green beans and two small ramekins. 'For dipping,' he said as he put them on the table.

It didn't make sense until I picked up a green bean, dipped it in the ramekin of thick, satiny, almost black sauce, and then into the other one filled with what looked like toasted bread crumbs.

'Oh my god,' I said, the flavor memory smacking me in the face as I took the first bite. 'It's green bean casserole.' The sauce was an intensely flavored mushroom, the crumbs pieces of deep-fried shallots. Murmurs of appreciation and surprise rose from the tables around us; like me many of the people in this room had grown up with green bean casserole. 'Now I'm curious to see how she can manage to elevate a hot dog.'

I didn't have long to wait. Shortly after they picked up the plates and ramekins the waiter arrived with the next course.

'Corn dogs, with three mustards and a sampling of Chicago microbrews,' he said as he put the plate down in front of me, along with a small wooden plank containing three shots of beer.

'This is delicious,' I said. 'I've never had a corn dog this good.' The beer was perfectly matched to the food, like all of the rest of the bubbly, whites and reds that accompanied the meal. Nowicki's benefactor had spared no expense.

'I'm not surprised. It's a smoked carrot,' said Sags.

'What?'

I turned the corn dog around to look at the inside. Yep, a carrot. *Damn.*

No midwestern meal was complete without Jello, typically served in a mold that encased nuts, cheese, fruit, shredded carrots, or whipped cream. Accordingly, once the tables were cleared of the corn dogs and beer, small glass goblets appeared in front of us. A palate cleanser, according to the waiter.

Three perfect squares in three colors. Bright red quince Jello was infused with small yellow bubbles, which turned out to be bursts of Meyer lemon; a single large, purple marionberry rested in the center of yellow passionfruit Jello; the third square was a dark orange persimmon Jello, holding Fraises de Bois, small wild strawberries, that tasted like the essence of strawberry.

No food coloring in sight, and a long way from the 'red' and 'blue' flavors I grew up with.

As always Gavin was charming and funny, entertaining the two of us and everyone within earshot throughout the meal. His accent didn't hurt. I glanced at Jeb a few times, sitting at a table near us. Each time he looked away.

The main meat course was served family style, platters of thick, brined and grilled pork chops, and stacks of wagyu beef tomahawk steaks. A few individual bowls of pasta circulated for the vegetarians, which were few in this crowd. The meat was accompanied by generous bowls of lightly dressed radicchio and fresh dill salads.

The low cacophony of voices in the room disappeared. Sags had always said silence was one of the most accurate signs of a successful meal.

Near the end of the meal the chef, an attractive, surprisingly young woman, came out of the kitchen. She received a heartfelt applause, which wasn't surprising. Most of the people in the room had never had a meal like this in their lives, and probably never would again.

She announced the dessert, 'Coffee and donuts', in an obvious acknowledgement of the evening's customers. Coffee and donuts turned out to be a small layered parfait of frozen custard and espresso ice cream, accompanied by freshly fried, hot donut holes, served with three sauces: basil raspberry, a slightly smoky charred rosemary and sage caramel, and cinnamon chocolate fudge.

As we were finishing dessert Carter stood up and gave a few words on Nowicki's behalf. Even though it was near the end of the meal, and people were liquored up, they paid respectful attention. Nowicki had been a solid, hard-working Chicago cop. A man who did a dangerous, largely thankless job, and who'd made it through unscathed, at least physically. Alcohol-fueled calls of speech forced him to mumble a few words of thanks before he was rescued by Carter, who took the mike and said, 'No more speeches, just dancing and drinks. We have another two hours on this thing, let's make the most of it.'

There was some whooping and most of the guests stood up, a lot of them heading for the bar. It was about to get rowdy.

I used the opportunity to excuse myself and go to the ladies room with Sags.

Tunnel Vision

'So, what's the deal with you and Outlander?' she asked.

'He's cute,' I said. 'Don't be surprised if you see a sock on my door tonight.'

'I'm not sure Smith is too happy about it,' she said.

'What do you mean? We're broken up.'

'Does he know that? I mean, if looks could kill, Outlander would be dead a bunch of times over.'

'I doubt it,' I scoffed. 'Jeb and I are friends now. But it's over.'

'Whatever you say.'

'That chef is cute,' I said, reapplying lip gloss.

'Nicola Bullware. And she's a terrific cook,' she said.

'Do you know her?'

'We just met when I poked my head into the kitchen. But I've heard of her. Nikky is one of the hottest chefs in the city right now.'

I didn't miss the fact that she was already on a nickname basis with the chef. 'What's her restaurant?'

'She doesn't have one. She doesn't need it. She takes exclusive bookings from the wealthiest people in the area. Whoever paid for the food tonight laid down a bundle.'

'Is she as good as you?' I said, joking.

'I don't know.'

In response to my raised eyebrow, she said, 'She's *really* good. She doesn't do the molecular gastronomy stuff, but, yeah, she thinks of things I wouldn't dream of.'

I found that hard to believe. 'She looks young for that.'

'She is. We're meeting later,' she said with a small smile.

Cooking was too important to Sags to allow her to date a chef who was less than stellar. And it was probably a huge turn-on for her. 'Of course you are.'

Sags rarely was turned down when she hit on someone. She was charismatic and really pretty, her cool grey eyes and wavy reddish hair framing great bone structure. And she was in great shape from being on her feet all the time. If I were gay I'd be into her.

We were just about to leave when I heard low voices, and turned my head to the stalls. One of them was closed, and from behind came a man's voice.

THIRTEEN

Sags and I looked at each other. I was about to leave and find the steward when I heard muffled giggling, and the sound of a zipper.

The door opened, and a woman walked out, smoothing down her skirt. Behind her came a smiling Martinez, in the process of fastening his belt.

'Oh, hi Kaminski,' he said, tucking his shirt in.

'Martinez.'

After a brief patting down of hair they both washed their hands and left.

'Speaking of the *Love Boat*,' Sags said as we walked out of the bathroom. 'I have a date on the deck.'

'Knock yourself out,' I said. 'Maybe we'll both get lucky tonight.'

The tables in the dining room had been taken up and moved to the sides, leaving a respectable-sized dance floor. A few couples were already doing their thing to 80's covers underneath a disco ball.

In the back corner of the room was a large and growing group of people. I walked over and saw Gavin in the center. He was in the process of placing men in two short lines.

I knew what he was doing and walked away. I had no desire to be in the center of a drinkfest. I looked around, and spotted Deputy Chief Jefferson nursing a drink by himself, at a table near the window. I walked over to him.

'Mind if I join you?' I said.

He nodded to the empty chair next to him.

'Not in a dancing mood?'

He smiled tightly and shook his head.

'Where's Maxine?'

He pointed towards the dance floor, where his wife was dancing with one of the commanders.

'What about you? Not interested in the competition?' he asked, looking towards the rowdy group at the other end.

I shook my head. 'No, it's going to get ugly. Like a slow motion

Tunnel Vision

train wreck. You know how it's going to end, and there's nothing you can do to stop it,' I said.

I noticed for the first time how tired he looked. His job wasn't easy, but one of the things that made him so effective was his ability to stay calm and confident, even under the most stressful conditions. It was unsettling to see him like this.

'Are you all right, sir?'

He sighed. 'I'm worried.'

He wasn't in the habit of sharing that kind of sentiment with his staff. But he'd known me since before I'd started on the force, and I wasn't a direct report, which made me a little safer to talk to. And he knew I kept things to myself.

'The cartel is ramping up. Three more dealers have been murdered since last week.'

'Three?' I'd only heard about two.

He nodded. 'One of them was dumped in broad daylight in front of Macy's today.' He shook his head. 'The cartel's not going to stop until we shut down the Greenpoint Crew.'

Chicago had been living with entrenched gang violence for some time, but bodies dropping around the city in public places was on a whole other level.

Jacobs had warned us about an 'explosion of violence' at the first meeting if the cartel's income stream was threatened. She hadn't been wrong.

'I'm guessing you're getting pressure from above to make this stop?'

'Like you can't believe. Everyone knows we're not going to solve the gang problems overnight, or, ever. But they expect me to contain it. And we're not doing that right now.'

He looked over at the crowd of people whooping it up. 'I'm glad they can blow off some steam, relax for a night. I don't know when any of us will be able to do that again.' He took another sip of his drink. 'Go on, have some fun.'

I got up and wandered towards the crowd in the corner. Sags was standing at the back of it.

'No luck?'

She smiled. 'She's meeting me on the deck in thirty minutes.'

I was happy to hear that. She hadn't dated for months, ever since things had ended with Ekaterina Belyaev. Ekaterina was a world-class beauty, and their affair had been intense and passionate. But she was also a high-ranking member of one of the city's most dangerous Russian gangs, and had put Sags' life at risk more than once. I was glad to see Sags finally moving on.

The rowdy crowd parted like the Red Sea as Gavin and Renfro walked through them, balancing trays of beers.

'One more time!' Gavin shouted, lining up the drinks on the table. 'Who's up? We need eight solid souls.'

Five of the men stepped forward.

'We need two more!' Gavin said, looking to see who else wanted to hurt themselves with alcohol.

Sagarine surprised me by raising her hand and stepping forward. 'I'm in,' she said.

'Wonderful!' He looked around, his eyes landing on Jeb.

'Mr G Man! Join us!'

'No, thank you,' Jeb said stiffly.

'What're you, chicken? We'll take the lass on our team. Surely you can stand up to that?'

Take the lass? He was going to be in for a surprise.

Several of the men at the table started to snigger. Even though Jeb was a good guy, there was always a fair amount of good-natured competition between the FBI and our guys.

Not to mention that unlike cops, who could be adrenaline junkies, and knew how to have a good time, even outside of work FBI agents tended to stay buttoned-up.

Jeb was no different. I'd rarely seen him cut loose, and never in public.

He surprised me and stepped forward, joining one of the two lines that Gavin had formed, he and Gavin taking the last place in each one.

'Fantastic! May the best man . . . er team, win!' said Gavin. 'On your marks, get set, go!'

The first man in each line stepped forward and chugged a beer. The guy in Jeb's line finished first, held the beer upside down above his head to show it was empty, and stepped to the back. Then the next man stepped up.

Four people in each line, I counted thirty-two beers on the table. Four for each person.

The women in the crowd cheered when Sags put her beer away in a flash. Somewhere she'd learned to suppress the gag reflex. Despite that, Gavin's team was falling behind. But when it was his

Tunnel Vision 93

turn he chugged his beer like he was dumping it down the sink. Jeb's team was faster, and he'd gotten to the table before Gavin. But while he enjoyed beer, he wasn't much of a chugger. The onlookers groaned as he slowly made his way through the beer, drinking instead of chugging. Three more times through the line and Gavin's team won easily.

'Better luck next time!' said Gavin. 'Who wants to go again?' he said, looking pointedly at Jeb.

Don't do it, I thought. Jeb didn't stand a chance against Gavin in a drinking game.

'Sure,' he said.

Oh, no.

Gavin left for the bar and came back shortly with another set of drinks. But instead of beers it was dark amber liquid in shot glasses.

'Who else?' he said.

Most of the drinkers including Sags stepped out at the sight of the whiskey. Two of them stayed.

Four people; I counted twelve shots.

'Grand,' said Gavin. 'Here's where we separate the men from the wee'uns.' He stepped to the back into his line. 'Ready, set, go!' he said, looking at Jeb.

The first two shots went down quickly for everyone, including Jeb. I'd never seen him drink like this. But by the time the first drinkers in the two lines got to their third shots, they were slowing down, and getting as much on the front of their shirts as they were in their mouths.

It was a dead heat when Gavin and Jeb stepped up to take their last shots. Gavin put his down just before Jeb.

He put his arms up in victory, whooping and slapping Jeb on the back. I saw him stiffen.

'Don't touch me,' he said, his voice dangerously low.

'Hey, now, take it easy,' said Gavin, putting his hands on Jeb's shoulders.

'Take your hands off me,' said Jeb, raising his arms up quickly to shrug them off.

Jeb was good at hiding his feelings, and Gavin didn't realize, nor likely did anyone other than me, that he was furious. I'd never seen him this mad. The jaw muscle in his face was pumping like a jackhammer.

The alcohol probably had a lot to do with it. He didn't drink a lot, and when he did he watched himself. Four beers, and as many shots in five minutes, on top of whatever he'd had earlier, was way over his limit.

'It's just a bit of fun, mate,' said Gavin.

'Fuck off,' said Jeb, his eyes glassy.

'Hey now,' said Gavin. 'There's no call for that. It's just a wee drinking game. Not a test of anyone's *manliness*,' he said, goading him. He was grinning as he jabbed Jeb lightly on the chest.

That was the straw that broke the drunken camel's back. Jeb grabbed Gavin's wrist and twisted, turning his arm upside down.

He'd learned that move at the National Academy, and I'd seen him bring criminals to their knees with it. But right now he was too drunk for it to be effective.

Gavin regained control of his hand easily, and backed up a step, putting his hands up in front of him.

'No need to get all worked up,' he said.

Jeb's eyes were burning into him. He took a step forward.

'You don't want to do this, mate,' said Gavin, his grin fading.

People were backing away, leaving a circle of space around the two men.

Jeb was too far gone at this point to listen to reason, and he stepped forward and took a swing at Gavin's face. Gavin backed up and Jeb missed, and stumbled. He was even drunker than I'd realized.

He righted himself, then turned back to Gavin with his hands curled into fists.

'That's enough, mate. Next one I'm taking you down.'

Gavin was still smiling, but it wasn't even close to friendly, more like a challenge. Like an ape.

I'd gotten up and pushed my way through the circle of people. I leaned in and put my hand on Jeb's arm. 'Let it go,' I said.

He looked at me like a crazed animal and shook off my hand.

'It's your funeral.' Gavin put his hands up, and when Jeb threw a punch Gavin sidestepped it easily again, this time round-housing a punch to the side of Jeb's face.

It decked him immediately. He lay on the floor for a moment, dazed, before he got to his knees.

'What the hell is going on?' Jefferson was pushing through the crowd. He looked at Jeb on the floor and back at Gavin.

'Knock it off, both of you,' he said.

Tunnel Vision

'Nothing,' said Gavin. 'Just a wee bit of fun.' He turned away from Jeb and walked through the doors to the outside deck.

I followed him out. 'Did you really have to do that?'

'What? He came after me,' he said.

'You provoked him.'

'C'mon,' he said, reaching for me.

I pulled away, and we stared at each other. My desire to get him back to my place had evaporated, and I was about to leave when we heard laughter.

Sags and Nicola were a few yards away from us, standing by the railing, talking. The way they were leaning into each other made it obvious that at least one of us would be getting lucky tonight.

'I wouldn't mind partaking of that chef's tasting menu,' Gavin said, staring at them.

Jesus. Sometimes I wished I were into women.

The doors to the main room banged open, and Jeb staggered out. He saw Gavin and rushed at him like a drunken bull, trying to headbutt him.

Gavin stepped to the side and grabbed Jeb's waist, using his own momentum to throw him into the railing.

Jeb flew forwards, tumbling over the railing and down towards the water. I heard a splash.

I ran over and looked down at the dark water. Jeb was nowhere in sight.

I turned to Gavin. '*Do something!*' I yelled. 'This is your fault.'

'Bollocks.' Gavin took off his fly plaid, grabbed one of the life preservers and jumped into the water. It was full moonlight, and well lit enough I could see his kilt fly up as he went down. He wasn't wearing anything underneath it.

'*Oscar, Oscar, Oscar,*' came over the ship intercom.

Sweeping floodlights shone over the dark water. With relief I saw Jeb's head bob to the surface. Gavin swam with strong strokes over to him, dragging the preserver. Jeb grabbed on and they waited for the lifeboat that would bring them in.

Things quickly calmed down on the boat, which by now had turned and was headed back to shore, no doubt at the request of Jefferson who'd seen enough for one night.

When we docked I joined the line to get off the boat, and followed the crowd to the shore to call a Lyft home.

My phone buzzed. 'Got lucky, See you tomorrow' from Sags.
At least one of us had.

'*Maude*!'

Gavin was coming down the pier, dripping wet. Behind him on his knees on the pier was Jeb, vomiting.

'Fancy a nightcap?' Gavin said, smiling broadly.

'You've got to be kidding. Did you really have to do that?'

His eyebrows went up, surprised.

'Does that macho shit impress *anyone*? You completely goaded him into that.'

'No nightcap then?' he asked, disappointed.

I shook my head and walked away from him.

Dammit. I wasn't ready to go home. I was too full of pent-up energy I'd intended to spend on Gavin. But not after watching him beat up Jeb and send him overboard.

I considered visiting my favorite adult book store, DJ's Sin City, on Wells. I went there occasionally, to peruse titles and get ideas for my books. But it was late, we had a task force meeting in the morning, and the thought of walking by the Museum of Medieval Torture that was on the way was too much. Instead I walked down to the Jane Addams park. I could wander around and burn off some energy, maybe give myself a chance to get some sleep tonight.

The park was just over four acres in size, more of a small green space, that nevertheless made it easy to forget that it was close to the center of the third largest city in the country. Pathways crisscrossed lawns punctuated by trees, some of them huge, the whole place dotted here and there by benches.

The park closed at eleven, and by the time I'd walked off my frustration it was deserted. Time to head back to the road to call a car.

I was passing under a short covered walkway when I noticed two men approaching.

I quickened my pace, holding my breath as they came closer.

I tensed, then breathed a sigh of relief when they passed me. I was pulling out my phone to call a car when I heard footsteps. As I started to turn around I felt a blinding pain in my head. There was a flash of light, and then black.

FOURTEEN

I woke up on the ground. As I sat up I felt a piercing pain in my head. I moved my hand to my skull and felt the start of a bump. My fingers came back wet with blood.

Not gushing, thankfully. My face was sore too, from landing on it on the stone walkway.

I stood up unsteadily. My purse was on the ground next to me, and my phone a few feet away. I picked them both up and opened my purse.

My wallet was still there. It didn't look like anything had been taken.

I looked around. I was alone, in the distance I could see the lights of Navy Pier and car headlights on Lakeshore Drive. All I wanted to do was go home, but it felt wrong to not report the attack. I called 911.

A patrol car showed up in a few minutes. I gave my statement, then let myself get checked out by paramedics, turning down the offer of a trip to the hospital to be looked over more thoroughly.

By the time I made it home it was after three in the morning. The apartment was empty, which was no big shock. Sags had probably spent the night at Nicola's place. I called her and left a message, letting her know what had happened, that I was OK and to be careful herself.

I made it in to the task force conference room the next morning just before ten. I was surprised to see Nowak in the room, her arm in a sling, even though she'd made it to the cruise. She looked pale but surprisingly well for someone who'd been shot a few days ago.

I was more surprised to see Jeb there. He was slumped in a seat in the back, looking like he'd been rode hard and put away wet. His face was puffy and ashen, his eyes bloodshot. His hair, normally with not a single strand out of place, looked like it had been combed with a leaf blower.

The entire team looked ragged and hungover, which matched the faint stench of the incident room, that was now starting to reek with the smell of stale sweat and Italian beef sandwiches.

Deputy Chief Jefferson was standing in the front talking to Jacobs and Bowles.

'Ms Kaminski. Are you OK? Should you be here?' he asked.

'I'm fine. I got mugged. It happens.'

'Have you been checked out by a doctor?'

'Paramedics, yes, I'm fine, sir. No nausea, headache, blurry vision, I'm not dizzy. Really, I'm fine.'

Gavin looked at me, his eyes growing wide as he took in the scrapes and growing bruises on my face.

'Jesus, Maude, what happened?' he whispered as I sat down on the empty seat next to him.

'I'm fine.' I didn't want to answer his questions and pulled out my laptop. If he hadn't been such a competitive macho jerk I might have spent the night having sex with him, instead of getting mugged.

Jefferson gave me a long look before leaving the room.

'Officer Nowak, you were shot,' Bowles said, putting extra emphasis on the word 'shot', 'two days ago. Are you ready to participate?' Clearly he wasn't impressed with me being here after merely being mugged.

'Yes sir. I'm not cleared for field work but I can continue to help the team.'

'Thank you, officer. We all appreciate your dedication.' He turned to the rest of us. 'Listen up. This is the second time in as many days that our task force members have been targeted.'

I frowned. There was no indication that my attack had anything to do with the task force. I raised my hand but he ignored me.

'From here on out, I want everyone taking extra precautions. Buddy up. No one goes anywhere alone if you can help it.'

'Kaminski, do you think you'll be able to contribute today?' he said, perfunctorily.

I was going on almost no sleep. The adrenaline from the night before had worn off, and I was bone tired and sore. Still, I was excited to share what I'd learned from the network mapping. 'Yes sir.'

He didn't wait for my answer, and sat down, leaving the floor to Jacobs.

'Ms Kaminski, we'll start with you. What did you find from the network map work?' she asked.

I pulled up my program and connected to the monitor in the front.

Tunnel Vision 99

'This is what we know so far,' I said, using the laser pointer to highlight the network map I'd created. 'We've used the cell phone data and our photo surveillance to identify members of the gang and how they're connected. These circles,' I said, pointing to the circles at the bottom of the graphic, 'indicate lower level gang members, you see that we've identified many of them.' Some of the circles were filled in with faces. 'There are others who we've only identified by their cell phone use. You'll also see that many of the circles – the gang members – have lines connecting them. These lines represent phone calls between the members. Thicker lines mean more calls, thinner lines mean fewer contacts – fewer calls.

'The cluster of five circles at the top of the diagram represents Brajen Krol, and who we believe to be his lieutenants. You can see,' I said, indicating the many thick lines between them, 'that they are in regular contact with each other.

'The interesting thing is that there is another layer to the gang structure, a middle management one, here, above the rank and file.'

I pointed to a cluster of circles between the low-level recruits and Brajen Krol and his lieutenants. Six additional circles, with no names or pictures. Thick lines connected them to the rank and file, and another set to Krol and his lieutenants. There were no connections between Brajen Krol, or any of his lieutenants, and the low-level members.

'I'm not sure I understand,' said Jacobs.

'What it means is that Brajen Krol and his lieutenants aren't the ones communicating with the rank and file. See, here,' I said, pointing, 'there are no connections – no phone calls, at all – between the street-level guys and Krol and his leadership team.'

'That means that we can't just pull in the rank and file, and get them to flip on Krol,' murmured Jeb.

He'd immediately understood the most important implication of my findings. 'That's right. Not just that, it means there's still an important group within the Greenpoint Crew that we haven't identified.'

'This doesn't make any sense,' said Jacobs, frowning. 'This isn't how the Greenpoint Crew has worked in the past. Brajen Krol always has a direct hand in the operations.'

I'd known she wouldn't like this. It meant that we had to go back and identify a whole other set of players before we could move forward with any arrests. Among other things, it would delay our plans to roll up the gang.

'Have we identified any of these so-called middlemen?' she said.

'No, ma'am, but given this, I think—'

'This flies in the face of everything we know about the Greenpoint Crew,' she interrupted. 'Krol likes to have his hands in the business, he deals directly with his gang members, top to bottom. This middlemen theory just doesn't jibe with what we know about how he works.'

'Ma'am, I don't think—'

She stood up and took the laser pointer from me. 'How do we know,' she said, pointing to the middlemen cluster of circles, 'that these aren't spurious phone numbers? Or friends, or girlfriends? Given that we've not seen anyone else in the proximity of Brajen Krol, do you really think it makes sense that there's an entire other tier of gang members operating at this level? And that we've not captured *any* of them on camera?'

'Even if that were true, ma'am, there are no connections between the lower level gang members and Brajen Krol. And these phone numbers aren't spurious, we used the same procedure to capture those as we did—'

'Thank you for your report, Kaminski,' interrupted Bowles. 'There are times when you have to understand that it's not all about computers, and that your little program doesn't have the same level of insight as on-the-street cops who have been intimately involved with the targets for years.'

Jacobs looked at him and nodded. 'We'll keep our eyes open for these so-called middle managers, but in the meantime we'll move ahead with our original plan.'

Outside of Bowles, the vast majority of the people I'd worked with in law enforcement were appreciative of analytical work, and took findings seriously. But while Jacobs herself had made a point to get me on her team, this result was not only against what she'd experienced, it meant that the work of the task force was much further away from completion than she'd anticipated.

Nevertheless, I hated it when people asked for data, and then ignored it when it went against what they already believed. She shouldn't have brought me on the team, if she was going to ignore my findings.

'Now that we have many of the gang members identified, we need to surveil the dealers, and catch them exchanging money and drugs with those gang members. Then we'll pick them up, and get them to flip on Krol and his lieutenants. At the same time we'll be tracking the money, so we can nail Krol when we bring him in.'

Whatever. I'd done my job. If she was going to ignore the data it was on her.

'Do we know where Brajen Krol is?' Nowak asked.

'Yes. He's in a house on Menard Avenue, in Jefferson Park.'

It was maddening that we couldn't just go there now and take him. But I'd worked enough with gang operations to know that we needed hard evidence linking him to the criminal activity, specifically testimony from lower level guys, and information on how and where Krol was laundering his money. And until Gavin could untangle his financials we wouldn't have that. On top of that, if we picked him up before also finding the manufacturing site, we'd risk not being able to tie him to what would be the essential criminal enterprise needed to prosecute money laundering.

It wasn't a complete deal breaker; after all, they'd convicted Al Capone on tax evasion. But with what we had now, at best Krol would get a slap on the wrist, not enough jail time to matter.

'Detective Renfro, you will continue to work your CIs. I want to know who the most promising dealers are to surveil. We're short on staff, so pick the one that is the most active and located in an area conducive to that kind of work: somewhere large enough we can insert an undercover officer without drawing attention, and where they're moving a lot of Red. Once we've found a replacement undercover officer for Officer Nowak, we'll set that piece up.

'Ms Kaminski, I think we have all we need from the network mapping. You and Officer Nowak work with Mr McCullom to go over the financials that we've acquired, and identify the gaps in our information so we can execute any warrants we might need for the remaining material. Do whatever it is that Mr McCullom needs.'

At the sound of 'whatever he needs' Gavin turned his head slightly and looked at me with a smile. I found myself smiling back. It was hard to stay mad at the guy.

Over Gavin's shoulder I could see Jeb, watching us, the muscle in his jaw working overtime.

'I'll be looking into finding a replacement for Officer Nowak. Dismissed.'

Jeb tried to catch my eye during the meeting. I was still mad at him for being such a Neanderthal the night before, and ignored him. As everyone shuffled out of the room he walked over to me.

'Are you OK?'

'I'm fine. Better than you,' I said, looking him over.

'Look, I'm really sorry about last night. I don't know what happened.'

'I do,' I said angrily. 'You were a macho jerk.' I sped up and walked away from him.

Gavin pushed by Jeb and followed me to my cubicle.

'I'm sorry about last night,' he said, leaning on my desk.

'It wasn't completely your fault. You're not the one who got stinking drunk and picked a fight.'

'I know, but I should know better not to involve someone like him in those kind of games.' A not-too-subtle dig at Jeb. 'But I did enjoy parts of the evening,' he said, smiling.

'Me too,' I said, resisting the urge to not smile back, and failing.

'I'd love another opportunity to spend some time with you. I promise not to sponsor any drinking games. Are you available this Saturday? I mean, if you feel like going anywhere, after, you know,' he said, pointing to my head.

I needed a distraction, and couldn't think of anything I would like better.

'Sure.'

'Great. I'll pick you up at two thirty.'

'That's a little early for dinner,' I said, surprised.

'I've got something special planned. Dress for outside.' He winked and walked away.

FIFTEEN

Gavin picked me up on Saturday casually dressed, wearing a wind breaker over a sweater, jeans and a pair of sneakers. When I opened the door he leaned in and kissed me on the cheek.

'Ready?'

'I don't know, where are we going?'

'Let's see how long it takes you to guess,' he said. We left the apartment, and instead of going to his car we started walking.

We walked to Portage Park, and then south through the park to Irving Park Road and the bus stop. When the 80 bus came we got on and headed east.

We got off at Sheridan, and went south to Addison, where we joined a stream of people wearing blue and red, all heading towards Clark Street.

'A baseball game?' I asked.

'I thought you'd enjoy it, and I've not been to many games, and none at Wrigley.'

We waited in line to get in as the game was almost sold out. Not only were the Cubs good this year, but they were playing the Red Sox, which always brought out a crowd. We showed our tickets, and were early enough to walk around the stadium, grab some beers and hot dogs, and take our seats in the bleachers before the first pitch.

'I heard these seats were the most fun,' he said.

'They're definitely the most interesting.'

I wasn't a big sports person, but as a kid my dad had taken us to a few Cubs games every summer. We'd always sat in the bleachers. They were the most affordable, important when you're bringing the whole family. They were also at times a little sketchy. Increasingly rowdy behavior and intoxication had led the stadium to enact a number of rules to try to contain the amount of extreme drinking that the bleachers were famous for. Beer vendors were no longer allowed to bring beer to sell to people in bleacher seats, and each person was limited to purchasing two beers at a time at the stand.

104 Wendy Church

Extra security staff circulated, ready to pull out anyone who was obviously inebriated.

Still, those committed to drinking their heads off and going nuts wouldn't be deterred.

'See those two?' I asked, nodding my head discretely to two men three rows in front of us. 'The guys with their shirts off?' They'd been drinking two-handed since we'd walked in, and I watched them each chug six beers since we'd sat down.

'The sweaty fat one, and the skinny one, wearing the "ShitHead" hats?' said Gavin.

'Yeah. I'd bet a hundred bucks they'll be gone by the fourth inning.'

'Gone? Why?'

'Just wait.'

It turned out I was wrong by two innings. By the end of the second inning the two men started a drunken fight with each other, from the sound of it about whose turn it was to go get more beer. They were shouting and throwing punches when two beefy security guards made their way down the aisle. They corralled the two drunks and escorted them out.

After the Shithead guys were taken away things settled down. And while I usually got bored in the middle of baseball games, I was surprised when everyone stood up to sing 'Take Me Out to the Ballgame', signaling the middle of the seventh inning. I hadn't thought about Michael, or work, for the entire time.

I was surprised again when the game ended, a shutout win for the Cubs. We trudged out with the crowds. 'What now?' I asked.

'I was thinking we'd go for a wee drink.'

'Sure.'

We crossed Clark Street and he moved towards a relatively new, chrome and glass bar a little north of the stadium.

'Not that one,' I said. 'C'mon.'

I turned us in the other direction, down the sidewalk and into an old brick building. Sluggers.

Like always, right after games, Sluggers was standing room only. We waded through a sea of people, servers making their way through the crowd, some holding up trays of Jello shots. I waved my hand at one of the Jello shot women and grabbed two, then continued to push through the crowd.

'Where are we going?' he yelled.

Tunnel Vision

'Upstairs,' I yelled back.

We walked up the ancient staircase to a large room, filled wall to wall with people, some playing air hockey and skeeball, most just standing and drinking.

'What's this?' he said, pointing to an area separated from the main space with floor-to-ceiling metal fencing.

'Batting cages.'

The cages were first-come first-serve, and while we waited our turn we bought some Old Style beers and leaned against the cage, watching people in various stages of inebriation try to hit baseballs.

Gavin had never been in a batting cage, and when our time came he went first, looking slightly hopeless. But eventually he got the hang of it, and started to make contact.

'Not bad for a guy who's never played baseball,' I remarked.

'From my shinty days,' he said.

'Shinty?'

'It's a little like baseball, but instead of standing in a box by yourself hitting a ball, you're running around getting mangled by other guys while you try to do it.'

When our time ran out we went back down the stairs and on to the street.

'You hungry?' he asked.

'Definitely.' All we'd had up to now were hot dogs.

'I was thinking,' he said, 'we could take the L downtown, and find some place to eat. Somewhere by the river?'

'There are plenty of places nearby, how about we walk somewhere?' I said.

Several of the L stations on the Red Line were underground. I was having a great time with Gavin, and was hoping the day would end the way the dinner cruise should have, with us in bed. I didn't want to blow it by advertising my neurosis about being underground. It might make him wonder what other weird shit was going on with me. For now he could believe I was a relatively normal person.

'Whatever you want, you're the local.'

'There's a pizza place not far from here that I like, does that work?' I asked.

'Absolutely.' He grinned and grabbed my hand, and we walked back towards Addison.

We didn't get far before we were slowed by a growing crowd of people. Up ahead I could see blue flashing lights, close to the

Addison L stop. At the same time I felt my phone vibrate in my pocket.

'Hello?'

'Maude, are you OK?'

'Jeb? I'm fine, why?'

'There's been another murder, near Wrigley. You're over there, aren't you?'

'Yes, we're fine.'

'OK, uh, good.'

'Is there anything else?'

'No.'

I hung up.

'What is it?' asked Gavin.

'Another murder. Let's take a look.'

We pushed our way to the front of the crowd, and showed our identification to the officers who were putting up police tape around the scene.

It didn't take a forensic genius to see what had happened. The torso of a man was laying on the street. Several feet away were his limbs, laying in a line. There was no pool of blood; he'd obviously been killed elsewhere and dropped here.

A drive-by body dump, under the Addison L stop in Wrigleyville, shortly after a game with thousands of people in the vicinity. This was about as public as it gets. The cartel was ramping up.

All of a sudden I lost my taste for pizza.

'Gavin, can we go home? I'll make us something at my place.'

'Sure,' he said, taking my arm. 'But you can let me cook. I'm not bad.'

We took the bus and walked back to my apartment. When we walked in he took his jacket off and folded it neatly across a kitchen chair. He pulled up his sleeves and opened up the refrigerator, looking inside.

I walked up to him, reaching around to shut the refrigerator door, then took his hand and led him to my bedroom.

It was hours later when Gavin eventually turned his attention from me. 'What's this?' he said, pulling a book off of my nightstand. 'You must really like Betty Phang,' he said, looking at the stack of books.

'Betty Phang is my pen name.' Anyone who made it into my bedroom was privy to that secret.

Tunnel Vision

'Pen name? Did you *write* these?'

I nodded.

He looked back at the stack. '*All* of these?'

'Yeah. It's kind of a . . . uh, hobby.'

'I had no idea I was in the presence of a published author. Can I read one?'

'Sure. Take whichever one you want. Just . . . uh, I'd appreciate it if you keep it to yourself. My pen name, I mean.'

'Sure.' He looked through the stack and pulled out two.

'*Doggy Style Afternoon* or *Rear Entry Window*?' he asked, holding them both up.

'Definitely *Doggy Style*.'

He flipped through the pages, pausing occasionally to read. 'This is inspiring,' he said, putting the book aside and rolling on top of me.

An hour later we were laying on our backs, panting. Gavin looked at the clock.

'Shit.' He got up and started looking for his clothes, which were scattered around the room.

I rolled over, propping my head up with my hand, and watched him as he dressed.

Damn, he was built. Like Jamie on *Outlander*, but a little less beefy. And, as I'd learned, way more flexible, and with apparently unlimited stamina. With the added benefit that he wasn't fictional, and currently in my bedroom.

'Hot date?' I asked.

'I wish,' he said, leaning down to give me a soft kiss on the mouth. 'I've got more work to do on the financials. Jacobs'll have my bollocks if I don't get through it.'

'You could do it here,' I said.

He laughed, a sound I was coming to love. 'No chance. That would be *way* too distracting.'

I put on a pair of shorts and T-shirt and walked him out of my room.

Sags was sitting at the kitchen table drinking coffee. Standing next to her putting on her coat was Nicola.

Both looked like they'd got no sleep, but weren't too unhappy about it. A lot like we looked, I imagined.

'How are you, Sagarine?' said Gavin.

'Great. You?'

'Very fine.'

'This is Nicola,' she said.

He reached across the table to shake Nicola's hand. 'I'm Gavin.'

'Nikky,' she said back.

'Aren't you the chef, from the boat?'

'I am.'

'That was an amazing meal. I'd love to see what you can do with haggis.'

'Maybe I'll give that a try,' she said, leaning over to kiss Sagarine. Gavin did the same to me and we walked the two of them to the door.

When they were gone Sags and I went to the other side of the room and looked at them through the window. They were walking together, smiling and chatting. We watched them until they disappeared out of view.

'At least we don't have to worry about them cheating on us with each other,' said Sags.

'How do you know?'

'Based on last night I'm fairly certain she's a one-way girl. And before you ask, yes, she's as fun as her food. What about him? Should we expect a line of Scotland-themed books from you? Let me guess . . . *Fucklander? Bravehard? Mary, Queen of Cocks?*'

I shook my head. 'I don't know if I could do it justice.'

'Good?'

'Indefatigable. Exactly what I needed.'

Her eyebrows went up. 'Smith level?'

'Hmmm . . . more like different.' Jeb had felt like a connection. Gavin was a physical force. 'What about Nikky? Is she going to be a thing?'

She shrugged. 'I don't know,' she said, looking away.

'You still miss her,' I said.

She didn't answer me. It had been eight months since Sags had been with Ekaterina. I wasn't sure she'd ever be over her, despite the fact that the last time they were together Ekaterina had tried to kill her. She was in the wind now, living wherever Russian mobsters go when they're trying to avoid jail.

'I'm starving,' she said, changing the subject. 'Wanna go get some breakfast?'

'Sure. Then I need to get some sleep.'

SIXTEEN

I slept most of the day on Sunday and as a result didn't sleep at all Sunday night. When Monday rolled around I struggled to get up, and barely managed to make it to the task force meeting on time.

Gavin was there when I walked in. He looked fresh and gave me a conspiratorial smile and a wink. I smiled back. Jeb was in a chair against the wall, making a point, I thought, to not look my way. Nowak and Renfro were in their usual seats in the front.

The gang network and information that we'd gathered about them and pinned on the wall had been updated since we'd been in the room last, several new photos and names replacing the empty circles that had designated some of the lower level gang members. All four of Krol's lieutenants had been identified, their names and cell phone numbers next to each face.

I wasn't sure that Jacobs ever took a day off. If so, she sure didn't look like it. The pressure that Jefferson was getting from Chief Jennings had obviously made its way down to her and Bowles. They both had dark circles under their eyes, and he looked like he'd slept in his clothes.

As usual Jacobs started in at ten on the dot, addressing the team without preamble.

'There have been two more murders since Friday,' she said, pointing to two images on the wall of disjointed bodies.

'A very public body dump under the Addison Street L station.' She pointed to the picture of the body parts laying on the street, the ones Gavin and I had seen up close and personal. 'And another one in Logan Square, behind a gas station.' She pointed to a second image of a dismembered torso, this one next to a dumpster.

'Mr McCullom. What do we have on Brajen Krol's financials?' He shook his head. 'Fuck all, ma'am, if you'll excuse my French.' 'Nothing?' she said, incredulous.

'We've estimated that the gang is bringing in somewhere between fifty and a hundred thousand dollars from Red sales each month, but we can't find a dime of it in Krol's financials. There's no sign that he's moving large amounts of cash in or out of his accounts, or from any of the businesses he's running.'

'Do you need more warrants? This task force is a high priority, we can get more warrants.'

'That won't help us, ma'am. We have everything we know to ask for. As far as we can tell, not a cent of what they're making is going to Brajen Krol.'

'What about his lieutenants? Could he be using one of their accounts?'

'We've looked there too, ma'am.' Gavin was nothing if not thorough. I was glad he'd left early on Sunday to finish his work; if not she'd be letting him have it. 'There's nothing associated with any of his top men that indicates they're moving large sums of money around.'

'So they must have hidden accounts, or businesses?'

Gavin shrugged his shoulders. 'Presumably. I've looked through all of the SAR reports, transactions in Krol's accounts, and his lieutenants', that are just under the ten-thousand-dollar reporting limit, everything we normally do to uncover secret accounts and money flow. There's nothing.'

'Then do something that you don't normally do,' Jacobs snapped. 'Look, people,' she said, putting both hands on the table, 'bodies are dropping all over the city. Everyone is watching this task force, and we've got to move this forward. Detective Renfro, where do we stand on the undercover sites?'

He nodded. 'We think the best site for surveillance of a Red dealer is the encampment in Lower Wacker. Everything's set up, ma'am. We just need a UC officer.'

Jacobs pressed her lips together tightly. 'It turns out we're short on female UCs.'

I wasn't surprised she was having trouble finding one. There was in general a dearth of female UCs in law enforcement. I knew we had a few of them in the PD, and those we had were almost always working on existing projects.

'I'm ready, ma'am,' offered Nowak.

'Even if you were ready, Officer Nowak, which you're not,' she said, pointing to her arm, which was still in a sling, 'we can't put you out in the field after a shooting. You know that. Not to mention that your cover might be blown to this group.'

We still hadn't figured out why she'd been shot. Even though

Tunnel Vision   111

Nowak had said they were just trigger-happy, there was still the possibility that they'd recognized her as law enforcement.

Jacobs looked at me briefly, then looked away.

I was perfect for what we needed, but there was no way I was going into the field. I had no desire to put myself in any more danger. If I'd been reluctant before I'd gotten mugged, I was steadfast now.

'Anything else?' Jacobs asked.

'My sources tell me they're seeing an increase in the amount of Red on the street. It looks like the Greenpoint Crew is ramping up production. And we've identified a few more new gang members,' said Renfro, pulling a small stack of pictures out of a folder, and walking to the wall to pin them up. I noted that Jacobs hadn't updated the org chart to include any of the middlemen whose phone numbers I'd identified.

'Krol is still recruiting,' he continued. 'These three men are associated with relatively new phone connections to . . . uh . . .' He hesitated, knowing Jacobs' aversion to the middle management idea. 'To other gang members.'

The three men were hard-eyed, with dirty stubbled faces framed with greasy strands of unkempt hair.

'Who's that?' I asked, pointing to a third picture he'd pinned up.

'We don't have names yet. We could get them soon, if they're in the system.'

I continued to stare at the man on the right. Something about him looked familiar.

'Do you know this man, Ms Kaminski?' asked Jacobs.

I shook my head. 'No, I don't think so.' I might have seen him before, but I couldn't place where.

We were dismissed, the meeting petering out as there was nothing to do other than to continue to try dig up any traces of money laundering, and find a UC for the next phase.

I got the cell phone information about the three new gang members from Renfro, and spent the next few minutes putting it into my network database and updating my graphics. Not that Jacobs would care at this point. The big takeaway from my work had been identifying the existence of a cutout layer of gang members, middlemen who separated Brajen Krol from the day-to-day activities of the gang. If she didn't accept that, there was nothing else for me to do.

Once I updated the database I pulled up my work from the SK

task force. I was still technically on that team, and while my portion of the work had slowed, the team now focused on the final takedown portion of the operation, I could get a jump on putting together my section of the final report.

I got through the report in an hour. With nothing left to do I shut down my computer. I was getting ready to leave when Renfro came by my desk.

'Hey,' he said.

'Hey,' I said, not looking up.

'We have the names of the three new gang members. Cam Weathers, Lester 'Skink' Williams, and the one you thought you recognized. Luke Roberts.'

Sheila Johnson's dead son.

SEVENTEEN

I grabbed my bag and headed for the empty conference room. I took the picture of Luke Roberts off of the wall and left the station. On the way out I passed Gavin in the hallway.

'Want to get together tonight?' he asked, smiling.

'I can't, I'm sorry,' I said, barely registering the look of surprise on his face as I turned away.

I drove home as fast as I could. When I got there I went to my room and pulled a box out of the closet. I rifled through the contents, a stack of cards, papers and old photos.

Halfway down the stack I found what I was looking for. A faded envelope, tied with a disintegrating rubber band that had long ago lost its elasticity. It broke off as I pulled it off the envelope.

Inside were old pictures. My mom and dad, a few wedding pictures, group shots, some of Nana and a gaggle of relatives, most of whom I'd never met.

I really needed to get these into an album, I thought as I flipped through them.

Eventually I found what I was looking for. Senior photos, head-shots of each of my parents.

I put my dad's senior photo on my bed, and next to it laid the picture of Luke Roberts I'd taken from the conference room.

Dad's photo looked like any other senior photo from the eighties. He was wearing a jacket and tie, and had longish, wavy, slightly shaggy blond hair in the MacGyver style of the time period. He was handsome, with a slightly dimpled chin, straight nose and high arching eyebrows that gave his face an open, happy expression.

At first glance Luke Roberts looked nothing like my father. Where dad was clean-cut, Luke's chin and cheeks were covered in stubble, his sullen face framed by loopy strands of hair that covered his ears and ran down to his shoulders.

But there was no mistaking the distinctive eyebrows, the striking blue eyes, the waviness of the blond hair and slight dimple in the center of his chin.

There's no way this could be a coincidence.

114 Wendy Church

I went back to the station and straight to the incident room. Jacobs and Bowles were huddled over some documents.

'Ma'am, Commander.'

'What is it, Kaminski?' Bowles said, irritated.

'I'd like to volunteer for the undercover portion of this operation.'

Jacobs looked up, eyebrows raised.

'We need someone reliable in the field,' snapped Bowles. 'And we don't use untrained, part-time employees in undercover work.'

I looked at Jacobs. 'You need me. You said it yourself, we're dead in the water until we can bring in a female UC. And as I understand it, for this part of the operation there will be no contact with anyone. Just living on the street for a week or so.'

She looked at Bowles, who shook his head. 'No. No way. I'm not putting her distracted ass back on the street, even for something like this.'

Jacobs shrugged her shoulders, shaking her head. Even though she was the titular head of the task force, and was desperate for a UC, Chicago PD staffing decisions were firmly in Bowles' purview.

I left the room and went to Jefferson's office.

'Sir, may I have a moment?' I said, leaning in through the slightly ajar door.

He waved at me distractedly, looking down at some papers with a pen in his hand. I waited, standing, until he signed what he was reading and looked up.

'What is it?'

'Sir, I'd like to work undercover on the Meatless task force.'

He frowned. 'Why are you telling me? Talk to Jacobs,' he said.

'I did, sir. She wants me. Bowles is blocking it.'

Jefferson knew my history with Bowles, and what an asshole he could be. At the same time, he viewed him as a competent and loyal commander, and he wasn't in the habit of overturning his employees' decisions.

'He's in charge of his own personnel. If he says no, it's a no. Not to mention, you're not an employee, nor are you trained in undercover work, as far as I know,' he said, looking back down at his stack of papers.

Jefferson and I had a special relationship, but that didn't extend to me questioning his decisions.

'Sir, if you get me on as UC on this task force . . . I'll move to full-time here.'

Tunnel Vision

He looked up and put his pen down. He'd wanted me on as an employee, asking me about it regularly since I'd started at the PD. He wanted to grow the analytics department, and had hinted at putting me in charge of it.

I'd put him off, relishing my schedule and the freedom that came with it.

'You mean that? Join the Chicago PD, as a full-time employee?'

I nodded. 'I already have the clearance.'

He sighed. 'OK. If SSA Jacobs wants you in that role, and believes that your lack of field experience won't be a barrier, I'll clear the way with Bowles.'

'Thank you, sir.'

He pointed a finger at me. 'You'll start as an employee as soon as we clear the paperwork. I'll make sure it's expedited.'

He followed me out of his office. As I walked back to the incident room, I heard him tell his assistant to send Commander Bowles to his office.

I went to my cubicle and waited. It turned out I didn't have to wait long. Thirty minutes after sitting down I got a message to meet Jacobs in the incident room.

She was there, standing next to a red-faced Bowles.

'Is this true, Ms Kaminski, that you're interested in being our UC for this operation?'

'Yes, ma'am.'

'Can I ask, why the change of heart?'

I'd thought about how I would answer this on my drive down. I didn't want to let anyone know yet about my suspicion that Luke Roberts was Michael. If they did, they'd take me off the case. We weren't generally allowed to work cases where family members were involved.

'I've thought it over, ma'am. We're not likely to find anyone else to do this any time soon. I might be the only option, for weeks, or months.'

She didn't need much convincing. I was telling her what she wanted to hear.

She nodded. 'OK. We'll let the team know tomorrow.' She turned to Bowles. 'What do you typically do to train your UCs here?'

'There's a two-week UC course that qualified and experienced officers take,' he said, emphasizing 'qualified' and 'experienced'. 'We can trim that down. I'd put Nowak in charge of getting Kaminski ready. She's been through the course and can streamline it for this operation,' he said.

I knew he was furious, but if Jefferson had told him to let me do it, he would. He was nothing if not a loyal soldier.

Jacobs nodded, looking relieved. 'OK. We'll see you here tomorrow morning, Ms Kaminski. Get yourself ready.'

'Thank you ma'am. Sir,' I said.

I wasn't sure what Jacobs meant by 'get yourself ready', and thought it probably meant to get my head ready, but I had my own ideas about that.

The next morning I got to the station early and went down to the property desk.

Sergeant Slivey was back at it. Apparently no learning had taken place.

'This is the form,' he said, leaning over the counter, and waving a piece of paper in Linda's face. 'It's fucking signed, right here,' he said, jabbing a fat finger at the bottom of the page. 'Now bring me my stuff! You shouldn't even be making me go through this!' he yelled.

Linda took the paper from him and looked down at it critically. 'We want to keep things by the book, Sergeant Slivey, so yes, I do need your form. But as far as I can tell, you don't have the correct paperwork,' she said in an even voice, as she handed it back to him.

'What the fuck are you talking about? Form twenty-three – one nine six.'

'There's a typo in the last paragraph,' she said, pointing to a section at the bottom.

'You're holding me up for a fucking *typo*?' He looked at her, incredulous.

To the untrained eye redoing a form to remove a typo didn't seem like much. He could easily make the change on his computer and print out a new copy. But the new form would have to go through the same level of signatures that he'd gotten for the last one, and whatever supervisor he'd asked to sign it the first time wouldn't appreciate being bugged twice because Slivey had made a mistake. Linda knew how a simple thing could make him look really bad in front of his superiors.

'You fucking bitch. Too bad that bullet didn't hit you in the head.'

She looked at him dispassionately. We both watched as he stomped away, sputtering down the hallway.

'Hey, Linda.'

'Hi doll. What can I do for you?'

Tunnel Vision 117

'Can I buy you a coffee? I'd like to pick your brain about something.'

'Sure. Hang on a sec.' She closed down her computer and verified the lock to the evidence room was engaged, then came around from behind the counter.

'Do you mind if we go outside? I try to spend as much time as I can outdoors.'

'Of course.'

We went outside and to a nearby coffee shop, grabbed a couple of drinks and walked a few blocks to a small park. We sat down on the bench, where she relished a deep breath and looked back at the sky before turning to me. 'What can I do for you?' she said, taking a sip from her latte.

'I'm going undercover.'

She frowned. 'They only allow trained officers to do that. And never contractors.'

'I joined the force. And it's either that, or we have to close down the operation. Nowak's out of commission. There's no one else.'

We didn't need to say what we were both thinking. If Linda hadn't gotten shot she'd be the one doing this.

'I know about the shooting.' Her expression became serious. 'Maude, you need to back out of this. This is real. If an experienced officer like Nowak got herself shot during this operation, what do you think is going to happen to you, with no field experience, and no training? No offense.'

'None taken. They're going to put me through a crash course.'

She rolled her eyes and shook her head. 'The normal training is two weeks, and most undercover officers spend their whole lives training. It never stops. When does the op start?'

'Next Tuesday.'

'*Jesus*. That means at most you'll get a few training days. That isn't enough. Even two weeks isn't enough. You have no idea what you're getting yourself into. Undercover operations that involve narcotics are the most dangerous. Unbelievably dangerous.'

She didn't add what we both new, that in addition to not enough training I was epically unsuited for undercover work. I was a terrible liar, had no physical skills or firearms training, and had little experience with field surveillance. My job to-date had been to take the data from those operations and do magic with it. Not gather it myself. Prior to yesterday I'd been all in favor of dropping the operation if we didn't have a UC.

Now this operation looked like my only potential link to Michael. And really, how hard could it be? I'd have to sit at a homeless camp for a few days, a week at most. Go without a shower, eat shitty food. Fake getting high. I'd done most of those things before, albeit not with the specter of a murderous drug gang at the center of it.

'I know, I know. But . . . there's a chance it could lead to finding Michael.' Linda was one of the few people I'd told about Michael's disappearance. 'Please, Linda. I *am* going to do it. And I'll have a better chance of success if you help me.'

She sighed. 'Is there at least an operational plan for this op? Have you seen it?'

'Yes, there's a plan.' Jacobs had drafted one earlier, when they thought Nowak would be doing this part. 'I haven't seen it yet. I'll probably get it at the meeting today.'

'OK.' She sighed again. 'I'll meet with you over the weekend. Send me the plan when you get it. Come over to my place after work on Friday, and be prepared to stay through Sunday.'

I leaned over and hugged her. 'Thanks, Linda.'

We went back to the station, Linda to the basement and me to the incident room. Jacobs was standing at the front. She looked energized. Bowles looked like he'd swallowed a bug.

'Everyone, listen up. We're back on with the undercover phase of the op.'

Nowak looked up sharply.

'Who's the UC?' asked Gavin.

'Ms Kaminski is stepping up.'

'Are you kidding? She almost blew the last one, and that wasn't even really undercover,' Renfro scoffed.

'I am not kidding, Detective Renfro,' said Jacobs. 'The fact of the matter is, we don't have a choice. We either drop the operation, or put Ms Kaminski in the field. It's a simple surveillance op, and she won't be interacting with any of our targets.'

'I have to agree with Detective Renfro, ma'am. Analyst Kaminski doesn't have the training,' said Nowak.

'I'm glad you brought that up, Officer Nowak. You will be in charge of making sure Ms Kaminski is up to speed. You have the rest of the week to do it.'

'The UC training is a two-week course, ma'am.'

'I'm aware of that. You will take the salient elements of the training and use the remaining time to share those with Ms Kaminski. You

Tunnel Vision 119

know this op better than anyone, and you should be able to communicate the critical pieces. It's not difficult, and as I said, she won't be interacting with the targets. It's a light lift, undercover-wise.'

'There are no "light lifts" in undercover work, ma'am,' said Nowak, persisting. I wasn't thrilled with her uncertainty.

Jacobs ignored Nowak's comment. 'The basic outline is this: Ms Kaminski will be inserted as an addict into the encampment at Lower Wacker. She will observe and take pictures of the local dealer, and the gang members with whom he interacts. Once she gathers the evidence of the gang members involved in supplying the dealer, we can start picking them up.' She turned to Bowles, who distributed binders to everyone in the room. 'This is the operational plan, with details. Everyone familiarize yourself with it by Monday.

'Officer Nowak, you'll be in charge of the training and making sure Ms Kaminski looks the part. Detective Renfro will set up field communications protocol. Mr McCullom, please outfit Ms Kaminski with the appropriate surveillance equipment and other technical devices.

'We'll be establishing a temporary ops center at the CTA office on Lake. They've agreed to give us space. As needed Ms Kaminski will be flagged to visit the building for updates and to share information. Questions?' She looked around the room for a half second. 'Good. Dismissed.'

Jeb walked over to me at the end of the meeting. 'Maude, are you sure you're up for this?'

'I'm not a child,' I snapped. 'By the way, how did you know I was in Wrigleyville?'

'What?'

'You called me, Saturday, about the body dump on Addison.'

'I was worried about you.'

'How did you know I was there?'

'Oh. Gavin told me.'

'Gavin? What did he tell you?'

'Just that he was taking you to the game.'

They weren't friends. The only reason Gavin would tell Jeb we were going on a date was to rub it in his face.

Whatever. I couldn't think about any of that right now. I needed to get going on my training. I waited for Nowak, who was at the front of the room, arguing with Jacobs.

Apparently she lost the argument. Sour-faced, she walked to the door and waved at me to follow her to the training room.

EIGHTEEN

The next few days were a whirlwind of activity. Nowak got me outfitted in appropriate clothes, and put me through a condensed version of the department's undercover training course. 'I've taken out the parts about recruitment and utilization of informants, prosecutorial guidelines, and anything to do with eventual prosecution and evidence collection, since you're not going to come into contact with the targets,' she said. 'We're going to focus on your safety, behavior in the field, and risk management.'

Despite her earlier objections to my taking part in the operation, her instruction was focused and intense. 'Before we get into all of that, you need to understand that the paramount element of any undercover work is safety. It needs to be the top consideration for you, and for whoever is supervising you. I can't stress this enough: if things start to go sideways, if you ever feel unsafe, you need to abort. Don't think about it, just get out. Live to see another day.'

I nodded. I'd heard enough safety lectures to last me a lifetime.

She must have sensed my lack of enthusiasm, because she said, 'This isn't just talk, Maude. It was learned after years of mistakes that resulted in the deaths of cops and witnesses. Safety is the foundation upon which everything else in undercover work is built. I mean it. There is no operation that is worth your life. You need to commit that you're willing to get out.'

She waited for my 'OK' before continuing. Even with the stripped-down course content I understood that she'd been right. A two-week training, at least, for this kind of work seemed more appropriate than the few days I was getting. I was a little surprised she didn't offer to extend it over the weekend, even though I knew I was already scheduled with Linda. But on Friday afternoon she pronounced me done.

Afterwards I met Gavin at his desk to get my equipment. He smiled broadly when I walked up.

'What have you got for me?' I asked, not returning his smile.

'These are cameras,' he said, holding up a baseball hat and a pen.

Tunnel Vision

'Very James Bond.'

'This is a standard camera pen. You click it once to take a photo, twice to take a video, twice more to stop the video. It has pretty good resolution, you should be able to capture facial features from about thirty feet away.' He demonstrated by clicking the pen, then handed it to me.

'Does it work at night?' I said, turning it over in my hands.

'Not well. For obvious reasons there's no flash on it. But if you're close, and there's enough ambient light, it might.'

'Do addicts carry pens with them?'

'I don't know. The pen actually writes, you might want to get a journal or something, and write in it, to help your cover. This hat is a camera too.'

'Why do I need this, if I have the pen?'

'It's a backup. You turn it on and off by pressing this button underneath the bill, the camera operates out of the logo on the front. There's no photo option, it will record whatever you're facing. It has enough memory for about thirty minutes of recording.'

He turned it upside down and pointed to the center of the cap. 'The SIM card is sewn into the bill. There's no easy way to replace it in the field. So, like I said, only use it as a backup.'

He leaned close, and whispered, 'Do you want to get together tonight?'

'No,' I said, standing up.

He frowned, looking confused. 'I thought we had a good time.'

'Was it really necessary to tell Jeb we were going on a date?'

'We were just talking, and—'

'*Bullshit.* You wanted to rub his face in it.' I was angry. We'd had a great time and he'd ruined it by being a competitive macho jerk. Jeb and I weren't dating anymore, but that didn't mean I wanted to hurt his feelings.

'I'm sorry. Let me make it up to you.'

'I have to go. Thanks for this,' I said, picking up my bag and walking away.

Renfro was in the incident room, standing at the center table looking down at a map.

'Here,' he said, putting a small red sticker on the map, 'is the encampment on Lower Wacker you're going to be staying in. During the day the people who live there make their way out to panhandle, or go to one of the shelters for food or medical attention. The closest shelter to the camp is here,' he said, putting another sticker on the map a few blocks away from the shelter. 'And this,' he said, adding a sticker north of the river, 'is the CTA building where the team will be located.

'Each day you'll make your way out of the camp. Take this route.' He ran a line with a red sharpie from the camp to the river. 'You'll pass by a bench here,' he said, placing another sticker. 'If we need to talk to you urgently, there will be someone sitting there wearing a blue jacket and green baseball cap. If you see that, go to the CTA building right away. And I mean, right away. Got it?'

He waited for my nod. 'We'll be watching for you. When you come in wait in the lobby, and someone will meet you and escort you back.

'You'll have your phone, but best not to use it, unless there's an emergency. If there is, call this number.' He gave me a sticky note with a number on it. 'If you make that call in view of anyone the operation will be over, so don't do it unless you think you're blown, or there really is an emergency.'

Unlike the others, Renfro was far more worried about the operation than he was about me.

'We won't call you on it. Again, unless there is an emergency.'

I left and drove home, packed an overnight bag and went to Linda's, a modest two-flat in Uptown.

She met me at the door and gestured me into her living room. We sat on the couch, next to a small coffee table, on which was a small box and the operational plan, whose pages were now marked with colored tabs.

'Where's Bill?' I asked, looking around.

'Boys' weekend in Vegas.'

'Your idea?'

'Yeah, but it's not like I had to twist his arm. He loves it there.' She looked at my bag. 'Tell me what you have so far, in terms of equipment and comms procedures.'

I showed her my equipment and shared the communication setup that I'd gone through with Renfro.

She nodded. 'Renfro's a jerk but he's solid at this. What training did you get from the team?'

'Nowak put me through a condensed undercover course.'

'Nowak's good,' she said, nodding. 'What did she cover?'

'Safety, mostly. A little bit about the op. And she gave me some clothes.'

Tunnel Vision 123

'That's it?'

'That's all we had time for.'

She took a deep breath. 'OK. The first thing to know is that my focus is going to be different than what you went through with Nowak. It's not by the book, or based on the department's training. It's entirely taken from my own time working undercover.

'In my experience there are three key aspects to this kind of work. First is general UC best practices. Second are things related to your particular role – in your case, a drug addict who's been living on the street. Third are the particulars of the op you're working.

'I've read the ops plan, and we'll start there since it's the simplest piece. Your goal is to get some pictures of specific people engaged in specific actions. That's it.

'It's really important –' she leaned forward, looking me in the eye – 'to concentrate on what it is you're trying to accomplish. It's easy to get distracted in the field, but you have to stay laser-focused on your goal. Anything else you do that doesn't serve that goal is not your friend.'

She stared at me until I nodded.

'Next. UC best practices. We'll do more of this tomorrow, but the most important part is this: you don't need to be a superhero, robocop, or anything like that when you're undercover. Exactly the opposite, in fact. Unlike what you see in the movies, where impossibly attractive and fit people go undercover and successfully take down hardened criminals, the best UCs are utterly unremarkable in how they look, and act. Their hair, voices, accents, and manner of dress are completely forgettable, their emotional affects casual. You can spend an hour talking to one, and five minutes later can't describe them, or even recognize them from a photo.

'I was under once as a diner waitress,' she said, smiling as she remembered. 'I served our target breakfast every day for three weeks. When they finally took him down and brought him to the station, I passed by him as he was being processed. He didn't recognize me.

'We'll practice some of that tomorrow. The third aspect is the particulars of the role you're adopting. This is the hardest part. You have to become that person, for the length of the time you're undercover. I mean that you live and breathe your character. You need to be in that skin, so when the shit hits the fan, and it always does, you can fall back on it like muscle memory.

'We'll start with your clothes. What do you have?'

I pulled the clothes out of the bag. 'Nowak gave me these, said they were taken from the evidence room.'

She shook her head. 'These are too clean. We need them lived-in. Dirt, vomit, urine, the works. People living on the streets don't have regular access to washing machines.' She set them aside on the couch. 'We'll take care of that tonight.

'Next is your body. Same thing as the clothes. I recommend you not take a shower, or brush your teeth or your hair between now and when you go in the field.

'Those are the parts that go with living on the street. Now the addict part. Have you ever been addicted to opioids?'

'No.'

She picked up a remote on the coffee table and turned on the TV on the wall across from it, then started a documentary that she'd cued up. 'This is the best thing I could find. Keep your eyes on the couple in front of the blue tent.'

As we watched she paused numerous times to point things out. 'Look at her eyes. She's always tired, her eyes are red, and at the same time, she's hypervigilant, although she never stares at anyone directly. That comes from living on the street, and the paranoia from long-term drug use.'

She pulled a small bottle out of the box on the table and handed it to me. 'These will keep your eyes red, put drops in every four hours or so.'

We watched the couple on the documentary meet with a dealer, then fast-walk their way back to their tent, where they injected the drugs.

'Watch how long it takes for the drugs to hit them. How are you going to pretend to take the drugs?'

'I hadn't thought about it.'

'I recommend you fake snort them. Easier than fake injecting.'

We watched the couple lean back, eyes barely open.

'That's it,' she said. 'They're like that for hours.'

She paused the show, the image stuck on the man and woman, sitting on the ground next to their tent, their heads dropped between their knees.

All of a sudden it was real. I would have to be those people. How was I going to do that?

'Are you having second thoughts?' she asked, looking at my face.

Tunnel Vision 125

'No . . . I just . . . I don't know how I'm going to be convincing, as an addict.'

'I think you'll be fine. No one will be paying that close attention to you. From my experience, the danger will come from your own feelings, rather than being found out by people watching you.'

'What do you mean, my own feelings?'

'I mean that the biggest challenge in undercover work is loneliness, and paranoia.'

She looked up at the clock above her fireplace. 'That's enough for tonight,' she said, standing up. 'You can sleep in the guest room.'

We spent the next day and a half diving into my character, spending extra time on addict behavior, as that would be the toughest thing to fake. Sunday night came quickly.

'Who's your control officer?' she said, as I was putting on my coat to leave.

'Mike Renfro.'

'Do you trust him? Your control officer will be the most important person to you in the field.'

Renfro was an ass, but a decent officer. And while we'd never liked each other, I couldn't believe he would do anything to put my safety at risk.

'Do you?' she persisted.

I nodded.

'OK. How do you feel?'

'Nervous. The more I learn, the more I think I'm not cut out for this.'

She put her hands on my shoulders and looked in my eyes. 'This is different. You're more prepared. And you have an entire team behind you.'

I looked down at the ground.

'You do have one big advantage. You don't look like a cop. There's a reason they don't put beefed-up specimens of muscle out in the field as UC officers. People would never buy the fact that they're desperate criminals. Desperate people don't work out religiously.

'And it's not like you're going into this with no skills. You have plenty of them to bring to the party.'

'Yeah, I'm sure my computer acumen will be a big help in the homeless camp,' I snorted.

'More than you think. You're detail-oriented, and observant. And you have the most important thing you need.'

'What's that?'

'You're highly motivated to succeed. You know the old saying, "No battle plan survives first contact with the enemy"? The same holds true for undercover operations. It's almost a certainty that something will come up that forces you to throw the original game-plan out the window. And when that happens, your intelligence and ability to want to succeed will force you to be flexible to get the job done.'

I nodded uncertainly.

She sighed. 'There is one more thing you can do, but I don't know if there's time.'

'What's that?'

'Most successful UCs have someone specific in mind who they try to model during the operation. If you happen to know a female fentanyl addict living on the street, someone you could spend some time with, and try to keep that person forefront in your mind while you're undercover, it would help. Know anyone like that?' she said, joking.

'Funny, it turns out I do know someone.'

NINETEEN

I got home on Sunday night and waited up for Sags. I hadn't yet told her I'd be gone for a few days, much less living on the street as an addict.

'This sounds dangerous,' she said, after I explained what the week was going to look like. 'Are you really cut out for this?'

'I'll be fine. But I could use your help. Linda told me that the best way to prep for undercover work was to model someone you know. Any chance you can get a hold of Gigi, so I can talk to her?'

She frowned. 'I don't want to cause more trouble for her.' One of the reasons that Sags hated Jeb so much was that he'd used the threat of jailing Gigi to make Sags help him bring down the Russian gangster. I wondered if Gigi might not have been better off if Sags had let that happen. At least in prison she wouldn't be doing drugs every day, and having to prostitute herself.

'I just want to talk to her for a few minutes, ask a few questions. Jeb's not involved in this part.'

'I'll try. You know her, it's hard to track her down.'

Sags did manage to track her down, and Gigi agreed to meet us on Monday, on the promise of cash.

'I feel a little bad about this,' I said to Sags on our way over. 'We both know she's going to use the money to get high.'

'Yeah, I know. But that's one fewer guy she'll have to sleep with.'

We met Gigi in Logan Square at noon, at a coffee shop on Armitage. It was the best time of day to meet her. By later in the day she was either high, or hooking.

Sags bought us all coffee and we went outside to sit on one of the street benches. She'd also bought Gigi a donut, which she didn't eat, instead chain-smoking. Every time I saw her she looked skinnier. The bruises on her face we'd seen before were fading, a few fresh ones taking their place.

Gigi was Sags' older sister by two years. When they were children they spent their summer vacations at their aunt and uncle's lake house, and the whole family visited them at other times of the year, including a two-week stay every fall. But unbeknownst to their parents, Sags' uncle was a pedophile. He started abusing Gigi when she was eight, and it went on for years.

It finally ended when he died suddenly, from anaphylactic shock, but by then the damage was done. In junior high Gigi started skipping school and drinking, eventually moving up to drugs. By the time she was seventeen she'd developed an addiction to heroin, and when it became widely available, migrated over to the cheaper but more dangerous fentanyl.

Their parents tried putting her into rehab, but finally gave up when she was eighteen and had run away for the third time. They'd washed their hands of her, a constant source of animosity between them and Sags. Gigi now lived on the street, turning tricks for money to support her habit.

Sags did what she could to maintain a relationship with her, or, at least, a line of communication, giving her a safe place to sleep when she'd accept it, and occasionally money. She knew Gigi would spend it on drugs, but she looked at it as one less trick Gigi would have to pull.

'What time of day do you usually get high?' I asked.

Gigi looked at Sags, with her hand out. Sags handed her the sixty dollars they'd agreed to.

'I start looking for it when I get up.'

'How long does it last?'

She shrugged her shoulders. 'Never long enough,' she said, her eyes darting around. She was already thinking about where she was going to buy her next fix with the money we'd just given her. 'A couple of hours, I think.'

I asked as many questions as I could think of. How she made the exchange with her dealer, what she said, how long the high lasted, how she felt when she was doing it, and what she felt as it wore off.

'Have you done any Red?' I asked.

'I don't touch that shit,' she said. 'Philly Dope turns people into zombies. I can't work like that. And it gives them sores. But . . .'

'But, what?'

'The high lasts longer. And everyone trusts Red. No one has died from it. I mean, none of the regular users. They're getting sores, and all, but no one's OD'ing on it. At least not that I know.'

She stubbed out her umpteenth cigarette. 'I gotta go,' she said, standing up.

Tunnel Vision   129

'Thanks,' I said to Sags, as we watched Gigi walk down the street.
'It's fine. It's good to see her, even like this. Did it help?'
'Yeah. I mean, everything helps at this stage.'
We were walking back to my car when my phone rang.
'Hello.'
'Maude Kaminski?'
'Yes?'
'This is Dr Alvarez. The medical examiner,' he added, when I didn't immediately respond.
'Oh, yeah,' I said, distracted.
'I've found something interesting about the woman you were looking into, Sheila Johnson.'
'Yes?'
'It's . . . uh . . . it might be better if we meet in person. Can you drop by this afternoon?'
I could use a distraction right now. 'Sure. I've got a meeting in a few minutes, I'll come by after that.'
Our Monday task force had been rescheduled to the afternoon, one last meeting before the op was starting and I went into the field.
'So, Ms Kaminski, any last questions?' said Jacobs, kicking off the meeting.
'Ma'am, I need to register my objection, again, to sending Analyst Kaminski into the field for this op,' said Nowak.
'Did you complete Ms Kaminski's training, Officer Nowak?'
'Yes ma'am, but—'
'Ms Kaminski, do you feel you're ready?'
'Yes ma'am,' I said, with more conviction than I was feeling.
'That's good enough for me,' said Jacobs. 'There is one change to the plan. SSA Smith is going to be Ms Kaminski's control officer for this op.'
That was a surprise, and not an unwelcome one. Regardless of anything that had happened since we'd broken up, I trusted Jeb more than anyone but Sags.
'SSA Smith will pick you up tomorrow at four a.m., then drop you off at—'
She was interrupted by the squealing of tires, the sound of a car door slamming, then tires squealing again. Someone screamed.
Everyone got up and went to the long window. Below us on the street, in front of the building, was a man's torso. His head, arms and legs were scattered not far from it down the street.

Uniformed police were streaming out of the front door, pushing their way through a growing circle of bystanders. Bowles' phone rang, and he left the room in a hurry.

Gavin and Nowak rushed downstairs to take a look. I didn't need a close-up of yet another limbless body, and walked back to my desk. On the way I passed Jefferson's office. The door was closed, Bowles was standing in front of Jefferson's desk. I rarely saw Jefferson visibly mad, and he never yelled, but I could hear him through the door.

Bowles was getting his head torn off.

'I wonder what that's about,' said Renfro, heading in the same direction as me.

'What are you talking about? They just dumped a body in front of *police headquarters*,' I said, incredulous.

'I know, but who really cares if they kill dealers?'

'We do, because the cartel's not going to stop as long as the Greenpoint Crew is taking business from them.'

'So, we're doing the cartel's work now?' he said, shaking his head.

What a moron. I grabbed my bag, left out the back door, and drove to the medical examiner's building.

'We've been seeing an uptick in dead homeless people,' said Alvarez, wasting no time once I walked into his office. 'I did an autopsy on a man that came in yesterday. We do a sampling of them, a small percent of the ones we get. He had high levels of fentanyl in his system, mixed with xylazine.'

'So he died of a drug overdose?' I wasn't sure why he'd called me in, and why he was telling me this.

'That's what we thought at first. But it turned out that isn't what killed him. My examination uncovered petechial hemorrhaging.'

'I don't know what that is.'

'Broken blood vessels in the eyes. It indicates he died from asphyxiation.'

'Isn't that a byproduct of xylazine use?' I'd heard it caused respiratory paralysis.

'No. Petechial hemorrhaging in the eyes is caused by something external blocking the airways.'

'You mean he was strangled?'

'Yes, or somehow asphyxiated. I went back and reexamined Sheila Johnson's body.'

Tunnel Vision   131

'You still have the body?'

'Depending on the circumstances, we keep bodies up here for months, on the chance that they will be identified and claimed. In this case, I'm glad we did. I found petechial hemorrhaging, as well as bruising around her neck, and upper arms.'

'Bruising?'

'Yes. It could be consistent with restraint and manual strangulation. I won't know for sure until I do a full autopsy, but at the moment we're backed up and it's not a priority.'

'You're saying Sheila Johnson could have been *murdered*?'

'Yes.' He nodded. 'Along with several other indigent people that have been brought in over the last two months. More than usual.'

This changed everything. *Dammit.* 'How could you not pick this up before? You'd said you'd done an examination on her.'

'I said I'd done a *preliminary* examination, Miss Kaminski,' he said, his voice officious. 'The bruises often don't show up right away, and the petechial hemorrhages can be missed without a close examination. I only found them on her because I was looking for them. In any case, I thought you would want to know.'

I noticed for the first time how tired he looked, and wondered when he'd last slept. Autopsies on people living on the street weren't a high priority for the city; he must be doing these on his own time.

'I'm sorry, yes, you're right. Thank you. I'm . . . uh . . . a little distracted right now with another case.'

'You're on the meat puppet task force, aren't you?'

I nodded. 'Meatless.'

'That one's interesting. From what I can tell, you have at least two killers.'

'It's the cartel, there's probably a lot of people doing it. Anyone who wants the money.'

He shook his head. 'No, I mean, there are two *completely* different methods to these killings, and different causes of death.'

He motioned to his computer and pulled up some photos. 'See,' he said, pointing to an image and zooming in, this one of the dealer they'd found in Avondale. 'Look at the body, and the cuts on the torso.

'There's blood everywhere, and these are jagged cuts,' he said, pointing to one of the shoulders. 'A real hack job.'

He changed the image, to the one they'd found in Logan Square. 'This one, this one is completely different. There's minimal blood loss, and the cuts are clean, precise.'

'So?'

'So it means that whoever did this,' he said, pointing to the second man, 'used a sharper instrument to dismember the body, like a scalpel. And he or she was skilled handling a knife.'

'You think a doctor killed them?'

'Hard to say. But maybe most significantly, he was dead before he was dismembered. Otherwise we'd see more blood.'

'Do you know what killed him?'

He shook his head. 'I'm going to do full autopsies on each of these men as soon as I have a chance.' I knew that was true; anything related to the task force was a priority.

I wasn't sure how much I cared about the cartel's varying methods of killing people, but I thanked him and left.

I was far more interested in the fact that Sheila Johnson had been murdered, and that I'd be spending the next few days in a place where the same thing could happen to me.

TWENTY

I didn't sleep much, my mind running back and forth between the news that Sheila Johnson had been murdered, and the fact that I was going to be spending at least the next few days living on the street.

When Jeb picked me up at four a.m. I'd had almost no sleep. I tried to put a positive spin on it; looking exhausted would help with my cover.

'You smell terrible,' he said, his nose wrinkling when I got into his car.

'How do you think I should smell?' I said, cranky. 'I'm supposed to be someone who's been living on the street. Where do you think I'd be able to take regular showers, or wash my clothes? All of my money would be spent on drugs, and maybe some food. There wouldn't be enough for soap, and fucking toothpaste, or a change of socks,' I said, irritably.

He put one hand up in placation. 'Sorry, sorry. Are you ready?'

As ready as I'll ever be. 'Yes.'

We drove in silence and he dropped me off on Upper Wacker, a few blocks away from the encampment. I grabbed my backpack and got out of the car.

'Maude,' he said, rolling down his window. 'Be careful. The only reason you're doing this is because there's no one else. Even so, you know you can't approach anyone who looks like a gang member. Stay away from people, take some pictures, that's it. OK?'

I nodded and walked down to Lower Wacker and the encampment.

Like the one I'd been to on Taylor, the smell as I approached almost knocked me over. And there was a depressing similarity between the encampments, this one littered also with needles, food containers, toys, and piles of fetid garbage.

Someone had written 'fentanyl = death' on one of the support pillars. It had been crossed out, and now said 'tranq = death'.

My instructions had been to establish myself in the camp, fake getting high, get pictures of the dealer selling drugs, and hopefully capture him interacting with his suppliers that hopefully would be known gang members.

I walked with my head down to the end of a row of tents and cardboard structures, then put my pack down. I pulled out a small tent and put it up, then went into it with the rest of my things. Linda had told me to do that right away, without looking at anyone.

I stayed in my little tent for a few hours, listening to the sound of cars above, and the occasional roar of a truck. *How did anyone get any sleep down here?*

After what seemed like an appropriate amount of time for a nap I came out of the tent, and sat down on the ground in front of it, looking around surreptitiously from under my baseball cap.

Gigi had said that most addicts either woke up to a fix that they'd saved the night before, or waited anxiously for the dealer to appear. A few people had already shot up, and were either laying down, or zombie-walking around the encampment. Others were watching the end of the underpass, their anxiety palpable.

I wasn't sure what time it was but estimated it was close to noon when a man walked into the end of the overpass. He stopped, and several people in the area got up and ambled towards him. He must be the dealer.

I had my journal in my lap, pretending to write. I was supposed to take pictures of the guy actively dealing, to give us leverage over him when we brought him in, but I wasn't prepared, and was fumbling with the pen and missed the first few transactions.

Shit, I'd really need to be on my toes.

More people approached the dealer, and I was able to take a few pictures. The exchanges were fast. The addict would pull out crumpled bills and put them into the hand of the dealer, who would pull out a single glassine envelope and hand it over.

Once the dealer was gone I pretended to snort my fake drugs. I mimicked the reactions of addicts, laying back on my pack and staring up at the concrete overpass.

Later in the day I joined the people who shuffled towards various street corners or to shelters for food. There was no man with a blue jacket and green baseball cap on my communications bench, so I didn't go to the CTA, having nothing to report. After what felt like the right amount of time I headed back to the underpass. I hadn't eaten, and had some power bars in my backpack, but the smell of the place was making me nauseous, so I just drank some water and waited for nightfall.

Tunnel Vision 135

They'd told me that the camps were relatively safe, that the addicts didn't care about anyone else, and any other people that were there were doing all they could to survive. Still, I'd never been on the street overnight before. It was beyond unsettling to be out in the open, surrounded by strangers, even though I knew I had support less than a mile away. How had Sheila Johnson done this for twenty years?

I was also exhausted, after spending the day trying to look tired, dragged-out, and high, while at the same time being hyper-observant. Nevertheless I couldn't sleep, laying down with my hand gripping the small flashlight that doubled as a stun gun I'd been provided by Gavin.

When I came out of my tent the next morning I was going on two nights of almost no sleep. I wasn't sure I'd be able to last three days, much less the week that the operation plan called for. Linda had said that field operations needed to be fluid, depending on the situation. My situation was that I didn't think I'd last much longer. I made the decision to change things up.

Around noon the dealer showed up again, and after several of the addicts made their purchases I put my journal down and walked over to him. I waited behind one of the other addicts until he shuffled away.

I stood in front of him and held out a handful of crumpled bills.

'Who are you?' he asked, looking me up and down.

'I want to buy.'

'I don't know you,' he said, starting to walk away.

'Please, c'mon, man,' I said, grabbing at his sleeve. I'd seen Gigi when she was desperate for a fix, and tried to emulate her pleading tone.

It must have worked, because he took my thirty dollars and gave me a glassine envelope with a small amount of white powder.

'I want Red,' I said, handing the drugs back.

He took the envelope, and fished around in his pocket, pulling out another one with an eagle stamped on it.

I reached for it, but he pulled it back.

'It's fifty.'

'Fifty?' Renfro had said the going rate for a single hit was thirty.

'New customer discount,' he said, smiling cruelly.

I reached into my pocket and pulled out another crumpled bill and handed it to him, and once he pocketed it he handed me the envelope.

I copied what I'd seen the other addicts do, grasping it greedily in my hands and fast-walking back to my tent, where I pretended to snort the powder, then leaning back against my pack and almost but not entirely closing my eyes.

Several more people ambled up to the dealer but he shook his head, apparently having run out. Nevertheless he stayed there, leaning against one of the pilings. An hour or so later a car pulled up near that end of the underpass.

Two men got out and walked towards the dealer. I thought I recognized one of them from the pictures of the gang members we had up at the station. I frantically pulled up my pen and took as many shots as I could.

After the two men got in their car and left, the dealer walked away. He returned in a little over an hour, and started dealing again.

Once he left I headed for the CTA office. When I got there I gave the prearranged signal to a woman behind the counter that I had information. She ushered me out of the lobby and down a narrow hallway and into a room.

In the small conference room were Jacobs, Jeb, Bowles, Renfro, Nowak and Gavin. They'd moved in, the wall covered with maps and the recreated gang org chart.

'You look like shit, Kaminski,' said Renfro, smiling.

'You try living on the street for two days, asshole,' I hissed back. I was in no mood for his shit.

'What do you have for us?' asked Jacobs.

'The dealer is selling both Red and the cartel stuff,' I said, handing over the packet of Red I'd bought. 'Around one o'clock a car pulled up to the site, and two men got out.' I looked at the wall. 'This guy,' I said pointing to one of the pictures, 'and this guy.'

I'd committed their faces to memory, and had watched closely in case one of them was the guy I thought was Michael. 'This one,' I said, pointing again to the first guy, 'walked up to the dealer, while the other one hung back. The one next to the dealer handed him a slip of paper. The dealer looked at it, then burned it up with his lighter. They barely talked; once the paper was burned the two of them left in their car.'

Bowles' face was beet red. 'You bought drugs?'

'Yes, uh, I wasn't sure the pictures would come out. I thought you could use some direct evidence.'

'You were given strict instructions to not interact with anyone.

Was any part of that unclear? That's it, Kaminski. You're—'

Jacobs interrupted him. 'So we've confirmed the gang is working directly with the dealers. As we expected,' she said smugly. 'Did you get pictures?'

'I'm not sure, it's a little dark down there, and I was pretty far away.' I handed Gavin my pen and he took out the SIM card, replacing it with a new one.

'What did you see happen between the dealer and the gang member?'

'Like I said, it looked like he gave him a piece of paper.'

Jacobs frowned. 'Paper? That's it? Did you see them hand him any drugs?'

I shook my head. 'No.'

'Did the dealer give him any money?'

'No.'

'You're sure?' she prodded.

'The only money I saw change hands was between the dealer and the junkies. The gang member didn't give him anything other than the piece of paper, at least that I could see.'

'What did the dealer do after he met with them?'

'He left.'

'Did he come back?'

'Yeah, about an hour later. He dealt for a little while, then left for the day.'

Jacobs frowned. 'You're going to need to go back.'

'I have to object,' said Bowles. 'Kaminski is not a fully trained field agent, she's shown she can't follow orders, and is potentially a huge liability.' I noticed he didn't mention anything about my own safety.

'I have to agree, Susan,' said Jeb. 'This is too dangerous.'

'We don't need her to interact with anyone,' said Jacobs. 'We just need to see an exchange of drugs and money between the dealer and the gang members. Ms Kaminski, if we send you back, do you think you can follow orders, to have no interactions with anyone?'

I couldn't imagine spending another night in that place. But I nodded.

'Ma'am,' said Renfro. He'd been quiet since I'd walked in.

'What?'

'I think they might be using dead drops for the drugs.'

'What do you mean?'

'The gang could be stashing the drugs somewhere, and the slip of paper is how the gang communicates the location to the dealer. Once the dealer gets the location he goes to the site and takes the drugs, and leaves the money.'

'You're telling me the gang is leaving drugs out in the open, in broad daylight?'

'Probably not out in the open. But yes, in public, places where no one would be likely to come across them.'

'Still, doesn't it make sense that someone else would find them?'

'Maybe, but even if so, these drugs are so cheap to make, if someone did stumble across them, it wouldn't be a big financial hit, replacing the odd batch. Far cheaper than getting caught.'

Jacobs looked skeptical.

'If you think about how the Heroin Highway works, it makes sense. There the addicts pull up in cars and give their money to one guy. That guy gives a signal to someone down the street, and when they drive down the street they pick up their drugs from the second guy. It's standard drug dealing procedure, so they're never caught with both the drugs and the money at the same time. It makes them almost impossible to prosecute.'

'What about the money?' said Nowak.

Renfro shrugged. 'What about it? The dealer's probably dropping off the money at the drug stash site. I'm guessing that none of the dealers would try to stiff the gang. At least not more than once. If the money *was* found, and taken by someone else, it's off the dealer, not the gang. And who knows,' he said, 'the gang might have someone else watching over the site.'

'They did work in three-man teams in Brooklyn,' said Jacobs, thoughtful.

Renfro nodded. 'It's kind of a perfect operation. They're not just avoiding being caught with both drugs and money, they're not handling either one at the point of sale.'

Jacobs turned to me. 'What time did you say the gang members approached the dealer?'

'Around one.'

'Middle of the day? That's odd.'

'Maybe not,' said Renfro. 'We know the lower level gang members are getting phone calls in the morning from the middle managers.'

Jacobs bristled at the mention of 'middle managers' but stayed

Tunnel Vision 139

silent. She still wasn't convinced that Brajen Krol wasn't dealing directly with the lower level members.

'Maybe those calls are telling them the location of the dead drops. The gang members pick up the drugs from wherever they're being made, and then they drop them off at the stash sites. By the time they do that, and then meet up to share the locations with the dealers, it would be about that time.

'It all fits, ma'am,' said Renfro.

He was a dick but he knew his stuff. He had me convinced.

Jacobs sighed. 'Let's suppose you're right.' She turned to the rest of the team. 'What's the play?'

'We could follow the dealer to the stash site,' said Jeb quietly.

'All that does is give us the dealer. We can pick him up any time we want right now. Besides, it's not likely they're using the same location twice. What would be the point, when they can change it every day?' said Nowak.

Jeb persisted. 'If Detective Renfro is right, the dealer will drop off the money at the stash site, and pick up the drugs. Someone from the gang has to come by and pick up the money. Possibly the third member of the team. And this way we can get her –' he looked at me – 'out of there sooner rather than later.'

I looked at him gratefully. Anything that would get me out of there sooner was a good thing.

'So we have one guy picking up a bag of money. What does that get us?' asked Nowak.

'We'll have evidence of a known drug dealer, based on Ms Kaminski's photos and interaction, dropping off money collected from drugs distribution, and that same money being picked up by one of the gang members,' said Jacobs. 'That's enough to bring him in, and depending on the amount of drugs, to at least threaten him with significant jail time.' She looked around the room. 'Any other ideas?'

No one said anything. I was usually one of the better idea generators, but I was too dragged out to offer suggestions. It had only been two days and I was already losing my shit. I looked at Nowak with growing respect. I had no idea how she did this kind of thing all the time.

Jacobs sighed. 'This is more sophisticated than what they were doing in Brooklyn. Brajen Krol is learning. In any case, the original plan was to pick up the lower level gang members, and get them to roll on Krol and his lieutenants. That's still the plan,' she said. 'Ms Kaminski, you go back to the camp.'

I stifled a groan.

'We'll post an unmarked car near the overpass,' she continued. 'The next time that Ms Kaminski sees the exchange between the dealer and the gang members, she'll alert the car to follow the dealer to the stash. Once he's left the site, the car will follow him and pick up whoever comes for the money. After that's done we'll grab the dealer.'

'The dealer's not going to talk, ma'am,' said Nowak.

'No. But we'll have him dropping off the drugs and leaving money, along with selling drugs. We'll also have at least one gang member, and possibly fingerprints on the money and the drugs. With those we might be able to get some of the other members.' She'd perked up. 'Detective Renfro, you work with Commander Bowles and organize the surveillance car at the camp and the pickup protocol. Ms Kaminski, go back to the camp today. The next time you see the exchange between the dealer and the gang members, take your pictures, and then alert the car. That's all you have to do. No interactions with the dealer, or anyone else. Understood?'

'Yes ma'am.'

She was giving out instructions to the rest of the team and I turned to go. Before I left I took another look at the wall of pictures. They'd updated the board since I'd seen it last, the latest dead drug dealers had been identified.

I startled when I saw the name of one of the dead dealers.

James Randall, aka 'Rando'.

Gigi's drug dealer and pimp.

I walked over to Renfro, and whispered, 'Mike, did you say that the last dead drug dealer wasn't selling Red?'

'Who?'

'James Randall.'

He looked up at the board. 'Yeah. All we found on him was the regular shit. Fentanyl mixed with laxatives.

'It's odd,' he said, scanning the wall of dead dealers. 'The cartel has been leaving the bodies in public places, for maximum shock value. But Rando and these guys,' he said, pointing to a few other dead dealers, 'were left in alleys.'

I wanted to ask why, but I thought I might know already.

A horrible idea was forming in my head. One I desperately wanted to ignore.

TWENTY-ONE

I walked slowly back to the encampment. I couldn't wait for this to end. Alongside the respect I'd developed for Nowak and other undercover cops was a growing empathy for people living on the streets. No shower, no way to wash my clothes or myself. I'd had my socks on for three days and my feet felt gross. I vowed to donate a load of socks to the shelter as soon as I got out of here.

The camp had pretty much packed it in for the night. People were asleep or high. The nights were starting to get cooler, and everyone was in their tents, if they had them, or huddled together, pulling blankets and comforters close to keep warm.

No one was setting fires. Nothing would get you booted from a homeless camp quicker than a fire hazard.

The quiet was broken by the sound of footsteps. I peered out of my tent to see a long figure approaching the edge of the camp.

As he got closer I could see he was carrying a bag, a bottle of water sticking out of the top.

He came to the edge of the camp, and looked around. When he walked to the center of the camp, his face was illuminated by the lone street light that still worked.

It was Luke Roberts.

'Mom?' he called softly, peering into each of the tents.

He made his way around the encampment, and I held my breath as he walked past. He glanced briefly at me and moved on.

'Are you looking for Sheila?' I asked, just after he passed by.

His eyes widened, and he turned away from me, and started to walk faster in the direction of the way he'd come.

'Wait,' I said, standing up. When I did that he set the bag he was carrying on the ground and started running.

'*Wait*! I just want to talk to you!'

I followed him through the camp and for a half block before I lost him. I walked back to my tent, stopping to pick up the bag he'd dropped.

In it with the water were a couple of apples, some cheese, a box

142 Wendy Church

of crackers, and a pair of socks. I put on the socks, took a drink of water, and tried to go to sleep.

The next morning I shuffled out of the camp with the rest of the camp residents, veering off to the bench to check for any signals. I planned to be back well before noon to watch for the gang members, and alert the team when they showed up. I didn't want to be gone long, in case either they or Luke Roberts showed up again. And I was ready to stay another night, or as many as it took, to see if I could get another glimpse of Luke Roberts.

When I walked by the signaling bench there was a man sitting on it reading a paper. He was wearing a green hat and a blue jacket, the sign for 'come in, urgent'.

I walked to the CTA building, and when I got there I was ushered quickly into the back room.

In the room were Commander Bowles, one of the station lab techs, and two uniformed officers.

'What's going on?' I asked.

The room had been cleared out. No one else from the task force was there, and all of the pictures and information on the walls had been taken down.

'Take off your jacket,' barked Bowles.

I took it off and gave it to Bowles, who handed it to the lab tech. He spread it flat on the table, then wiped a flat swab all over both sleeves. He laid the swab down, then added a number of drops from a small bottle to the end he'd rubbed on my jacket.

A few minutes later he peered at the flat stick. 'Positive for fentanyl,' he said to Bowles.

'Well, duh,' I said. 'Of course it's positive. I've been on the street, buying drugs from a dealer as part of an undercover operation. What the hell is going on?'

'You're done,' said Bowles. 'Report to Deputy Chief Jefferson,' he added, a malicious half smile on his face.

One of the officers gestured at me to follow him, and he drove me to the station. I didn't miss the fact that he put me in the back of the patrol car, instead of in the front.

He escorted me to Jefferson's office and left, closing the door behind him.

Jefferson was shifting in his chair behind his desk, looking as uncomfortable as I'd ever seen him.

Tunnel Vision 143

'Maude, is there a problem?'

'What do you mean, sir?'

'I mean, I know that finding your brother's backpack must have been a big shock to you and your family. And people, well, they handle that kind of thing in different ways. Do you, uh, do you need help?'

'Help?'

'There's no shame in it, Maude. You wouldn't be the first law enforcement person with a substance abuse problem.'

'*What*?'

'I've heard reports of you coming in late, being distracted, obviously hungover. Missing meetings. Someone made an allegation, and we had to investigate. We found this in your desk.' He held up a glassine envelope of white powder.

'Oh, for fuck's sake,' I said. 'That's not mine.'

'Your clothes tested positive for fentanyl.'

No surprise that Bowles hadn't wasted any time passing that along.

'Of course they did. I'm undercover, as an addict, remember? And I turned in the drugs I bought on the street, right after I bought them.'

He stared at me, then visibly relaxed. 'I believe you. But we have to investigate this. Until we do, and you're cleared, you can't be here.'

'What?' Just when I'd made contact with Luke Roberts, who might be my brother. 'No, sir, you can't take me off of this. Not right now,' I said, pleading.

'I'm sorry, Maude. Those are the rules. You need to report to the lab, and take a blood test. This isn't a request. Get your test, and leave the station. Don't come back until you hear from us.'

There was nothing left to say. I went down to the lab and took a blood test.

'How long for the results?' I asked the technician as he put the band aid over the puncture.

'Normally a day or two, but we're backed up at the moment. Could be longer.'

Dammit. I knew the results would turn out to be negative, but now I had to wait at least two days for everyone else to know it.

More importantly, why did they find drugs in my desk? And what had made them look for them in the first place?

Someone was setting me up.

I left and drove home. On the way I called Jeb but it went to voicemail.

I needed a shower, but on the way home I detoured to his apartment in Andersonville.

Maybe he would know what was going on.

He answered the door, looking surprised.

'Maude. What are you doing here?' he said, peering over my shoulder into the hallway.

'Can I come in?'

'Sure,' he said, after a short hesitation.

'What the hell is going on?' I asked.

He shook his head. 'I don't know. This morning they told us the op was over and to go home. And, uh, that we weren't supposed to be in contact with you. I thought you might be able to tell me.'

'I have no fucking idea. They tested my clothes for drugs, and I had to take a blood test.'

His eyes widened.

'For Christ's sake, Jeb, I'm not doing drugs. And they're going to find that out when the blood test comes back,' I said, exasperated. 'Do you have anything to drink?'

'Sure,' he said, walking into the kitchen and opening up the refrigerator.

'I have beer,' he said, moving things around. 'And beer.'

'Beer's fine, thanks.' He pulled one out and opened it, handing it to me. I took a long drink. It tasted really good. I realized I hadn't had anything other than water to drink in days.

'I'm suspended until I get cleared.'

'Suspended? Why?'

'They found drugs in my desk. Someone is setting me up.'

'Why would anyone do that?'

'I don't know,' I said, shaking my head.

'Without a UC the op is dead,' he said. 'We needed the location of the stash and money to make anything stick on these guys.'

'I know.'

The op is dead. 'Doesn't it seem like a big coincidence that this happened the day we thought we were going to break it open, and follow the dealer back to the cash?' I asked.

'I don't know. I'm not sure it matters.'

Tunnel Vision 145

'It would matter if we were getting close to something. And if someone wanted to stop that from happening.'

'Someone? Who?'

'Someone who knew what was going to happen.'

'How would anyone know that?'

'*Anyone* wouldn't. It had to be someone who knows what's going on with the task force.'

'You mean someone on the team?' he said, frowning. 'No.'

'There's no other explanation. And the timing is just too coincidental. There's a rat on the task force.'

'Like who?'

'Well, there's a finite list of people involved in this. You, me, Renfro . . . and how well do you know Jacobs?'

He put his hands up. 'I know how you feel about Renfro, but he's pretty committed to the job. And Jacobs, well, we go back a long time. I wouldn't say we're friends, but I'd be shocked if she was trying to ruin this operation. She's one of the most committed law enforcement people I know, not to mention that her career is tied to the success of this task force. As a woman she's had to work twice as hard for promotions, this is her big chance. I can't see her sabotaging her own team.

'There are a few others that knew what was going down today,' he offered. 'Two detectives were in the surveillance car.'

'They didn't know about what was happening until today. I don't think that would have been enough time to set me up.'

'Maybe McCullom . . .' he said, musing. 'Jacobs brought him over with her from Philly. So he's got a history with the Greenpoint Crew. And what do we know about him, really?'

I had no doubt that if we had a mole, Jeb would want it to be Gavin. But he was still right that we couldn't rule him out. I'd slept with him, but I really didn't know much about him.

'Jefferson, Nowak, Linda, Bowles . . .' I continued. I'd love it if it were Bowles. 'I think we can rule out Jefferson, and Linda. And Nowak was shot.'

'Can we?'

'Can we what?'

'Can we rule anyone out? Really?' He leaned back against the refrigerator. 'I think you're right. People turn for all kinds of reasons. Money, obviously, but sometimes they get blackmailed. Or their family gets threatened. People will do anything to protect their family.'

'So, what do we do?'

'I don't think *you* can do anything. You're *persona non grata* until you're cleared. I'm not even supposed to be talking to you.'

'OK, but then what?'

He looked down. 'I don't know. Even if, uh, I mean, when, you get cleared, I doubt they'll put you back in the field. And until Jacobs can put another UC out there, the task force is basically on hold.'

'I'm not talking about that. How do we find out who is setting me up?'

'I don't know that, either. But if it has something to do with the task force, then you're probably in the clear if it gets shut down.'

The last thing I wanted was for the task force to get shut down. Michael might be in the gang, and rolling them up was how I was going to find him.

He looked at the empty bottle in my hand. 'I'd offer you another one, but I'm not even supposed to be talking to you . . .'

'I know, it's OK. I've got something I have to do, anyway.'

Something I had to do. Not something I wanted to do.

I left his place and drove home. When I got there I dropped my bag and coat on the floor by the door and took a long hot shower. Then I sat on our couch and waited.

At midnight the front door opened.

'Hey,' said Sags, as she shut the door and put her bag down.

I had thought of a million ways to start this conversation. In the end I just came out with it.

'Please tell me you didn't murder Gigi's drug dealer.'

She ignored me and walked into the kitchen. It was all the confirmation I needed.

'God*damn*it, Sags!' I yelled, following her.

She pulled a beer out of the refrigerator and opened it. She took a long drink and then turned towards me, leaning against the counter.

'He was beating up my sister,' she said. 'Selling her to his friends. What would *you* do?'

'I wouldn't be murdering people!'

'Really? Are you sure? What if it were Sophie? Your little sister? What if someone got her hooked on drugs, and then shopped her around like meat to his friends? What would you do to protect your family? You're really saying you wouldn't do *anything*?'

'Really,' I said, although imagining Sophie going through all of that, I wasn't one hundred percent sure. 'And he wasn't the only one, was he?'

The ME had said there were several bodies with clean cuts, cuts that were made after death, by someone who was skilled with a knife.

Like a chef.

'They're scum. Every one of them has sold drugs to my sister, and to lots of other people. They deserved to die.'

I shook my head. 'Do you realize what you've done to the investigation? The ME has figured out that some of the dealers were killed by different people. The task force now has to reconsider our earlier assumptions about the cartel, and the Red, because you decided to piggyback on the cartel's murders with your own. This could set the investigation back months,' I said, leaving out the fact that it was dead in the water now, anyway.

'They'll figure it out,' she mumbled, walking towards her room.

'They sure will if I tell them,' I shot back.

She stopped, her hand on the door. 'You wouldn't.'

'*Wanna bet?* The team is going to waste resources tracking down this new development. Resources we need to put this gang out of commission. Other people's lives are going to be lost because of your actions.'

'Other *people's*?' she sneered, turning to look at me. 'You mean drug dealers.'

'Whatever. They were people. People that you cut up into pieces.'

'I only did that to throw the blame on to the cartel,' she said, shaking her head. 'And only after they were dead.'

'So how did you kill them?'

Most of the men she'd killed before this were victims of various kinds of food-related poisons, like death cap mushrooms, or kitchen appliances, and toxic cleaning products, none of which would be viable on the street.

'Do you really want to know?'

Her eyes were glittering, and her cheeks were flushed. Exactly the way she looked when she was lost in her cooking.

'You *like* it,' I said, aghast. 'You actually enjoy doing it.'

She shrugged. 'It needs to be done.'

'It's not your job to decide how to punish people.'

'You don't get it, do you?' she said, her voice rising. 'Rando was a murderer himself. The cops take months, or years, to put a few of them behind bars. *If* they get lucky. Then they're out a few years later, dealing, and pimping out young women. Sometimes young *girls*. And all the while, people like my sister are dying by the thousands.

'Face, it, Maude, the police aren't staffed to even *begin* to deal with this problem. I'm not willing to sit around and hope that at some point they'll get around to arresting the guys who were beating up and abusing my sister.'

We stared at each other, neither willing to back down.

She was the one to finally break the silence. 'What are you going to do?'

I shook my head, looking down. 'I don't know.'

I went into my room and slammed the door. I needed sleep. I'd deal with this later.

Driving home from Jeb's I'd made a decision.

I wasn't going to wait for the results from the drug test. Michael was out there. I was going to find him.

TWENTY-TWO

I was off the task force, but there was no law saying I couldn't hang out at the encampment. The man I thought was Michael might come back.

I knew I could get in trouble doing this, being on suspension and acting alone, but what did I have to lose? Even when they cleared me from the drug charge, the stench of it would linger. I'd known people who'd undergone those kinds of investigations. Even after they were found innocent, the rumors never went away.

My career as I'd known it was over. And as far as friends went, Sags was back to murdering people. Bad people, sure, but still . . . I didn't know if I could live with her anymore. I thought she'd given all of that up. Could I have a best friend who was a serial killer? I didn't know.

Gavin was fine for a few dates. And while we'd had a pretty epic night in the sack, that was all it was ever going to be. I knew enough about him now that I knew we'd never be close. The amount of energy he'd put into taunting Jeb was really unattractive.

And Jeb. *Shit.* Abby was right. I'd really blown that one.

All there was left was my family.

I put my dirty street clothes back on and drove downtown, then parked a block away from the encampment. I wasn't too worried about running into anyone working with the task force. They wouldn't have been able to find another UC this quickly, and surveillance cars were too expensive to leave out on the street for a dead operation.

I walked to my old spot at the end of the line of tents and tarps and waited. Someone had taken my tent, no big surprise there. I sat on the ground on a piece of cardboard, and leaned against the wall, feigning sleep.

About an hour after I set up two of the gang members showed up. One of them gave the dealer a slip of paper. When they walked away I followed them around the corner.

Parked down the street on the corner was a white van. The two men got in and drove off.

150 Wendy Church

I ran to my car and pulled out behind them.

I followed the van to Upper Wacker and then down Clark and on to the Dan Ryan Expressway. It drove through the city and took the exit to Taylor, then stopped near another encampment under the expressway.

The men got out and repeated the exercise with another dealer. Then they got back in their van and drove south again, leaving the streets with planters and well kept, windowed office buildings, and on to bleak, unpopulated blocks dominated by abandoned warehouses and vacant office buildings.

We were only a few blocks away from the UIC campus, but it felt like we were in a different world. Graffiti marked most of the buildings and doors, and the few windows that were intact were boarded over. Decrepit metal fencing with green shade covers leaned in various directions underneath sections of the expressway. I glanced back towards the center of the city, the skyscrapers, and in the center the twin spires of the Willis Tower. It seemed like a million miles away.

Eventually the van slowed and stopped on the side of the street. Both men got out, and one of them opened the back. They pulled out a hand truck, then a number of cardboard boxes that they stacked on to it. They closed and locked the van, then walked to the narrow recessed doorway of one of the buildings.

They unlocked the door and went in, closing it behind them.

I waited. Five minutes passed. Then ten.

The street was empty, no cars or people had passed since the van had stopped. I got out of my car and walked to the door.

I assumed they'd locked it when they went in, but to my surprise when I pulled on the handle it opened. I leaned in, listening.

There were no sounds, so I stepped in and closed the door.

I waited for my eyes to adjust to the dark but it didn't happen. I turned on my phone light.

High ceilings looked over tall metal shelves that were leaning against the walls on two sides, and in lines on the floor in between them. The shelves were empty, save for a few boxes. Everything was covered in dust, and it smelled musty, like my parents' attic.

I walked down the center aisle until I could see the far side of the space, and a small hallway.

The hallway dead-ended after about twenty feet. On either side were doors. Two were offices, one was an old bathroom. The other was a stairway.

Tunnel Vision 151

I turned off my phone and slowly opened the door to the stairway, and listened.

Faint footsteps, below me.

I turned my phone back on, and saw that the stairway went down two floors, each with a landing and a door.

I could feel my heart beat faster as I peered over the railing down the stairs. I avoided basements the same way I avoided underground L stations. Our apartment was the exception, primarily because it was only a half floor down, and it had windows.

I took a big breath and walked down one floor. Then I turned off my phone again and carefully opened the door on the landing.

No sounds, no voices. Another large room with some counters and shelves. I walked down the aisles, hoping that whatever it was the two men were doing would be on this floor. I didn't want to go any further underground.

There was nothing. I walked back out the door to the stairwell.

I heard faint noises, coming from below. I took a big breath and walked down to the last stairwell.

It occurred to me that I was now two floors below the surface, and no one knew where I was. Maybe it was time to get the hell out and tell them what I'd found.

Somehow I couldn't imagine Jacobs checking out this building purely on my suggestion of watching two men who might be gang members walk into it. Even if she wanted to, Bowles would put the kibosh on anything coming from me.

I'd just check out one more floor by myself. I opened the door and peered in, focusing my phone light on the ground.

I was in a basement. Dusty wooden shelves, stacks of bricks and old machinery were scattered around the room, resting on a cracked cement floor surrounded by brick walls that were crumbling in the corners.

Where the hell had those guys gone?

Wherever it was, it was time to leave. I could feel my heartbeat pounding in my chest, and my breathing was getting shallow. My hands and feet were freezing. Jacobs might not act on what I'd found, but I wouldn't do anyone any good by having a heart attack down here.

Just as I was closing the door I heard a slamming sound from across the room, and the murmur of low voices.

I looked around wildly and fast-walked as quietly as I could over to one of the counters. I ducked down behind it.

The footsteps came closer.

'*Skończyliśmy na dzisiaj?*' (Are we done for the day?)

'*Tak, zjedzmy coś.*' (Yeah, let's get something to eat.)

I held my breath and waited until they passed, going through the door I'd just come through. They were dragging the hand truck, which was now empty.

I crouched there for what seemed like an eternity but was probably a couple of minutes.

What had they been doing?

I wanted to get out of there, but I couldn't go back up right now, anyway, or I'd run into them.

I took a deep breath and held it for a count of four, then let it out to a count of eight. Abby had taught me the technique to help quell panic attacks. I'd found it to be marginally helpful in the past. Right now it was useless.

I turned my phone back on and walked across the room, to a wide metal door set against the back wall. I turned off the light and cracked open the door.

More voices, too far off to hear what they were saying, and a regular 'clank' from some kind of machinery.

I stepped through the door on to a narrow platform with a low metal railing. A few lights were set up on the floor below me, and I heard the low hum of a generator.

I was one level above a large open space. A sub-basement by the look of it, surrounded by more brick walls, and littered with rusted generators and stacks of crates. Old scaffolding leaned against the railing, rusted pulley fixtures hung from the ceiling, from a few of which hung frayed wires.

At one end of the platform rested a gleaming metal ladder that led to the floor. Across the sub-basement floor from the ladder was a large opening in the wall.

I estimated that by now I was thirty or forty feet underground. Even though it was cold in here I was starting to sweat. I felt light-headed, and my stomach was turning over.

The voices were coming from the opening in the wall. Whatever those two men had been doing had to do with what was down here. I should go back up and tell Jacobs.

This might be enough to get her to check it out, but I couldn't take the chance. This gang was my only link to Michael.

I took a big breath and slowly climbed down the ladder to the bottom.

Tunnel Vision 153

A very old, very large furnace took up one side of the space. Coal burning, I thought, given the state of the ceiling and surrounding areas. On the ground leading up to the furnace was a set of narrow, rusted metal tracks. They led across the room and into the opening in the wall, which I could now see was a tunnel.

I walked towards it, and as I got closer I could see the glow of lights coming from the other end. Stacked against the wall near the opening were boxes that looked like the ones I'd seen the two men carrying.

I heard footsteps, and ducked behind the furnace. Peeking over the top I saw a man come from the opening and walk to the stack of boxes. He picked one up and disappeared back through the hole.

My curiosity overcame my fear and I walked over to the cardboard boxes. On each box was a shipping label, to a Chicago PO box. The return address was in Chinese, and there were shipping stamps, also in Chinese.

I peeked down the opening. No one else was coming. I'd take one last look to see if I could tell what was going on, and then get the hell out of here. Whatever was going on was illegal as hell, and the PD could check it out themselves. Jacobs and Bowles wouldn't be able to dismiss this.

I went into the opening, walking next to the wall. After fifteen feet it dead-ended into the T of a larger tunnel. I stopped and looked around the corner.

The metal tracks led in both directions, through an oval-shaped tunnel, less than ten feet wide. I realized now where I was.

Several years ago I'd attended a lecture at the architectural institute on Chicago's underground. Forty feet below the surface, underneath both the Pedway and the L stations, lay Chicago's freight tunnels. They'd been built in the early part of the twentieth century by the Chicago Tunnel Company to haul coal and ash to and from downtown buildings, collect and distribute mail, and house communications cables.

The tunnels were built in response to increasing traffic on the surface. The city was growing quickly in the early 1900s, and snarling traffic was slowing down the transport of goods to and from the businesses and government institutions in the heart of downtown. The thought was that an underground tunnel system would be a profitable and efficient addition to the city's infrastructure.

154 Wendy Church

The narrow gauge railway tunnels were built and then linked to business and government buildings, including the Merchandise Mart, City Hall, the Board of Trade, the Federal Reserve Bank, the *Chicago Tribune*, the Field Museum, and dozens of others. At one point the Chicago Tunnel Company was even marketing 'Tunnel Air', where they pumped the cool, fifty-five-degree air from below up to the buildings during the summer months.

The tunnel business peaked in the forties and fifties, and then dropped due to competition from the trucking industry. The Chicago Tunnel Company went bankrupt in 1959, and the tunnels were abandoned, other than for a few special operations, including the transport of newsprint from the *Chicago Tribune*'s warehouse to Tribune Tower. The tunnels remained something of a hobby for underground enthusiasts, and there would be the occasional tour. But in the early 2000s, in response to potential terrorist threats, real and imagined, the city closed the tunnels to public access, at which point the only government entrance was from City Hall. From then on access to the tunnels from public buildings was tightly controlled, and granted only to city employees.

People forgot about the tunnels, including those that owned buildings that connected to them.

Until 1992.

One morning in April 1992 workers at Merchandise Mart noticed water filling in the building's sub-basement. They thought that a pipe had broken, until they discovered fish in the water.

It soon became obvious that Merchandise Mart wasn't the only building that was flooding, as the city was flooded with urgent calls. Utility crews scrambled to find the source of the leak, but it wasn't until someone noticed a sizable whirlpool on the Chicago River near the Kinzie Street Bridge that they realized what was happening.

Construction workers installing a new piling for the Kinzie Street Bridge had unknowingly punched a hole into one of the freight tunnels. The Chicago River was now emptying into the sixty-mile tunnel complex that ran underneath the city, flooding dozens of government buildings and stores throughout downtown and near the river. In some buildings the water in the basements and sub-basements rose as high as forty feet.

Affected buildings were evacuated, and utilities were shut off as a precaution. Employees in downtown businesses who made it in to work that day were told to go home.

Tunnel Vision   155

Determining the source of the problem was just the first step. Once they found the leak, they had to figure out how to plug it. It took several tries, including an attempt to stuff the hole with a set of mattresses, before they finally poured in tons of special concrete that filled the hole. But not before doing close to two billion dollars worth of damage to the city.

I was standing in the sub-basement of one of the private buildings that connected to the freight tunnels. But as interesting as that was, my curiosity was fighting with the growing panic I was feeling about being this far underground.

Panic was winning. I'd take just a quick look and then get the hell out of here.

Down the tunnel about twenty feet from me were two banks of lights, set up on either side of the tracks. They illuminated a long table in the center, containing pots, beakers, and other lab equipment. A man in a white coat wearing a respirator mask and gloves was standing at the table, opening up one of the boxes I'd seen the two men take into the tunnel. He pulled out a plastic container and opened it, then dipped some kind of measuring cup into it, and carefully added the amount to a bowl that was on the counter.

Next to the lab station was another table, this one with two small machines, and a cardboard box.

Two beefy looking men were leaning against the tunnel walls, on either side of the table. Both were wearing cloth masks, and had what looked like machine guns lazily hanging from straps around their necks.

Two other people were sitting at the second table on crates. I recognized the bearded homeless man I'd spoken to at the camp where they'd found Sheila's body, the one who'd recognized the Spiderman backpack. The white-coated man poured powder into a funnel at the top of a small machine on the second table, under which the homeless man placed a glassine envelope he pulled out of the cardboard box. He pressed a button, and a small amount of the powder dropped into the envelope. Once the powder was in, he folded the envelope to seal it and handed it to a woman. She placed it underneath another machine, and then pulled a lever. The loud clanking sound I'd heard was the stamp machine slamming into the envelopes. Once it was stamped she placed the envelope into a black leather gym bag sitting on the ground.

Another man and a woman, looking like they were also from the encampment, sat on the ground, leaning against the wall, eyes locked on the bags filling with powder.

It was a largely silent operation, other than the occasional comment in Polish from one of the men with guns, and the regular 'clank' of the stamp machine.

I'd found the location of the Greenpoint Crew's Red lab. Or, at least one of them. With sixty miles of these tunnels underneath the city, who knows how many of these labs were down here? And they were using homeless people to help them operate it.

It was time to call in reinforcements. I stepped away from the tunnel opening and walked back towards the ladder.

I turned on my phone and hit Jeb's number.

No signal. Not a big surprise, we were forty feet below the surface. I'd have to go back up at least one story to get service.

I put the phone in my pocket and started up the ladder.

'*Kim jesteś*?' (Who are you?)

I looked behind me. One of the goons with guns was standing at the opening, his gun up and pointed at me.

TWENTY-THREE

'*Zatrzymywać się!*' (Stop!) he said, as he walked closer, his gun pointing at me.

I turned and scrambled up the ladder as fast as I could. '*Hej, chłopaki, chodźcie tutaj!*' (Hey, guys, come here!) he yelled, now letting go of his gun and starting up the ladder.

I was almost to the top, reaching for the ledge when my foot slipped on one of the rungs. I dangled for a moment, then managed to get it back on.

My slip gave the gunman time to catch up. He'd let his gun go and was using both hands to follow me up the ladder. As I was pulling myself over the top I felt him grab my ankle. I held on as tight as I could but he was too strong. He pulled hard, and my hands slipped off of the platform. I fell.

I would have hit the floor except for his grip on my ankle. I dangled, upside down.

I thought he was trying to keep me from falling, but that only lasted until his friend showed up. Then he dropped me.

I hit the floor hard. I lay there, gasping for breath, when the other one grabbed my arm and pulled me roughly to my feet.

'*Kim jesteś?*' (Who are you?)

I was still trying to get my wind back.

'Who are you?' he said, in heavily accented English.

I couldn't think of anything to say that would help my situation, so I stayed silent.

A bad idea, as it turned out, as he slapped me hard across the face.

'*Nie krzywdź jej jeszcze. Musimy wiedzieć, kim ona jest i co tutaj robi.*' (Don't hurt her yet. We need to know who she is and what she's doing here.)

'*Co powinniśmy z nią zrobić?*' (What should we do with her?)

'*Trzymamy ją tu do przyjścia szefa.*' (We keep her here until the boss comes.)

The one who'd followed me up the ladder was clearly in charge, and the one who hit me nodded. They frog-marched me back into the tunnel.

They dragged me past the two tables to a spot further down the tunnel, near the edge of the reach of the lights. The first goon pushed me down roughly on to the floor.

'Not move or we shoot.'

I didn't think they'd shoot me, given their earlier discussion. But I wasn't about to take the chance. Even if they didn't kill me they could still shoot me in the leg, or anywhere else, to keep me there until the boss showed up.

I sat down and leaned against the wall.

The two workers at the table didn't even look up as I went by. Now that I was closer I could see that their faces were bruised, the woman bleeding slightly from a split lip.

Next to the table they were working at were two wheeled platforms, with hand levers. Old time railcars. On one of them rested a black leather gym bag.

There was nothing to do but wait. I looked down the tunnel, rough cement walls curving up to a slightly rounded ceiling. Not too far away from me the tunnel disappeared into inky blackness. I could feel the panic welling up again and tried to control my breathing.

I didn't know how long I sat there, the only measure of time the periodic 'clank' of the stamp machine. I was exhausted, but the adrenaline and the fact that I was expending a lot of energy trying not to freak out was keeping me awake.

At one point the man in the white coat stopped what he was doing. He said something quietly to one of the gunmen, who walked the few paces to the workers. He picked up the last two envelopes that had been filled and stamped, and handed one to each of them.

They both got up and walked to the side of the tunnel, where they sat down and eagerly opened the envelopes, quickly snorting the contents. In a few moments they both leaned back against the wall, closing their eyes.

The white coat guy took his mask off and leaned against his table, pulling a sandwich and a container of milk out of a brown bag. He slowly chewed while he watched them.

Fifteen minutes later he said, 'It's good.'

One of the gunmen barked at the other two people leaning against the wall. They got up quickly and moved to the table, taking the place of the two who were now slumped against the wall.

My stomach turned over as I realized what they were doing.

Tunnel Vision 159

Renfro had said it was unusual, that the Red drug formulation among batches was more consistent than normal.

It was consistent because they were testing each batch on addicts. It wasn't precise, but the lab guy had probably watched enough of them to identify reactions that indicated his formula was drifting. And if it did, and someone died, who cared? There was no shortage of addicts who would do this work in exchange for a steady supply of drugs.

I felt the floor start to vibrate.

There was a chattering sound of metal, coming from down the tunnel.

Whatever was making the sound was getting closer, and soon out of the darkness came another one of the handcars, this one propelled by a single man pumping a hand lever, wearing a headlamp that shed just enough light to illuminate the immediate area around the handcar.

He stopped just short of the packing table. One of the gunmen picked up the recently filled gym bag and placed it on the car, along with another one. After they were loaded the man on the car changed sides, adjusted something on the center column, and pushed the lever up and down, moving the car back in the direction he had come from. Only moments passed before I watched him disappear from sight. They'd said nothing to each other.

So that's how it worked. They made the fentanyl here at this lab, and then took it somewhere else to distribute. No wonder the cartel couldn't find them. And that explained the new-looking tracks. They'd replaced the old ones in the areas they were working, to facilitate moving the drugs from place to place.

This was a well-thought-out operation. If anyone did manage to find the manufacturing location, the gang would have little trouble packing it up and moving it. With sixty miles of pitch-black tunnels, and no cell or other electronic capabilities, it would take a major effort by the authorities to find it, much less close it down. Or, close *them* down. Who knew how many of these were down here?

And using homeless people as workers and as quality control was horrifyingly efficient. They wouldn't need to pay them, just guarantee them a few hits a day of the product, which was cheap until they marked it up and sold it on the streets.

I slowly reached up to the bill of my hat and turned on the recording function. Gavin had said it would be good for thirty minutes. I didn't need that long to get a good image of what was happening down here. I just needed to find some way to get out and get it to the task force.

I must have nodded off as I was staring at the lab, as I was woken up by a kick in my side. One of the gunmen was standing over me. Next to him was Brajen Krol.

Big, bald, and pockmarked, I recognized him from the pictures that Jacobs had shown us at the start of the operation. But the images hadn't captured his essence.

Like most mugshots, his eyes had looked dead. But now, in person, I could see that they weren't dead. They were shallow, more thought-less . . . un-human looking. The eyes of every dog I'd ever met showed more intelligence than this guy's. Seeing him up close I had no trouble believing he would happily kill someone with a golf club.

An uninvited guest to the tunnel must be a big deal for them to call Krol. He couldn't be happy about having to come down here.

'Who are you?' he said, his voice low and gravelly.

'Betty. Betty Phang.' Might as well use the pen name. If he was a porn consumer maybe he'd heard of me, and would take pity. But he didn't look much like a reader.

'Are you with police?'

'No, no, I'm just, uh, I'm a tunnel enthusiast.' I wasn't sure anything could be further from the truth than that. 'I've heard about the tunnels, I wanted to see them.'

'*Przeszukaj ją.*' (Search her.)

The gunman roughly pulled me up to my feet and started frisking me, patting me down everywhere and emptying my pockets. I was glad I'd left my wallet in my car.

When he was done, Krol stared at me a long time without speaking. Then he turned and walked away, the gunman following.

They stopped to converse at the tunnel entrance for a few seconds. Krol looked at me one last time, then disappeared into the sub-basement.

The gunman spoke to the other one, and they walked back to me, gesturing for me to get up.

'You come,' he said.

A reprieve? If so, we were going in the wrong direction. They were escorting me away from the lab, and down the tunnel.

Soon we were out of reach of the lights. Both men pulled out flashlights, pointing them at the ground in front of us.

Tunnel Vision 161

We walked for several minutes, my apprehension growing. If they were taking me to the other end of their operation, they would have taken me on one of the handcars.

Sure enough, we stopped nowhere near any kind of opening. There was a break in the tunnel wall, a small recessed area, that looked like it might once have been a maintenance bay. On the ground in the center was a metal plate, surrounded by broken cement and puddles.

In the back corner of the space was a single shoe. It looked familiar.

Oh no. I broke free of the man holding me and started to run out of the space and back down the tunnel.

The other one grabbed my arm and swung me around easily. He pointed his gun at my head.

The other one put his hand on the barrel, pushing it down.

'*Jak myślisz, co do cholery robisz? Chodzi o to, żeby nie straszyć innych.*' (What the hell do you think you're doing? The whole point is not to scare the others.)

'*Masz rację.*' (Right.)

They were going to kill me. They'd walked me down here to not upset the workers while they did it.

The man who'd held down the other's gun reached into his back pocket.

'*Trzymaj ją za ramiona.*' (Hold her arms.)

The other one let go of his gun and pinned my arms to my side, while the first one unfolded a plastic bag. He opened it and fitted it over my head, closing it tight around my neck.

TWENTY-FOUR

I reflexively gasped a big breath, and discovered immediately that the seal was complete. There was no air, and the breath sucked the bag into my mouth.

I struggled, but it was hopeless. The second man had my arms pinned to my sides while the first one held the bag tight around my neck.

Think. I only had a few seconds.

I sucked the bag further into my mouth, and started chewing on the dirty plastic. I ground my teeth into it as hard as I could, as fast as I could. All I needed was a small hole.

I kept chewing, and taking small breaths to test if I'd broken through. I was starting to feel faint.

Finally, a bit of air. I resisted the urge to take a huge breath.

I used every bit of control I had to take tiny breaths, even though my chest wanted to heave. Then I stopped struggling, and let myself go limp.

The first man held on to the bag a few moments longer, probably seconds but that seemed like an eternity. Then he let go, and the other one let go of my arms.

You're dead, I said to myself. I let my legs go boneless and I dropped to the ground. My head bounced on the concrete, and everything went black.

When I came to the bag was still covering my face. I tore at it with my hands and pulled it off, gulping deep breaths. My panic was at bay for the moment, as I appreciated the simple act of being able to bring air into my lungs.

The gunmen were gone. I was far enough down the tunnel that I couldn't see any signs of light, the only indication that I wasn't alone the 'clank' of the stamp machine.

I tried to stand up, then fell back down. The darkness was disorienting, and I was dizzy. Possibly from a concussion, I thought, feeling a sore bump forming on my head.

I waited a couple of minutes, then tried again. I managed to stand

Tunnel Vision

up, and immediately reached for a wall to steady myself. I reached into my back pocket for my phone.

Not there. I didn't remember them taking it. Maybe it fell out during the struggle. I dropped back to my knees, landing in the puddle, and reached around to feel for my phone.

I tried not to think about the fact that I was forty feet underground, but I couldn't help it. Joining the 'clank' of the stamp machine was the sound of my own frantic breathing.

I was going to die down here. Forty feet underground, in pitch blackness. Maybe I should have let them suffocate me. At least it would have been over quick.

I leaned over from my kneeling position and stretched out on the ground, feeling for my phone. I'd recognized the shoe that was on the ground, it was a match to the one I'd found in the box with Sheila Johnson's things. They'd killed her down here, and eventually had moved her body to the surface. Along with a number of other homeless people, the ones that Alvarez had said had been asphyxiated.

They'd be back to do the same with me. I didn't know how long I had before they'd come back for my body, and then discover I was alive.

That might not be so bad. A bullet to the head, or suffocation – both sounded better than a slow, dark death in an underground tunnel.

My hands closed on a piece of cloth. My hat. I put it back on, then reached around for several more minutes. No phone. They must have taken it. I gave up looking and stood up and leaned against the wall. *Breathe two, three, four . . . exhale five, six, seven, eight.* I went through several cycles until my heart started to slow and I could breathe without hyperventilating. Then I reached for the wall, running my hands along it, looking for the opening to the tunnel.

I couldn't give up yet. My mother would be devastated. Not just losing a second child, but having yet another just disappear.

There was at least one other opening down the tunnel. Hopefully there were others, too, ones that didn't have drug-running gang members in them.

I found the opening to the tunnel from the alcove, and turned to walk away from the drug lab.

It quickly became apparent that walking in the dark was far more difficult than it seemed. It wasn't just dark, like a moonless night, or a basement. It was the complete absence of light. I took a few steps and immediately tripped over an uneven mound of dirt on the ground, landing painfully on my hands and knees.

I stood up, and after two steps I pitched forward again, my foot tripping over one of the tracks.

Get a grip, Maude. This is what blind people experience every day. They get through life without light, and you can stand it for a little while.

I got up and moved away from the tracks, towards the wall. I placed my hand on the rough cement and used it as a guide. It wouldn't prevent me from uneven ground, but at least I wouldn't be tripping over the tracks in the center of the tunnel.

I racked my brain trying to remember what I knew about the tunnels. They were connected to dozens of buildings. One of them must be open. On the other hand, there were sixty miles of them, and I could wander down here for weeks without finding one.

I didn't think I would last weeks. I wasn't sure how long I could go without food, but water, was . . . three days? Four? There were puddles on the ground, but it would be pure luck if I found one of them. And right now I could walk right by an opening to an exit and not realize it.

It felt like hours, walking in the dark, when I heard a familiar chattering rumble. The handcar was coming.

The light on the driver's headlamp wasn't much, but it would be enough for him to be able to see me. More importantly, the tunnel was narrow, and I could get pinned between the car and the wall.

I'd passed another maintenance bay somewhere behind me. As much as I loathed giving up the ground I'd gained, I turned and started walking back.

The handcar was getting closer. I had no idea how far back the bay was. Time seemed to stop in here.

I started to run, keeping my hand on the wall.

I ran about forty yards when I tripped on something, and fell flat on my face. I stood up quickly and kept running, ignoring the warm trickle of blood making its way down my face.

I glanced behind me and could now make out the soft glow of the light from the handcar.

I kept going, keeping my hand on the wall, until the wall wasn't there any more. The maintenance bay.

I threw myself into it and lay down, making myself as small as

Tunnel Vision 165

possible against the back wall. Moments later I felt a pulse of air as the handcar went by. I listened to it recede into the distance. I stood up, and started back down the tunnel. Then I stopped. He'd be back soon. Better to wait until he made the return trip.

I went back to the bay and knelt against the back wall until I heard the car come back again. Then a small growing light, and a puff of air.

I estimated it was about two hours in between trips to the drug manufacturing site. At least, that's what it felt like. If he kept to that schedule, that's how long I had to find an exit, or another maintenance bay.

I started back down the tunnel, my hand on the wall, walking faster now.

To keep my mind off of where I was, I focused on what I would do when I got out of here. The first thing would be to contact the PD. They needed to know about the drug lab. Maybe they could roll up the whole gang in one fell swoop. If they did that, there was a strong chance Luke Roberts would be in the bunch, and I'd have a chance to confirm my suspicion that he was Michael.

Thinking about that took my mind, however briefly, off of my current situation. I couldn't imagine it: my brother, alive, after all of this time. It was almost too much to contemplate. What would my mother do? There wasn't a word, I couldn't think of one, to describe what I imagined her reaction to be. 'Happily ecstatic' didn't even begin to cover it.

They'd take me off of the task force. I couldn't continue to work with it, if I had a family member involved. I didn't care, I'd want some time off, anyway. I wondered what Michael was like now? It was exciting, to think about getting to know him.

I walked for what I estimated was an hour, my hand scraped rough from where I'd been keeping contact with the wall.

It was a relief when my hand left the wall and found empty air.

A turn, to the right. Possibly to the left as well, but one direction was as good as another.

I took the turn, reestablishing contact with the wall.

Every now and then my fingers ran over what felt like metal plates. Electrical boxes? I didn't know.

Another hour or so went by, and the wall opened up again. I traced my way around it. It was an opening, about three feet off of the ground.

I ran my hand across the back wall of the opening and felt metal against the back of it. A door?

There were hinges on one side. Definitely a door!

I searched for a handle. I found it and pulled.

The door didn't budge.

I felt for the door seam and ran my hand over it.

It was welded shut. Would they all be sealed?

Nothing to do but keep going.

It was cold down here. Not freezing, but probably in the fifties. And I was still wet from laying in the puddle. I pulled my jacket tighter around me.

I walked until I found another maintenance alcove. I turned into it, and immediately tripped and fell down to my knees, landing on a metal plate.

I felt around the plate for the relatively warmer ground on each side of it and laid down. I needed to rest, just for a minute.

I woke up, freezing cold. It took a few moments to remember where I was. Then I heard the rumbling chatter of the handcar. More distant than before. I must have turned into an offshoot of the main tunnel they were using. That meant I was out of danger of getting discovered by the handcar.

It also meant I might not find an exit. The only ones that I knew existed for sure were the two ends of the drug operation.

I had no idea how long I'd been asleep. It could have been minutes, could have been hours. My head was pounding, I ran my scraped fingers over another tender egg-sized bump starting to form on my forehead.

Maybe a concussion. I should try not to fall asleep again.

It was hard to imagine that forty feet above me was a bustling city. Forty feet didn't seem like much, but right now it might as well be a light year. I wasn't sure what part of the city I was under, or what time it was, but even in the middle of the night there would be cars, and lights. The glitz of the city, people in expensive shoes, smelling of perfume or cologne, window shopping for Gucci bags, or buying Italian beef sandwiches.

Italian beef. I couldn't remember the last time I'd eaten. How long had I been down here? At least eight hours. And on the street for most of the day before that.

I stood up unsteadily. I was hungry. And so tired.

Tunnel Vision 167

How long could I keep this up? Not long, I thought.

I had to make a choice.

On the one hand, I could go back to the tunnel with the handcar. I knew there would be an exit there. I was also more likely to get caught.

The other option was to keep going on this tunnel, and hope I'd find a door. One that would be open.

But what if there wasn't one? I could wander down here forever. No one would ever find me.

My legs of their own volition turned around and I started to plod down the tunnel in the direction I'd come, towards the line with the handcar.

Both of my hands were now raw and bleeding from rubbing against the walls. I put them up to my face. It was weird not to be able to see them. I could feel stinging, and warm blood dripping over my palms.

I dropped them to my sides.

That lasted only a short while until I tripped again over one of the rails.

'Ow.' The sound echoed off of the walls. It seemed like it was coming from someone else.

I stood up and reached back for the wall.

I walked for what could have been minutes, or hours, until I felt the wall turn. I was back at the intersection.

Which way had the handcar come from? I couldn't remember which way was back to the lab, and which direction the handcar had come from.

I had to choose one direction.

I could try one and hope, or wait until he came by again.

The thought of taking the wrong direction, and going all the way back to the lab, made me want to cry. There was no way I'd make it if I did that. I wasn't sure how much I had left in me.

I had to wait.

I estimated a half hour went by before I heard the rattling. I pulled back into the tunnel I was in, and waited for him to go by.

The puff of air hit me, as did the welcome sign of the tiny bit of light I was afforded by the passing car. The car did not have any of the black gym bags. So he'd come from the right.

The small bit of light lifted my spirits, and I started down the center tunnel from where he'd come.

I'd estimated that the handcar was doing about ten miles an hour. If he was going by every four hours, that meant the entrance was no further than . . .

Shit. This was simple math. My brain wasn't working right.

What if I went insane down here? How long does it take to go insane? Longer than it takes to die of dehydration?

In two three four, out two, three, four, five, six, seven, eight.

Ten miles an hour. If he was taking just a few seconds at each end, and coming by every two hours, that meant the furthest away they were was . . . twenty miles? No, that wasn't right. Ten miles? Not likely. The entire city was just over twenty miles long.

OK, well, it was less than ten miles. And I'd already covered some of it. And that was worst case. He might be waiting longer in between trips.

Normally I'd be more than capable of walking a few miles. Right now I wasn't so sure. I was probably making no more than a half mile an hour. That meant . . . no more than ten to twenty more hours, worst case.

Less than a day. I could do that.

Of course, once I got to the other end, I'd have to get by whoever was guarding it. But I'd cross that bridge when I came to it. I stepped up my pace.

I heard a sound. I must be getting close! The thought of getting out was almost too much to think about. I sped up.

As the sound got closer I realized with horror that it was the chattering of the handcar.

I hadn't come across any maintenance bays. He was going to get to me in seconds. And there was nowhere to go.

TWENTY-FIVE

There was nothing to do but go back to the intersection. I stifled a small sob at the thought of having to double back, and the energy I'd wasted getting this far.

I turned and started to walk back the way I'd come.

The rumbling chatter was getting closer. Soon I'd either get run over, pinned against the cement wall, or he'd stop and kill me. Even if he wasn't carrying a gun, I had no illusions in my weakened state about my capabilities.

I let go of the wall and broke into a full run. It was terrifying, running this fast in utter darkness.

I wasn't sure I imagined it, but I looked back and thought I saw light.

I wasn't imagining it. The prick of light was getting bigger. I put everything I could into my legs, running as fast as I could.

The light was almost to me when I slammed into a wall.

When I came to I was lying on the ground, on top of a rail.

My entire head was pounding. I felt my forehead. Another large bump had formed, this one just above my other eye. I could feel warm blood running into it.

I stood up shakily, then crumpled down from a sharp pain in my left ankle.

I stood up again, balancing on one foot, immediately feeling dizzy and nauseous. I'd given myself a concussion. Or maybe a second one. I sat back down, leaning against the wall.

I didn't trust myself to stand up. When the spinning in my head slowed I crawled around the space, feeling the wall.

I'd made it to the intersection, and had run into the wall on the far side.

I was so tired. I leaned against the wall, feeling the sticky blood drying on my face.

I heard the chattering of the railcar. Had it already been two hours? Or were they not on a schedule? How long had I been unconscious? I had no way of knowing.

I waited until I saw the prick of light, then backed away into the side tunnel, and felt the puff of air as it went by again.

I thought I'd started getting a handle on how long I'd been down here. But I'd fallen asleep, and knocked myself out. And even without that, the passage of time was starting to feel hazy.

I'd once watched a *Law & Order: SVU* episode, where Detective Stabler had had himself put into solitary confinement in a prison. He did it as an experiment, to see if a prisoner had been exaggerating about how being in solitary had driven him insane. When Stabler started banging on the door for them to let him out, he'd estimated he'd been in the room for days.

It turned out to have been four hours. It seemed unbelievable, that he could have misjudged the passage of time so severely. But now I had no trouble believing it.

I was parched, my lips cracked and bleeding. So, I'd been here at least a day. I realized I was laying in a puddle, and knelt down and put my face into it. I drank, taking in mud along with the water. Who knew what was in it, but at this point I might not live long enough to get sick.

All of a sudden I was overcome with exhaustion. I lay myself down and put my head on the track.

I dreamt of Michael. I took him to the park. He loved the slide. 'More, Maw, More.' Then peels of laughter as we slid down, and then he ran back to the ladder for another trip.

Was I awake, or was that a dream?

I reached behind me for the wall and stood up, leaning against it. Which way? *Shit.* I was turned around, again.

I stood there, paralyzed, looking in every direction.

Then I heard voices.

I followed the voices, keeping my raw hand pressed against the wall, until I could see a small bit of light.

The light was coming from a large opening next to the tunnel. As I got closer I could start to make out features on the ground. What a luxury, to be able to see where I was going.

This was the end of the line for the operation. Where they were taking the drugs for distribution.

I slowed down as I got closer to the opening. It was light enough now, that if anyone looked this way, they would see me. When I got to the opening I peered around the corner.

Tunnel Vision 171

A few bare bulbs hung down from the ceiling, dimly lighting the entire space. I could hear the low hum of another generator. The railcar was there, on newish-looking tracks, resting twenty feet or so into the opening.

There were a number of side tracks, the original ones, all of them rusted, broken and dirty. This had been some kind of staging area from when the freight tunnels were active, underneath who knows what business. Like the sub-basement at the other end of the tunnel, there was a newish-looking ladder leading up to a railed walkway, and then a set of stairs that went to the upper floors.

The man who'd been operating the railcar was talking to another one, who was in the process of gathering up two of the leather gym bags. He shouldered the bags and walked up the ladder, and then the stairs. I watched him disappear into the door at the top level.

The other guy sat down on a stone wall on the side, next to a cooler. He looked at his watch, then opened the cooler, taking out a sandwich and a Coke.

I would have been salivating if I wasn't so dehydrated. It was torture watching him eat. When he popped the top on the Coke I thought I was going to scream.

He finished his lunch and stood up. He grabbed the other two gym bags, presumably empty ones, and put them on the railcar.

He was going to go right past me, so I walked to the other side of the opening and crept a little ways down the tunnel. Then I stopped, holding my breath.

I heard the rolling rattle of the railcar as it came out from the entrance, then turn and go down the tunnel. I watched it until the light from the headlamp disappeared.

I went back into the room, my eyes watering from the first real, albeit dim, light I'd been exposed to in what seemed like forever.

I made a beeline for the cooler and opened it.

It was empty. I picked up the Coke and tried to shake the last few drops into my mouth.

The other guy had disappeared up the ladder. My way out.

The ladder looked impossibly high. I stepped on the first rung, and found myself swaying out to the side before I fell off.

I tried again, this time keeping both of my hands tight on the metal on either side of the rungs as I went up. Each step took a huge effort.

When I got to the top I used the last bit of energy to pull myself over and drop on to the floor.

I laid there, resting.

Now I just had to make it up the stairs, and I'd be out. It was hard to imagine, being out of here.

I stood up, and heard sounds.

Steps, from above.

. I looked down the ladder. There were lots of places to hide at the bottom. But at this point I didn't think I could climb down, much less make it back up.

There was a storage area underneath the staircase. I walked over to it, and knelt down next to a stack of old boxes, chunks of cement, and pieces of rebar.

The steps on the staircase came closer. I closed my hand around a piece of rebar and waited.

A man stepped off the bottom stair on to the landing. He turned the corner, and I realized I'd be well within his peripheral vision when he walked by me. As he approached I stepped out, and with every ounce of strength I had left I swung the rebar at his head.

He staggered back against the railing, his head and shoulders leaning over it. I hit him again, and he tumbled over the side, landing with a soft 'thud' on the floor below.

I didn't know if he was dead, or out cold. But whether or not he woke up, the other guy on the railcar would see him laying there as soon as he came back.

I dropped the rebar and moved as fast as I could to the stairs, intending to take them two at a time.

I missed the first step and dropped hard, my shin hitting the edge of the step. I stood up and took another one, more careful this time, my hand on the railing as I plodded painstakingly up the stairs.

Move faster. But my legs at this point weren't responding to my brain.

I waited at the first landing, leaning against the railing and catching my breath, when I heard shouting.

Two voices. Railcar guy was back, and the other one was still alive.

I didn't know if I heard footsteps coming up the stairs or imagined it, but I started running, using the railing to swing myself around at the second landing and scrambling up to the third level.

I finally made it up to the last landing and heaved open the door. I threw myself into the opening and was almost knocked over by the blinding light.

Tunnel Vision   173

I didn't have time to get acclimated. Closing my eyes into slits I ran at the source of the light, towards the front of the room and its large windows that were only partially boarded-up.

My hands closed on the handle and I turned it, launching my body at the door at the same time, and hurtling out on to the sidewalk.

Daylight. I stood there, relishing the light, until I heard running steps, and shouting.

I needed to get away, and find a phone. I had to call . . . who? I couldn't remember.

I ran into the street, looking both ways, for any sign of people or cars. There was nothing, other than boarded-up buildings and windowless warehouses.

I picked a direction and started to run, as fast as I could, limping on my bad ankle.

I ducked into a door well and stopped to listen. I thought I heard the low roar of cars.

The expressway. I couldn't run any more, but continued to walk towards the sound, keeping close to the buildings.

I walked for another few hundred feet until I saw something moving.

People.

As I got closer I saw there were many of them, underneath the overpass.

I walked to the overpass and stopped by one of the pilings. *I think I need to sit down.* I leaned against the piling and sank slowly to the ground.

I started to close my eyes when I saw the white van, on the street. The one with the two men that I'd followed. Days ago.

I couldn't let them see me. I started to get up but my legs gave out, and I dropped down to the ground.

'Miss, are you OK?'

A man was standing over me. He looked funny. His head was moving around his shoulders, like it wasn't attached.

'Miss?'

I'm fine. Why couldn't I hear my voice?

I was on my back, laying on the ground. People were standing over me.

They'd caught me again.

I wasn't going back down there. I'd die first. I stood up and started to run away. One of them grabbed my arm. I pulled it away and tried to scream.

'Maude, it's me, Jeb.'

I struggled to get my eyes to focus.

He had both of his hands on my waist, holding me firmly.

Jeb?

'I'm here,' he said.

Jeb. I collapsed into him, sobbing.

TWENTY-SIX

A nurse was adjusting the IV that was running from a stand next to my bed to a port in one of my bandaged hands. 'You're severely dehydrated, you have a broken nose, a sprained ankle, and you've been concussed, perhaps more than once. You needed fifteen stitches in your head. We've given you a tetanus shot.'

So that was the pain in my ass. But it was nothing compared to my hands, which hurt more than anything. Scraping them against the wall for . . . I realized had no idea how long I'd been in the tunnels.

'What day is it?'

'Monday,' said Jeb, sitting next to the bed, relief written on his face.

Monday. I was in the tunnels for almost three days.

'How did you find me?'

'There was a tracking device in your hat. We didn't realize you were gone until Saturday. No one was supposed to contact you, but I got worried when I hadn't heard anything. I looked up the tracking signal. We weren't getting a signal, but then it suddenly popped up near the encampment where we found you. Where were you all of that time?'

'In the freight tunnels.'

'What? The freight tunnels?'

'I'll explain everything. But can I get something to eat, first?'

The nurse picked up a tray that had been left next to the bed and put it in front of me. 'This is from earlier, I can get you something fresh,' she said.

'No, thanks,' I said, taking the cover off of the plate and picking up the sandwich that was sitting there. I finished half of it in three bites, and as I started on the second half I threw off the covers, swinging my legs off the bed and standing up.

'We've got to—'

The room spun, and I fell back on to the bed.

'You don't have to do anything, other than rest,' the nurse said.

'You're here overnight,' added Jeb.

'They're making the drugs in the tunnels, we have to . . .' I said, trying again to stand up, and failing. I couldn't believe how weak I was. 'They're murdering people down there. We've got to get the team on it. Where's my hat?' I asked, looking around the room. My clothes were piled on a chair in the corner, the hat resting on top of them.

'There will be time for all of that later,' said Jeb.

'I saw Brajen Krol.'

When he didn't respond, I said, 'Look. I'll stay here, I'll rest. Just let me talk to Jacobs. I'll do it from here.'

He looked at me for a long moment before pulling out his phone.

Thirty minutes later Jacobs was in the room, along with Deputy Chief Jefferson.

'Are you feeling up to telling us what you found?' asked Jacobs.

I nodded, taking one last big bite of another crappy but currently delicious hospital sandwich I'd requested.

'The Greenpoint Crew, they're making and packaging the drugs themselves. They're doing it in the freight tunnels, and—'

'Freight tunnels?' she asked, frowning.

'The tunnel system underneath downtown.'

'That doesn't make any sense,' she said.

'Actually it might,' I said. 'They set up the lab in the tunnels, and bring the chemicals down through one of the abandoned buildings. They make the drugs, test them, then take them out through another one of the abandoned buildings.'

'That seems unnecessarily convoluted.'

'No,' I said, shaking my head. 'It's brilliant. They drop off the precursor chemicals at one site, bring the drugs up through another one. No one goes in those tunnels, the city sealed them off years ago.'

'So how is the gang getting access?'

'The city officially sealed off access from public buildings, like City Hall, and the post office. But there are tons of private buildings with access.' I turned to Jeb. 'Can I borrow your phone?'

He handed it to me and I pulled up a map of the city. I zoomed in on the area where I'd gone into the tunnels. 'Here, this building, this is where I went in, it's got access to the tunnels. This is where they take in the precursor chemicals. The lab is in the tunnel pretty close to this building's sub-basement.' I turned to Jeb. 'Where did you find me?'

Tunnel Vision 177

He looked down at the map for a moment, then pointed. 'Here,' he said.

The underpass where he'd found me was less than a mile away from where I went into the tunnels. I walked less than a mile down there.

Jesus. I would have guessed it was much further. It had taken me over two days to walk that far.

'The building that they're taking the finished drugs out, it's close to there.' I didn't remember much from when I escaped, but enough to know that I hadn't made it far from the building I came out of. 'It shouldn't be too hard to find out which one it is, it will be one with tunnel access.'

'Did you confirm that it's the Greenpoint Crew making the drugs?' she asked.

I nodded. 'I saw Brajen Krol. And I recorded some of the lab work, it's in the hat.'

'*What*? Why didn't you say this at the start?'

Jeb frowned. 'Not appropriate, Susan,' he said to her.

'I'm pretty sure he gave the order to have me killed.' I took another bite of sandwich and several long sips of an ice cold Coke. 'Is all of that enough to bring him in?'

'The fact that he tried to kill you is iffy. You were alone, concussed, it was dark . . . the defense should be able to tear that apart. But if the recording confirms the drug manufacturing, and once we get a few of the gang members to implicate Krol's involvement, that's something else. The lab is the underlying crime that we'll need to get him on money laundering, if we can ever find the money.' Jacobs looked at Jefferson, who nodded.

'We'll send in a team right away to shut down the lab. Once we do that, the Red on the streets will disappear, and the cartel will stop throwing body parts all over the city. Good work, Ms Kaminski,' she said, for the moment at least forgetting that I'd been suspended, and had gone completely off-book.

'There's something else, ma'am. They're using homeless people to package the drugs, and to test them. I think they're—'

Jacobs wasn't listening, already walking out of the room and pulling out her phone.

When Jacobs left, Jefferson stayed behind.

'How are you feeling?' he asked, leaning against the bed.

'I'm fine, sir.'

'I wanted to be the one to tell you, your blood test came back negative. We've reinstated you.' He looked embarrassed. 'I'm sorry, Maude, I should have trusted you. In my position . . .'

'I know, sir.'

'Is there anything we can do for you?'

'Actually, there is one thing. Can you get an autopsy prioritized?'

'An autopsy?'

'Yes, on Sheila Johnson.'

'Didn't she die of a drug overdose?'

'I don't think so. The ME said it could have been asphyxiation, and I think it was done in the tunnels, by the Greenpoint Crew.'

When he hesitated, I said, 'I don't think she's the only one they've killed down there, sir.'

Jacobs walked back into the room. 'We're sending a SWAT team down to the tunnels tonight,' she said to Jefferson. 'Once we've done that we can pick the rest of the gang and Brajen Krol.'

She left. After an awkward pat on the shoulder Jefferson followed her.

'I should probably get going too,' said Jeb, standing up. 'Do you need anything?'

A shower. A gallon of water. At least several beers.

'No, thanks. I'll be fine.' I couldn't begin to communicate how overjoyed I was to not be in the dark, forty feet underground.

'Good,' he said, leaning over to give me a gentle kiss on the head.

'But you know,' I said, musing, 'now that I think about it, Jacobs was right. The Greenpoint Crew's operation is pretty complex.'

'But effective, as you said.'

'Right, yes. But do you think, from what we know about Brajen Krol, that he could have set all of this up? He's a thug, and this whole operation took a lot of planning. And there's nothing about Krol that suggests he's a careful planner, or sophisticated operator. I mean, he murders people with golf clubs.'

'What are you getting at?'

'I mean I met the guy, and he's a few gene sequences away from an orangutan. There must be someone else behind all of this.'

'You mean like one of his lieutenants?'

'Maybe,' I said. 'But from what we know about them, it's the same thing. Murderous, and violent, but not one of them is a rocket scientist. Or even a junior scientist.'

He shook his head. 'You heard Jacobs. Krol doesn't tolerate any

Tunnel Vision 179

kind competition at the top. He wouldn't have someone smarter than he is running things. Not to mention that the only people he really trusts are his relatives, and we've accounted for all of them.'

'Maybe Krol read a book.'

They released me from the hospital the next morning. I went home to take a shower and get the smell of hospital out of my hair.

Jeb must have given Sags a head's up when I left the hospital, as she was at the door when I walked in. 'Are you OK?'

I didn't know if I could live with a murderer, but I accepted her warm hug gratefully. 'A little sore, but I'll be OK.'

'Listen, I have to go out, but do you need anything?'

'No, thanks, I'll be fine.'

I didn't ask her where she was going. Maybe to the restaurant, or maybe out to kill someone.

Right now I didn't care. I'd need to do something about her, but I didn't have the energy for it at the moment.

I spent the better part of the next two days sleeping and eating. On the third day I drove into the station, arriving in the conference room as the daily task force meeting was getting underway.

'The SWAT team raided the tunnel at the location provided by Ms Kaminski,' said Jacobs. 'There was no one there.'

That wasn't a huge shock, they knew I'd gotten out of there.

'We did confirm they were manufacturing drugs there, and the lab will find out if it's Red. We believe it is; we found empty boxes of precursor chemicals and some stamped glassine envelopes. We also found the other end to their operation, where they were taking the finished drugs out. Also abandoned.'

She turned to Bowles, who said, 'We're in the process of sweeping up the gang. Uniforms will go to Brajen Krol's place today to pick him up, and shortly thereafter we'll get as many of the underlings as possible.'

'Detective Renfro,' said Jacobs. 'I'm assuming we're seeing the amount of Red on the street going away?' she asked, smiling.

'Not exactly, ma'am.'

'What?'

'I've spoken to my CIs. They haven't heard of any shortage. If anything, there's more of it now than there was last week.'

'Maybe it will take more time, maybe there was some storage . . .' she said, hopeful.

180 Wendy Church

Renfro shook his head. 'It's been about three days since they moved the lab. Based on Kaminski's descriptions we have an idea of how much they were making there. Any disruption from that would have been felt by now. That points to them making it somewhere else down there.'

'Or they've moved out of town,' offered Nowak. 'Now that they know you're onto them.'

'No,' I said, shaking my head. 'They've moved their manufacturing to somewhere else in the tunnels. Without missing a beat.' It was a simple operation that would have been relatively easy to pack up on a couple of railcars and move.

Jacobs was red-faced, but her voice was steady. 'So we go back to the tunnels, and look for the other site. Or sites.'

'There's sixty miles of tunnels down there, ma'am,' I said. It would take a while to do an inventory of the connected buildings. Then it would be a matter of checking each one, and sealing them up. 'It could take months.'

'So it takes months. Mr McCullom, get going on that,' she said. I doubted it would lead to anything, not to mention that it was unlikely the top brass would fund an indefinitely long search for drug sites.

'Should we still go ahead and pick up Brajen Krol and the gang members?' asked Bowles, after an uncomfortable silence.

'Yes. All of them,' she said angrily. 'Our job was to shut down the Greenpoint Crew. They're still manufacturing, but we have enough to get them off the street, and maybe enough to convict. It won't matter that they're still making it if everyone is in jail.'

'Ma'am?' said Gavin. He'd been silent since the meeting started, all but ignoring the discussion, focused on his computer. 'I think I might have found something.'

She nodded at him to continue, and he set up his monitor to show on the front screen.

'These two buildings,' he said, pointing to the map on the screen, 'were put up for sale the day before we raided the drug site in the tunnels.'

'So? Buildings are bought and sold all the time in this city,' said Renfro.

He replaced the first map with another one. 'This is a map of the freight tunnels. Each building that is known to have access to the tunnels at some point is marked with a blue dot.'

Tunnel Vision 181

'Now look.' He overlaid another image, this one of a map covered in red circles.

'Here are the buildings in this area that have been purchased in the time since we did the raid. I'm going to take away all of those buildings that were recently purchased, and that never had access to the freight tunnels.'

Only two red circles remained.

'I'd bet my last pound that this is where they moved their operations, to these two buildings. They're about a mile apart. Not only that,' he said, excited, 'this could be how they're laundering the money. What better way to launder large sums of cash than purchasing real estate?'

'Do we know who bought these buildings?' asked Jacobs.

He shook his head. 'Not yet, I've just started to untangle that. At first glance it looks like a Russian nesting doll of LLCs and corporations.'

Brajen Krol, setting up a maze of LLCs and corporations to hide real estate sales? That didn't sound realistic, but Jacobs was energized.

'Great work, Mr McCullom. Keep at it,' she said. 'It would be a bonus to have that in hand by the time we bring in Brajen Krol.'

We were dismissed, and I went back to my desk to clean out my inbox, which over the course of several days had bloated. I skimmed through them until I found one from the ME.

Jefferson had apparently granted my request, as the ME had done the autopsy on Sheila Johnson. As he'd suspected, she'd been asphyxiated. Likely the same way that they'd tried to kill me.

I wondered why they'd killed her. Did she refuse to keep working? Had she physically become unable to continue stamping or filling the glassine envelopes, or to be a test subject for their drugs? The trip down there for Sheila, and the people they brought in to work in their lab, was a one-way journey. Once the addicts had seen the operation, the gang would have no interest in letting anyone back up to the surface, and start any rumors about an underground drug manufacturing site.

With nothing left to do I went home. I was tired, still feeling the effects of three days in the tunnels.

When I got home I made myself something to eat and went straight to bed. I set my alarm for five a.m.

The next morning I left the apartment early and went down to the station, eager to start working again. When I got there I was surprised to pass by Renfro in the lobby, going out as I was coming in.

'What are you doing here at this hour?' I asked.

'I went with the team to pick up Brajen Krol last night.'

'Did you get him?'

'No,' he said, disgusted. 'It's like they knew we were coming.'

'They?'

'None of his lieutenants, or most of the gang members, were where we thought they would be. We did manage to get three of them.'

'Who?'

'Cam Weathers, Lester Williams, and Luke Roberts.'

I froze. 'Luke Roberts?'

'Yeah, a real dirtbag.'

'Where are they?'

'Downstairs, being processed.'

I ran down the stairs and to the door to the cells. Martinez was just coming out.

'Hey, Martinez.'

'Maude Kaminski, Analyst! What brings you here?'

'I need to talk to one of the guys you just brought in. Luke Roberts.'

'Sure.' He turned back to the door and started to unlock it.

'Uh, I'd like to do it when he's not with the others. Is there any way you can get him into one of the interview rooms?'

'I guess, sure. I think three is open.'

'Thanks. Can you bring him up there in about an hour?' I fast-walked out of the station, and ran to my car. I drove home, and then stopped at a burger joint.

Just over an hour later I was back in the station, standing in front of the door to interview room three.

I took a deep breath and walked into the room.

TWENTY-SEVEN

'Hi,' I said, sitting down on the chair across from Luke Roberts.

He didn't look up, scowling at the floor.

'I'm Maude. Maude Kaminski. I'm not a police officer.'

He continued to stare at the floor, his blue eyes darting back and forth.

'Can I get you anything? Some water? Something to eat?' His shoulder-length hair was dirty, hanging in greasy strands around his face. Stubble covered his chin and above his mouth. Now that I had a closer look at him, he looked his age. Twenty years old, albeit a very hard twenty years.

'Well, I'm going to have something.'

I opened the bag of fast food and pulled out a hamburger and a Pepsi. I took my time opening the burger, letting the smell emerge, then took a bite and chewed.

He was staring at the burger. I pulled the other one out of the bag and pushed it in front of him, along with a Pepsi and a straw.

'Help yourself,' I said between mouthfuls.

He stared at the burger, and then finally picked it up. He tore the wrapper and ate it in four quick bites, washing it down with the soda.

I finished mine and we sat there in silence.

'Look, I don't know how to tell you this . . .' I had no idea what to say. 'I, uh, I think I know you.'

He snorted and shook his head.

'From a long time ago. You might not remember. I'm your sister.'

He snorted again, and started to get up out of the chair.

'Your real name is Michael Kaminski. You were born in Chicago, and lived at thirty-five nineteen Ridgeway Avenue in Avondale until you were almost three. You were taken from your family by a woman, Sheila Johnson.'

'Sheila?' He lowered himself back into the chair, and looked up at me for the first time.

'Yes, Sheila Johnson. She took you from us, she was . . . confused.'

184 Wendy Church

He shook his head and looked away.

'I'm sorry to tell you, Sheila is dead.'

He looked at me again, then dropped his head.

'You might remember this,' I said, bending down to the bag I'd put on the floor. I pulled out the Spiderman backpack and set it on the table in front of him.

His eyes were riveted on the backpack. After a moment he reached out and pulled it towards him, pulling it open, and looking inside.

His eyes grew wide. 'Where did you—'

The door opened, and an angry looking Commander Bowles stuck his head into the room.

'You're done, Kaminski,' he said.

'Sir, I—'

'*Done.*' He stepped back and allowed a sheepish looking Martinez to enter the room, who grabbed Michael's elbow and escorted him out.

Bowles shook his head, muttering as he turned and left. I picked up the backpack and followed him out, not before I pulled an evidence bag out of my pocket and carefully bagged Michael's straw.

I went down to the basement to the property desk.

'Hey, Linda.'

'Hey, how are you?' she said, concern on her face. 'I heard about what happened in the tunnels. That must have been awful. Shouldn't you be taking some time off?'

'I did, I mean, I will, take more time. But, listen, I think I found Michael.'

'*Michael*? Really? Where? How? Is he, uh . . .?'

'Yes, he's alive. It's a long story.'

'That's wonderful!' She came from around the counter to give me a hug.

'Yeah. I'm ninety-nine percent sure it's him, I just need to confirm it, before I tell my parents. Can you help me get a DNA test?' I showed her the bag with Michael's straw in it.

Her brow furrowed. 'Those tests are expensive. And the lab is backed up.'

'I don't want to tell my parents unless I'm one hundred percent sure. But they've been waiting twenty years.'

Another person would have thought that after twenty years, a few more weeks wouldn't matter. Not Linda.

Tunnel Vision   185

She looked up at the clock, then reached for the bag. 'Theo in the lab owes me a favor. I'll catch him before he goes to lunch. I'll need something from you,' she said, going back behind the counter and reaching under it. She handed me a swab and a container. I wiped the inside of my mouth with the swab, put it in the container and handed it back to her.

She put her 'Back at one o'clock' sign on the desk. As she was shutting down her computer, Sergeant Slivey came down the hall. He leaned over the counter, waving a piece of paper at her.

'Here's the form. It's signed and there are no typos. I want my evidence box, now.'

'I'm sorry, sergeant, but I'm taking my lunch break. You'll have to come back in an hour.'

'You're supposed to be here until noon!'

'My contract, *Dick*, specifically section eight, paragraph four, states explicitly that "an employee can take a lunch break in and around midday, for no longer than sixty minutes". I'm sure you would agree it is "in or around midday".

'But you can put your form in my inbox –' she pushed a plastic basket towards him – 'and I'll be sure to get to it when I get back.'

Slivey was smart enough not to leave his form, which we all knew would somehow get lost. 'I'll be back at twelve fifty-six. If you're not here I'm reporting you,' he said and stomped away.

She winked at me and we walked up the stairs together.

'How long will it take?' I asked.

'They usually get the results back in a few days, but the test itself just takes a few hours. I'll encourage Theo to expedite it. I'll let you know as soon as I hear something.'

'Thanks, Linda.'

She left the building for the lab and I went to my cubicle.

The next few hours crawled by. I spent my time looking over my network analysis and checking my phone every fifteen minutes.

A little after four I got a message from Linda.

'It's him. Congrats!'

TWENTY-EIGHT

'Thanks for seeing me on such short notice.'

Abby smiled. 'It's not every day you recover a missing brother. I'm so happy for you, Maude.'

'I know,' I said, slumped back into the couch, looking down. I still hadn't completely processed the fact that my brother was alive.

'It wouldn't be unusual at all if you're feeling . . . many different things right now. This is a lot to take in. On top of everything else you've gone through.'

I'd started the session by sharing my experience in the tunnels. She knew more than anyone how being underground affected me.

'Yeah, I know. The thing is, now, how do I tell my parents?'

'Do you feel trepidation about that?'

Trepidation didn't begin to cover it. 'I mean, I should be thrilled. But I'm nervous.'

'Why?'

'I don't want to let them down again.'

'Why would you be letting them down? You found him, somehow, after all these years. After taking some extraordinary risks.'

'I know, I know. It's just, well, he didn't exactly warm to me. What's he going to do when he sees them? If he reacts the same way to them as he did to me . . . it might kill my mother, all over again. He recognized the backpack, and Sheila's name, but clearly didn't remember me. If he doesn't remember my mom . . .'

She nodded. 'You can't control his reaction, or their feelings. You have to let it play out. You've done what you can.' She waited a moment, then said, 'Tell me again how he seemed when you talked to him.'

'He didn't believe that I was his sister. The first reaction I got out of him was when I mentioned Sheila. But when I showed him the backpack, he definitely remembered that.'

'That makes sense. Most children start retaining their memories around three years old. Sheila Johnson was his mother for the first part of his life that he remembers.'

'Is there anything we can do, to help him remember? Maybe talk about what happened to him?'

Tunnel Vision 187

She leaned back, sighing. 'Normally when children are kidnapped, and then reunited with their families, we try to avoid making them talk about their experience. It retraumatizes them. Lots of intrusive questions can be harmful, and we like to wait to let them talk about it on their own time. In Michael's case, even though he's an adult now, he's been exposed to a lifetime of trauma.' She shook her head. 'Being kidnapped and taken from everything you know as a child is extremely traumatic. Living with an addict is traumatic. Living on the street is traumatic. Being taken from someone and placed into a foster situation . . . well, you get the idea. Each one of those things by itself can cause huge damage. All together? It's hard to say how to broach the subject with him.'

'Is there *anything* I can do?' I asked, exasperated. 'For my parents? For him, to make this . . . better?'

'You might want to tell your parents about Sheila Johnson.'

'Sheila? Why? Why would they care?'

'If you tell them about how she ended up on the street, losing her son . . . it might help them.' She looked at me for a moment. 'He was around three when he was taken, wasn't he?'

I nodded.

'I suggest rather than bringing your parents to the station, that you take him to their house.'

I couldn't imagine that would go well. 'Why would that matter?'

'Three years old is mature enough to remember some things. And he's more likely to recall his parents' faces than yours. He saw them more often, and you were a child when he knew you. You've changed more than they have.

'Also, the sense with the best recall is smell. You might have a better chance of jogging his memory if you can get him to a familiar place, with familiar smells. Are your parents by any chance living in the same house as they did when he lived there?'

'Yes.'

They'd thought about moving, but never did. They never said it, but I think they wanted to stay there, just in case Michael ever came back.

I stood up. 'Thanks. I gotta go.'

'We have another forty-five minutes.'

'I know.' I didn't want to wait another second.

* * *

I drove back down to the station. To get them to let Michael out of custody for a field trip was a long shot. I'd have a better chance in person than over the phone.

I knew I had no chance with Bowles or Jacobs, or the ADA. I went straight to Jefferson.

Possibly because he was feeling a little guilty for my suspension, he surprised me. 'I'll let you take him out for a few hours on these conditions: you find a law enforcement officer to go with you, someone who will be with him at all times. And he stays handcuffed. Neither of those things are negotiable.'

'Yes sir. Thank you, sir.'

I ran out of Jefferson's office and called Jeb. He was still in the building and I met him in his office. It wasn't a hard sell to get him to agree to escort Michael to my parents' house. He was well aware of what we'd all gone through over the years.

We went together to the lockup. I waited in the hallway while Jeb disappeared into the back area with the cells. Even with Jefferson's OK and Jeb's FBI badge, it took a couple of hours before he came back out, his hand on Michael's arm.

'He didn't want to come,' said Jeb. 'I convinced him it would be in his best interest.'

Michael's hands were handcuffed in front of him. He stared at the floor, scowling, as we left the building.

TWENTY-NINE

'd called my mom as soon as I got the OK from Jefferson, and listened to her stunned silence when I told her we were coming over with Michael.

We pulled in front of their house and were barely out of the car when the front door opened. My mom and dad stepped out on to the stoop.

Jeb got out of the back, leading Michael. The three of us walked up the driveway to the porch. As we got close my mother gasped.

I'd warned them about Michael's state of mind, that he might not yet really believe he was Michael Kaminski. I'd told them a smattering of what he'd been through, and that we'd have to be patient with him.

That all went out the window when my mom saw him. She rushed down the cement stairs, reaching up to touch his face.

He leaned back, then started to turn away.

'Maybe we should go inside?' offered Jeb, his hand firmly gripping Michael's upper arm, forcing him to face forward.

We followed my parents in, my mom's head turned back the whole time looking at Michael, causing her to stumble as she walked into the house.

Jeb led Michael to the couch and sat down, pulling him down next to him. Mom picked up a chair and set it as close as she could to Michael, my dad taking a seat next to her. Nana was in her chair by the fireplace.

I took a deep breath. 'This is Julia Kaminski, your mother, and Jan Kaminski, your father,' I said. 'And that's Nana, your grandmother,' I said, pointing to her in her chair. She smiled and gave him a small wave.

Sophie was at a friend's house. We thought it would be too much for her, and for Michael, on this first visit. I'd also told Mark and Lydia, but Abby had suggested that we keep the first meeting small.

'And this –' I waved my hand at the room – 'is where you grew up.'

He looked around the room perfunctorily before looking back down at the carpet, his eyes briefly resting on the mantel.

We sat there in uncomfortable silence for several moments. Abby had said not to rush things.

'You're so tall,' said my mom, finally. 'And skinny. Are they feeding you over there?'

'Over there' was her take on jail.

'I made dinner,' she continued, ignoring his silence. 'Are you hungry?'

Michael continued to stare at the floor until Jeb gave him a not-so-subtle jab in the ribs.

'Fine, sure,' he said quietly.

She got up and went into the kitchen. My dad stood up, awkwardly gesturing to the dining room, where Mom had set the table. Shortly after we sat down she started coming out of the kitchen with trays of food.

She'd apparently spent the entire time since I called her cooking. Plates of pierogis, pork cutlets, cucumber salad, and mashed potatoes. Once everything was on the table she sat down. When no one made a move for the food, she said, 'I didn't cook all of this food so you could look at it.'

We started passing trays and taking food. Jeb put little bit of everything on Michael's plate.

His handcuffs didn't affect his appetite, and once he started he ate like a man possessed. I was glad to see it, it always made Mom happy when we ate her food. And he needed the calories.

The table was largely silent, other than the occasional request to pass something. Despite her directive to the rest of us, Mom ate almost nothing, looking up from her plate constantly to look at Michael.

I could tell she had a thousand questions to ask him, and things to say, but I'd told her on the phone that we should try not to overwhelm him this first time, and that it would be a long process. Still, I was surprised at her restraint.

She was doing the thing that Abby always talked about with me. She was appreciating the moment. Her son was back from the dead, and at her table. Nothing else mattered right now.

We finished the meal and she cleared the plates. 'We'll have coffee in the living room,' she said, nodding her head indicating we were to leave the table. The rest of us stood up and walked back in. Jeb and Michael took their places back on the sofa.

A few minutes later she came back out of the kitchen with a tray, holding a coffee pot, cups, and a plate of warm kolaczki. She put them on the coffee table in front of Michael. 'These used to be your favorites,' she said.

He stared at the tray, his nostrils twitching. He reached his manacled hands to the tray and picked one up, bringing it to his nose. Then he put it in his mouth, taking a small bite.

His face changed and he dropped the rest of the cookie on his lap. His eyes moved to the pictures on the mantel. He looked at them for a long moment, then he dropped his head, and his shoulders started to shake.

I looked at Jeb, wondering what the hell we were supposed to do now. He shrugged his shoulders.

My mom moved her chair closer to Michael. Then she said one of the smartest things I'd ever heard anyone say.

'Tell us about Sheila.'

He started haltingly, his description of his life without us made up of partial sentences, and interspersed with long pauses. To their credit my folks didn't interrupt, and let him tell his story in his own time.

He didn't remember much from when he was taken. Blurry memories of being outside in strange places, wondering where his mother was. Then being outside, almost all of the time.

'Except when it got very cold we went inside, to the shelter.'

As he talked he gained steam, possibly helped by the energy from consuming the entire plate of kolaczki.

'Mom – I mean, Sheila, read to me, all the time. She said we were Hobbits.'

At some point my mom replaced Jeb on the couch. I saw her tentatively reach for Michael's hand. She didn't react when he jerked it away from her.

'Did you have enough to eat?' she asked.

'I don't remember being hungry. She said that my uncles were taking care of us.'

The 'uncles' were johns, presumably. What didn't go to her drug habit went to feeding Michael.

'One night the police came. They took her away, and took me to a big building with other kids. Then I went to a house with a family. I think I was seven. That was my first house.'

192 Wendy Church

Somehow Sheila had managed to care for him, and keep him alive and reasonably healthy, for over three years on the streets. Most astounding to me was that he wasn't addicted to any drugs, and never even used them. 'She made me promise to never do any drugs,' he said. 'Every night before we went to sleep.'

Even though she'd kidnapped my little brother, and caused my family immeasurable pain, I found I couldn't drum up much anger towards her. She'd done her best for him.

After she'd been taken away Michael had bounced from foster home to foster home, and eventually ended up back on the street when he was sixteen. He'd lived there ever since, occasionally getting picked up by the DCFS and put back into a facility. Once there he'd wasted no time escaping back to the street, where he'd occasionally visit Sheila, and formed bonds with other street kids, including his best friends Cam Weathers and Lester Williams.

The three of them had been recruited by Brajen Krol, and they'd been working for the gang for the last three months, dropping off drugs to dealers, and occasionally collecting money.

'It's been good,' he said, sitting up straighter, and looking at each of us, seeming to forget he was in handcuffs, sitting with law enforcement. 'And it's not hard, we get new phones all of the time, and money, just do some pickups and deliveries. Sometimes we can afford to stay in a hotel,' he said proudly.

'Where?' I asked.

His face clouded over, and he looked away. *Dammit.* I should have kept my mouth shut. Just because he was telling us about his childhood didn't mean he was going to start talking about the gang.

Jeb had been looking at his watch for the last thirty minutes, and said, 'I'm really sorry, we have to get back to the station.'

'Do you have to go?' my mom asked.

'I'm sorry, Mrs Kaminski. Michael is under arrest, we had to get special dispensation to let him come out today. You can visit him at the jail.'

Everyone stood up, and this time when my mom reached for him he let her, and she hugged him. Not the normal strangling, breath-stealing hugs that were the norm. She held him gently, like he was still three years old. He stood there, unmoving, but didn't pull away.

She stepped back from the hug, her hands still on his arms. 'I will come tomorrow, and every day after that. And when you are out you will live here,' she said.

Tunnel Vision

He looked down at the ground and shuffled out of the house, Jeb's hand on his shoulder.

The three of us drove back to the station in silence. Jeb took Michael down to the lockup, and then he drove me home.

'What will happen to him now?' I asked.

'I don't know,' he said, shaking his head. 'He was caught with a large quantity of drugs, and he's implicated in the gang. All of them are going to face charges of the criminal sale of a controlled substance and conspiracy, at least. The DA's not going to fuck around with this, Maude.'

'But he's low-level. Don't they make deals with the low-level members, to bring in the leaders?'

'Sometimes. This isn't an FBI case, even though Jacobs is running the task force. I don't know what your DA will do. But at the moment, they don't have any higher-level guys.'

'Can you find out?' I asked as we pulled up to my apartment.

'I will. But don't get your hopes up. A lot of resources have gone into this task force. They're going to want convictions. If they don't find anyone higher up, they're going to bring the hammer down on the ones they catch.'

'I know. Thanks.' I didn't really feel like being alone, and thought about inviting him in. But it would be cruel for me to string him along. 'Good night,' I said, closing the door.

He nodded, then waited until I was in the building to drive off.

THIRTY

I went to bed but slept fitfully. Something was niggling at my subconscious.

When the alarm went off I showered quickly and ran out the door and to the situation room at the station. I fired up my computer and spent a few minutes adjusting my analysis. Then I pulled up the file with the photos we'd taken from the festival.

Most of them were from Nowak, but they included a few other shots, from me, and Gavin, that we'd taken with our phones.

'Hey,' said Gavin, walking into the room.

'Look at this.' I brought my network map back up and pointed to the monitor.

'Yeah, I've seen it. The gang network map.'

'Now look.'

I brought up a second map, the one that I'd recently revised.

'Do you see?' I said excitedly. 'This layer of what we thought were middlemen, the guys between Brajen Krol and the rank and file. It's just one guy.'

He frowned. 'What do you mean?'

'I mean, we used the cell phone numbers to identify who was calling who. We put this together assuming these numbers –' I brought up the older map, with the line of middlemen – 'belonged to different people. What if this whole group of unidentified middlemen is actually one guy?'

His frown deepened. 'It looks to me like you're just making random changes to support your theory. What data do you have to support this?'

'No, look.' I enlarged the revised map and pointed to part of it. 'Look at the times. None of the calls the middlemen are making to the rank-and-file guys are at the same time. Not a single one.'

'I still don't get it,' he said.

Arghhh. 'Their operation has been up for six months. Twenty-four weeks. Don't you think, over twenty-four weeks, that these hundreds of calls would overlap, at least once? There are twenty-four different numbers here. We assumed it was six people, changing out their

Tunnel Vision

phones every week. What if it's one person, who's changing out his phone every week?'

I pointed to the wall, where we'd laid out a partial organizational chart of the gang, with pictures of the ones we'd identified. Brajen Krol and his four lieutenants at the top, various street workers including Michael at the bottom. In between were blank spaces for the six middlemen identified to date only by their phone numbers.

'It's not six guys. It's one. One guy is running this operation for Krol.'

Gavin still looked skeptical, but had stopped frowning.

'I was so stupid,' I said. 'We looked at the numbers, at the dates of the calls, but not at the *times*. When you add that in, it's obvious that it's just one guy. I went through the photos from the festival, and—'

We were interrupted by the rest of the team filing into the room, flanked by Jacobs and Bowles.

Gavin stepped away from me, and waved his hand, indicating I should shut down my computer. He knew that I was already on thin ice, and bringing up my 'single middleman' theory might get me in the doghouse again.

Jacobs strode to the front. 'So right now we have a few low-level gang members in custody, and we've shut down their manufacturing site. Renfro, what's the word on the street?' she asked, clearly hopeful that we'd been wrong before, and that the initial raid had stopped their operations.

He looked down. 'As far as we can tell, there's still no impact on their operation, ma'am.'

'*None?*'

He shook his head. 'If anything, there's been an uptick on the amount of Red available.'

'*Dammit.* So they've definitely moved their manufacturing,' said Jacobs.

'Or there were always multiple sites,' offered Gavin.

'Whatever,' said Jacobs, exasperated. 'It's obvious we're not going to take this gang down until we take down the top man. Nothing has changed, we still have to get to Brajen Krol. Mr McCullom, keep working that real estate angle. Detective Renfro, increase the pressure on your CIs, see if any of them have seen Krol or his lieutenants.'

Jacobs was grasping at straws. We'd gone over the financials

196   Wendy Church

several times, and Renfro had already been hammering on his CIs. Until or unless we could find the manufacturing sites, or Gavin could find a link between the real estate and Brajen Krol, we were dead in the water.

I opened up my computer and looked back at my revised network map.

'Ma'am, commander, I think I found something,' I said.

Out of the corner of my eye I saw Gavin drop his head, shaking it slightly.

'I believe we're not finding anything that links Krol to the operation, because we're focused on the wrong person,' I said. 'Look at this.' I put up the two network maps, the original one with the middlemen tier of six people, and the revised one, with one person in the middle.

Jacobs was frowning, and Bowles was shaking his head. 'I thought we put this bullshit to bed, Kaminski.'

Jeb had been leaning against the wall on one side of the room.

'I think you need to consider this, ma'am,' he said quietly, looking at Jacobs.

During the time we'd dated I'd shared my work with him, and he had more than a passable understanding of social network analysis. He saw the same thing I did on the map.

She frowned at him and turned back to me. 'Go ahead.'

I walked them through the discovery, and my realization that our group of middlemen was just one guy.

'This,' I said, pointing to the single circle in the center of the revised graphic, all alone between the leadership and the rank and file, 'is the guy we want. I think they've been setting us up, getting us to focus on Brajen Krol. What if he's just the figurehead? And their plan all along has been to distract us with him?'

No one said anything, afraid of getting on the wrong side of Bowles. But everyone was focused on the map intently.

'Think about it. There's not a *single* connection between Brajen Krol and the Red business.'

'That we know of,' said Renfro.

I rolled my eyes. How was someone so stupid able to walk upright?

'We haven't found any of the money. And not because we haven't tried. We've been all up in Krol's finances since the beginning.'

'Let's suppose you're right, Ms Kaminski. So what if it is one man? That doesn't get us anywhere,' said Jacobs, sighing.

'With all due respect, ma'am, it points us in a different direction. If we all believed this' – Bowles and Renfro both snorted – 'what would we do differently?'

There was complete silence in the room, everyone else looking anywhere but at Bowles and Jacobs.

'We'd go over our information from the festival. We'd focus our efforts on finding out who this man is,' said Jeb.

'Yes.' I nodded gratefully. 'And I've been going through the images we have from the festival. Who is this man?' I said, pulling up an image on the monitor.

It was a picture I'd taken with my phone, one of the few, from the line at Sagarine's food counter. I used the laser pointer to highlight a tall, slender man, with blond hair cut short above his ears. Then I put up two more pictures that had been taken of Brajen Krol. In them the tall man was in the frame. In one of the images he was seen speaking to men we now knew were recruits.

Jacobs looked at the images, transfixed. 'How did we miss this,' she said quietly. 'We went through hundreds of photos.'

'Let's assume, just for the moment, that I'm right,' I said. 'That Brajen Krol is nothing but a figurehead.

'This means the lower level guys in the gang get their daily instructions about where to pick up the drugs, and where to distribute them, from this one man. Then they drop off the money at dead drops, the locations also provided by this man. We've assumed whoever's picking up the money is giving it to Krol. What if it's going to him?' I said, pointing to the tall man in the image.

'This whole thing does seem beyond what we know about Krol's intellectual capacity,' Jacobs said. 'How would we proceed, if we believed that?'

'If she's right, it means that Krol's entire operation hinges on this guy. If he gets taken out, the whole thing might collapse,' said Jeb.

He was spot on. I'd done this kind of analysis many times, with other gangs. The primary function of applying social network analysis to gangs was to help identify the crucial members in an organization, so law enforcement could focus their limited resources on that person.

'All right, everyone. As of right now our main focus is finding out who this man is. Whether or not Ms Kaminski is right, he's a member of this gang who is unaccounted for. How do we do that?'

'I can check facial recognition,' offered Gavin.

I didn't think that would amount to anything, but it was worth a shot.

'I can circulate the image to my CIs,' said Renfro.

Jacobs nodded. 'The other thing we'd be doing is working on getting people that we've picked up to flip on him, rather than on Brajen Krol. And we *have* people. We've been interrogating them, but we might just not be asking the right questions. Commander Bowles will reinterview the seven men we have in custody.' Bowles was red-faced but kept his mouth shut. 'We'll reconvene tonight at five. Dismissed.'

Everyone filed out of the room. Jeb was last, turning to wink at me as he headed out the door.

I spent the rest of the day trying to wrangle a meeting with the ADA. I finally got her assistant to squeeze me in for a five-minute meeting.

'Meeting' was too strong of a word. I followed her down a long hallway in the courthouse building on California.

'What are you planning for the Greenpoint Crew prosecutions? I mean, for the men you've picked up?' I asked, struggling to keep up with her brisk walk.

'We're throwing the book at them. Everything,' she said, looking at her watch.

'They're low-level. The leaders will just replace them.'

'Well, I don't have any leaders, do I?' she said, stopping and turning to me. 'Your task force has been at this for weeks, and from what I've heard you're not close to any of the top guys. The best I can do is set an example, the most devastating one I can.' She looked at her watch again. 'I have to go,' she said, turning into a conference room.

Shit. Unless I could do something, Michael was going to prison.

The team reconvened at five o'clock.

As expected, nothing showed up on the facial recognition search. And Renfro's CIs claimed to not know the tall man. We looked expectantly at Jacobs.

'None of the seven men we have in custody claims to know this mystery man,' said Bowles, emphasizing 'mystery' to make it sound sarcastic.

'What did you offer them?' I asked.

Tunnel Vision

'The usual,' he said. 'Reduced sentences.'

Even if the gang members did know something, it was no wonder they hadn't talked. They were probably all in the same boat as Michael and his friends. They'd had an upgrade in their living conditions since they got involved with the gang. On top of that was the specter of Brajen Krol's retaliation on anyone he suspected was disloyal to him.

'That's not enough,' I said, turning to Jacobs. 'We're going to need to offer suspended sentences for anyone who helps us find the mystery man.'

Jacobs shook her head. 'The DA is hot to make a big splash with convictions. The city wants to believe we're doing something about these murders. There's no way they're going to drop the charges for seven men, on the off chance that they tell us something that may lead to this guy.'

'Not talk,' I said, taking a deep breath. 'What if we let one of them go?'

Bowles and Renfro both snorted.

'Hear me out. The man we let go goes back to working for the gang, but he's really working for us. At some point he'll be involved with the money, and will end up meeting with the mystery man. He lets us know when that's going to be, and we take the man down then.'

'Why would any of them agree to do that?' asked Nowak.

'Because we'll offer them complete immunity,' I said.

Bowles laughed out loud. 'You've lost your mind. Let someone we've picked up completely off? The DA will never go for that. You just want to get your brother off.'

I did want to get my brother off. I also wanted him to be safe, and the only way that was going to happen is if Brajen Krol was gone, and the only way we could get him gone was to take down his operation. The way we were going to do that was to pick up the mystery man, who I suspected was behind the whole set up.

Jacobs must have figured that out, too, because she nodded. 'I'll see what I can do. Dismissed, everyone back here tomorrow morning.'

Now I just had to hope that someone other than Michael would agree to be our bait.

THIRTY-ONE

Jacobs must have pulled some strings, because despite the ADA's previous stance that she was going to take down the gang's rank-and-file members hard, she made a generous offer to anyone willing to take part in the undercover operation. In exchange for help bringing in the mystery man, the participating gang member would get immunity from prosecution, instead of at least fifteen years at Stateville.

I was hoping one of the other men we had in custody would find the prospect of immunity enticing enough to do it. As it turned out, none of them found it even tempting enough to speak a single word to us. The fear of Brajen Krol's reprisal was too much.

All seven of the men in custody had been brought down to the station and put into interrogation rooms. The team split up the interviews. I'd been given Michael, and had found reasons to delay his interview so he would be the last one, wanting to give the others every chance to take the deal.

'Are you sure? You never saw this man?' I said to him, showing him an image of the tall man.

'No, I've never seen him before.'

'You were getting a call from this guy, every day. How could you not know who it is?'

'If he is the one who's been calling us, some of the others have seen him, when they've dropped off the money. Talk to them.'

'They're not talking.'

'All I know is I'd get a call, and a location. Then he hung up. I doubt I could even recognize his voice, even if I did want to help you. But I might as well shoot myself in the head. They don't tolerate snitches.'

'You know if we don't catch Brajen Krol, or this guy, it's all going to fall on you, and your friends. You'll spend at least fifteen years in prison. Not jail, Michael. Prison.'

'So you need to catch them.'

'We're trying. But we need some help. It's not a big lift. You just have to let us know when you meet with this guy.'

Tunnel Vision   201

I described to him what we wanted to do.

'No. No way,' he said, shaking his head vigorously.

'This is the only way. If we don't catch him, or Brajen Krol, there's no chance for you. I've talked to the ADA. They want to set an example.'

'Do you know what they'll do to me if I get caught?' he said, his eyes wide.

'You won't get caught. The whole team will be behind you. If you help us take them down the ADA will drop your charges.'

'And what about Cam, and Spink?'

'I'm sorry, Michael. They've already indicated they're not going to work with us.'

'What if I can get them to do it?' he asked.

'We only need one person for this operation. I can't do anything for them.'

He folded his arms across his chest. 'They get whatever I get. Or no deal.'

Nothing I'd said to him changed his mind. I finally went to Jacobs and laid out the requirements; Michael would do the op only if his friends would also be let out, and get the same immunity deal.

To my surprise she took the offer to the ADA, who agreed. While Michael was back in jail talking his friends into the deal, the team met in the conference room to go over the undercover op.

Jeb was sitting next to me. 'She must really be desperate to go along with this,' he whispered. 'She's way out on a limb.'

'I know. We all are.'

Jacobs went through the op, and dismissed us. As usual she didn't waste any time. Michael and his friends would be let out tonight.

'Pretty cold, Kaminski, serving up your own brother,' said Renfro as we walked out of the room.

'Fuck you, meathead.'

Gavin and Nowak met with Michael, Cam, and Lester before they left the station, going over the operation and getting them geared up. Each man received a phone. They were to text us with information on the mystery man's whereabouts as soon as they became aware of them. The phones also had a one-button notification feature, to be used if he showed up, and they needed to notify us quickly and quietly that they were in his presence. All three men were fitted with GPS tracking devices.

'Remember,' I said, as Gavin was fastening the small tracker on Michael's shirt. 'Don't take any chances. Do just what we tell you. We don't actually need you to do much. As soon as you see him, or know where he is, you're done. When that happens, get as far away as possible. Someone will pick you up. Just in case,' I said, handing him a slip of paper, 'here's my address. If things really go haywire, you can always go there.'

The ADA had let them all out on bail. We covered them by ginning up a phony legal aid rep, and a fake nonprofit who provided bail for low income criminals.

'What if they take our phones?'

'We'll deal with that. You've got the trackers, and watchers.' We'd begged, borrowed and stolen every officer in the station to help with surveillance. 'We'll know where you are at all times, and backup will be less than a minute away.'

We let them all out on the street, where they called a cab. The unmarked surveillance cars followed them at a distance, to a shitty hotel we'd designated.

Gavin, Jeb and I were in the situation room, watching the three men's GPS signals on Gavin's computer moving in real time. Jacobs and Bowles were on the radio, getting regular updates from the trailing cars.

And then we waited.

As the night went on we took turns taking breaks. At midnight we started taking shifts, allowing one person to sleep on the couch for a couple of hours at a time, while the two others monitored the trackers.

At six a.m. the next morning one of the radios crackled. 'I think we've got something.'

'What's happening?' said Jacobs. As far as I could tell she hadn't slept.

'Package delivery.'

I looked at Gavin. 'Burner phones?'

He nodded. 'Probably.'

We'd set up Michael's hotel room with a StingRay to capture calls. An hour after the package arrived Michael received a call on a new phone. In a few minutes Cam received a call, and shortly afterwards a call came in for Lester.

The calls were brief, lasting less than fifteen seconds.

'We're in business,' said Gavin excitedly.

Tunnel Vision 203

I nodded. 'Now comes the hard part.'

We waited, watching the GPS trackers as the three men left the hotel at the designated time. They drove south, and stopped, presumably to pick up a stash of drugs for delivery.

'Pershing and Damen,' said Jeb, pointing to the map. 'That's in the old Central Manufacturing District. That makes sense. Not a lot of people down there, and lots of abandoned buildings.'

Ten minutes later the trackers had moved, but only a short distance away from the original location.

'Something's wrong,' I said. 'They should just be picking up the drugs and taking them to a dealer. Why haven't they moved?'

'Maybe they had to wait for them? We don't know exactly what time they were supposed to be there,' Gavin said, not sounding entirely certain.

Thirty minutes later one of the trackers went offline. The other two were still live, but in the same location.

'This isn't right,' I said, my voice shrill. 'We need to get someone over there,' I said to Jacobs.

'Give it a few more minutes,' she said. 'Once we go in the whole thing is blown.'

I waited, my anxiety growing. My eyes were glued to Gavin's monitor and the two blinking, unmoving GPS dots.

Ten minutes later Jacobs sighed. 'Go in,' she said into her radio.

Minutes later her radio crackled. 'No one here, ma'am. Bystanders report hearing shots.'

She looked at Bowles who was already on the phone. 'All units, shots fired, go to Pershing and Damen. Be advised, three plainclothes in the area. Repeat, friendlies in the area.'

Jacobs was talking into the radio while I made my way out the door. 'Where are you going?' asked Jeb, who'd followed me out.

'Where do you think?' I said.

He grabbed my arm and I struggled to pull away. 'Let go.'

'My car's closer,' he said, joining me as I ran out the door.

By the time we got to Pershing and Damen several patrol cars had joined the surveillance team and were parked in an empty lot, lights flashing. Uniformed police were fanning out, several moving into an alley a few yards from the original location.

'*Here,*' one shouted.

The uniform stood near the side of the alley, leaning over a body. As I got closer I saw it was Lester Williams. He was laying on his

204 Wendy Church

back, his arms over his head. Shot once in the stomach, and once in the head. He'd been facing whoever had shot him.

A minute later we heard 'here' from another uniform, a little further down the alley.

I walked toward it, holding my breath.

Cam Weathers was still alive, but barely, his blood pooling around him on one side. He'd been shot in the back. Running away.

I continued down the alley, walking slowly, dreading the sound of the next 'here'. A simple word that would mean Michael was dead, or close to it.

Thirty minutes went by, then an hour. There was no sign of Michael. I was torn between relief that they hadn't found him dead, and dread that Krol had taken him, and was doing something worse.

Bowles called off the official search after two hours. I stayed, walking the alleys, calling Michael's name. Jeb had stayed with me. 'They'll pick it up again tomorrow,' he said, after we'd walked the alley and surrounding streets for another hour.

'Why aren't we getting his GPS?'

He shook his head. 'I don't know. But don't give up hope. He's a street kid. If anyone knows how to survive, it's him.'

He didn't add what I was thinking. Cam Weathers and Lester Williams had been street kids, too.

Jeb drove me home. I was exhausted. I put my key into the outside door and waved at Jeb while he drove away.

I screamed as a heavy hand gripped my shoulder from behind.

'*Shhhh*,' said a familiar voice, his hand over my mouth.

I relaxed, and his hand fell away. I turned to see Michael, slightly stooped over, holding his other hand over a dark red stain on his shirt.

Michael eventually relented to letting me take him to the hospital, only after I agreed to tell no one on the task force.

The bullet had grazed his side. As bullet wounds went it wasn't too serious, if painful. A few inches over and it would have killed him.

The doctor cleaned it and put in some stitches. I knew she'd have to report it, it was a requirement for hospitals to report all gunshot victims. But it would take some time to get back to the task force. She also wanted him to stay overnight, but he refused, and we left after she'd finished the stitches and given him something for the pain.

Tunnel Vision 205

'There were no drugs at the stash site,' he said, sitting next to me on my couch. We were both exhausted, but both too wired to sleep. 'We waited, we thought maybe they were late. Then a van pulled up. Two men got out, from the gang. At first we thought they were bringing the shipment. But they pulled out guns. Me and Cam took off. Spink tried to talk to them,' he said, looking down at the floor. 'Did you find Cam?' he said.

'He's in intensive care. They're, uh, they're not sure he's going to make it.'

'This is your fault,' he said, anguished. 'You made us do it. We *told* you what would happen.'

'I'm sorry,' I said again, knowing it sounded lame. Also knowing that whatever blame he was throwing at me, he'd eventually put on himself for talking his friends into it.

'Did they say anything?'

'Who?'

'The gunmen.'

'No. I mean, there wasn't a discussion. One of them just said something like, "Kres sends his regards".'

'Kres?'

'Yeah.'

'Not Brajen Krol?'

He shook his head.

Could this be the mystery man? It was something, at least.

'How did you get away?'

'Cam and I started running, and then we split up. He went down the alley, I went into one of the buildings. They shot at me as I was going in the door. They tried to follow, but it was dark, and that building's a maze. I knew my way around. Mom – uh, Sheila – and I stayed there once. I waited until they left, then took the L to your place.'

I imagined him, shot, bleeding, walking in the dark to the L station, riding the train to downtown, changing lines, then the long trip to Portage Park, then walking from the station to our apartment. It was a miracle he hadn't bled to death.

'What happened to your GPS tracker?'

'I crushed it.'

'Why?'

He looked at me like I was stupid. 'They knew what we were doing. Someone told them. How did they know?'

THIRTY-TWO

'd called Jacobs right away to tell her Michael was still alive, and to give her the name that he'd shared with me. She wasn't happy that he was staying at my place, and that I'd not let them know as soon as I'd found him. But she didn't belabor the point once I gave her a potential name for the mystery man. Now that they knew that Michael was alive, they'd want to put him back into custody, but for her that wasn't a priority right now.

'Nice work, Kaminski,' said Bowles sarcastically when we'd all assembled for the task force meeting the next morning. 'Two men are dying or dead and your brother is gone.'

'Actually, he's turned up,' said Jacobs. 'Alive.'

'Whatever,' said Bowles. 'It was still a clusterfuck.'

'Not completely,' said Jacobs. 'We have a name, for our mystery man. Michael Kaminski heard the gunman mention "Kres". I contacted a colleague of mine in Customs, he gave me a list of everyone entering the country from Poland in the last several years.'

She had dark circles under her eyes, but she was smiling. 'I believe we're dealing with Kresimir Skala,' she said, putting up a few photos on the monitor.

Did this woman ever sleep? It must have taken her all night to go through all of that.

'Kresimir Skala is one of Brajen Krol's cousins. He's forty-five, and has lived in Poland most of his life. He has a degree from Warsaw University in economics, and no record as far as we can tell.'

At first I thought Skala was bald, but it was just that his hair was shaved close to the skin. He'd grown it since this photo had been taken. Unlike Brajen Krol he was less thuggy looking, and more ascetic, with pale blue eyes above a thin nose and sharp cheekbones. His lips were so red they looked like they were bleeding.

'No one in custody has mentioned Skala, and there's no evidence of his activity, other than cell phone calls on burner phones to men who can't or won't identify him.

'This means that the only way we're going to get him is with his financials. The good news is that there is a ton of money, and

Tunnel Vision 207

all of it is going somewhere. We've been through Krol and his lieutenants' finances, and we've found nothing. Kresimir Skala is the only viable suspect left, and I'm optimistic that we'll be able to find the money in his accounts.

'Mr McCullom, you take the lead. Find the money trail that leads to Kresimir Skala. I've spoken to the ADA, and she's put together the warrants we need for his financials. Detective Renfro, Officer Nowak and Ms Kaminski, give Mr McCullom any help he needs going over the numbers, drag in whoever else you can get to go through it. Call me as soon as you find anything.'

Jacobs had apparently lit a fire under the ADA, who'd in turn lit one under Skala's bank, as we had his entire financial records provided to us by the time we left the meeting. Gavin called in Linda to help, and with his instruction the six of us spent the rest of the day looking at Kresimir Skala's financial records.

What started as optimistic enthusiasm faded to lethargy, as hours went by and no one had found anything.

'There's nothing,' announced Gavin, finally calling it at nine o'clock. 'Not a fucking thing. Wherever the money's going, it's not into this guy's pockets.' He slammed the computer mouse on the desk, breaking it into several pieces. 'I'm going home.'

The next morning Gavin kicked the meeting off with the bad news. 'Skala's squeaky clean. No businesses, no sales related to any real estate, no significant withdrawals or deposits. Not a goddamned thing.'

'Nothing?' asked Jacobs, incredulous.

Gavin shook his head.

The blood drained out of her face. She knew this meant that the investigation was dead in the water, again. We'd identified the lynchpin of the Greenpoint Crew's drug operation, the one who, if we caught him, would bring the whole thing to a grinding halt. And there was absolutely nothing we could do about it.

It was beyond frustrating. Two violent criminals, identified as being involved in a large scale drug operation, along with several murders, and we couldn't get them off of the street.

Worse, for me, was that they knew who Michael was, and that he'd helped us. It was only a matter of time before they got to him.

He didn't qualify for witness protection. And before too long they'd get around to taking him back into custody and charging him. The ADA would destroy him, not least because she'd been

208 Wendy Church

made to look foolish by letting three suspects go. She needed to prosecute the five men she had left in custody to the fullest extent, just to avoid looking bad.

Michael wouldn't last a week in prison. Brajen Krol could get to anyone, anywhere. Michael would be a dead man the second he was incarcerated.

We were dismissed, with vague instruction to 'keep pursuing leads'. But everyone knew it was over.

I wanted to go home, to sit with Michael, for what might be the last hours of his freedom, and possibly his life. But I was an employee now, Jefferson's promise to bring me on as soon as possible made fact the day after I met with him.

I sat at my office for a few minutes staring at my computer. I called Jeb but it went to voicemail. He was probably meeting with Jacobs to talk about how they would shut down the task force.

I really wanted to talk to someone. Normally I would call Sags. But it didn't feel honest, leaning on her for support, when I was considering throwing her out of the apartment. No matter what happened, I still cared about her.

I got up and headed downstairs. Linda had worked with us on the financials, but wasn't part of the team. Someone should give her the bad news. And it was close to lunchtime.

When I got to her counter she took one look at my face, and said, 'Let's go.'

We left the station and headed to our bench in the park, stopping at a gyro place on the way.

'What happened?' she said, taking a bite.

'The op was a bust. Michael's been shot.' Hearing her gasp, I added quickly, 'He's going to be OK. One of his friends is dead, though, and the other's barely hanging on. The gang knew what we were doing.'

She frowned. 'How did they know?'

'I don't know for sure, but I think we have a mole. That would explain how they knew our plans to hit the manufacturing site in the tunnels, too.'

'What's the next move?'

I sighed. 'There isn't one. They know we're onto them now. Jacobs might try to get more budget for surveillance on the dealers, in the hopes we'll get lucky. Or they may shut down the task force all together.'

I put my gyro back in the bag, not hungry. 'They're going to kill him, Linda. Michael's going to get a max sentence, and Krol will put the word out. Once he goes to prison he'll be dead in a week . . .'

I was choking up. This was too horrible, to get Michael back, after all these years, and then to lose him.

She leaned over and put her arm around my shoulder. We sat there in silence for a few minutes.

Her brow furrowed. 'What if we could get someone else to take Kresimir Skala out?'

'What do you mean?'

'What if his own men killed him?'

'That would be great, but why would they do that?'

'Brajen Krol values loyalty above everything else, right? This whole set up is new for him. Kresimir Skala's a distant cousin, and while he's related, they're not particularly close. But Skala's got a position of import in the gang. What would Krol do if he thought Skala was cheating him?'

I laughed, grimly. 'He'd kill him with extreme prejudice. But we don't have any evidence that Skala is cheating him. You were there, with us, going through his financials. There's not a shred of evidence that Skala has anything to do with the money.'

'I know, but, what if Krol *thought* he was taking the money?'

'I don't know what you're getting at. Why would Krol think that?'

'Because someone he trusts would tell him. You said you think there's a mole, right? What if you manufactured evidence that Krol was being cheated by Skala, and shared it with the task force?'

I nodded, catching on. 'And then whoever the mole is would share that with Krol. And,' I said, thoughtfully, 'it might even reveal who the mole is. Two birds with one stone.

'You're a rock star Linda.' This was a great idea. 'We're going to need to bring Jefferson in on this. He's the only one we can trust completely. I don't know Jacobs at all, and Bowles, Renfro, Nowak, even Gavin . . . I don't know any of them that well.' I really hoped it was Renfro.

'What about Jeb,' said Linda quietly.

'Jeb? No. No way.' I shook my head emphatically.

'Who knows what financial pressures people are under? Or other pressures? Some people turn because they're greedy, but some people are blackmailed, or their families are threatened. Until you know for sure, you can't trust anyone on the team.'

This was the same thing that Jeb had told me before. I didn't

210 Wendy Church

like it, but she was right. No one could know. 'OK. Let's go.' I stood up and we went back to the station.

When we got there I went straight to Jefferson's office.

'You realize what you're saying, Ms Kaminski?' Jefferson said when I'd explained what we wanted to do. 'You're accusing one of our own of collusion and murder. Multiple murders. Do you really want to go down this road?'

'I know, sir. But look at it this way. Whether or not we identify a mole in the department, if this plan works, we get Skala off the streets, and the gang's business likely collapses. Brajen Krol's not the brains of the operation, and probably doesn't even know how the day-to-day process works. At the very least, we'll get a pause in Red supply.'

'I don't like keeping my commanders in the dark,' he said, no doubt thinking about Bowles' reaction when he eventually found out he'd been included in the 'not to be entirely trusted' group.

'It's not ideal, sir. But it doesn't look like we have a choice.'

Jefferson sat, stone-faced, considering. He was under immense pressure from above. I'd seen Chief Jennings in his office almost daily since the body had been dumped in front of police headquarters, along with weekly visits by several aldermen and women who were no doubt tired of dealing with dismembered bodies in their communities.

'OK,' he said, finally. 'Do it.'

Whew. 'One more thing, sir.'

'What?'

'My brother. They want to bring him back into police custody. Since the last operation failed he doesn't get the immunity deal. It's not really fair, he did give us the lead to Kresimir Skala, and it's not his fault that we have a mole—'

'Alleged mole,' interrupted Jefferson.

'We might have a mole. I believe his life would be in danger if he goes into custody. I'd like him to be released into my care until we finish this op.'

'There's no remedy to "release him into anyone's care", and you're not a . . .' He was going to say, not an employee. But I was now.

He sighed. 'I'll talk to the ADA and Bowles, and strongly suggest that they release him on his own recognizance, pending a hearing.'

'What reason will you give to Bowles, sir?' I said, knowing that he'd object strenuously.

'That's the beauty of being in charge, Ms Kaminski. I don't need a reason.'

THIRTY-THREE

t took Linda and I two days to set everything up. Jacobs was still holding the ten o'clock task force meetings, which by now were perfunctory. Everyone knew it was going to be disbanded. Linda let me know when she was ready. I picked up a folder from her and went into the conference room.

'Ma'am, I've been working with Sergeant Cohen, and we think we've found something.'

'What, Ms Kaminski?' she asked tiredly.

'More social network do-dah?' scoffed Bowles.

'We've been going over the financials again,' I said, ignoring him. 'We've found evidence that Kresimir Skala was laundering money.'

'*What*?' she said.

Gavin's head whipped around.

'Yes,' I said, handing her the folder, at the same time showing the documents that Linda had created to the rest of the team on the monitor. I'd highlighted a few lines of phony transactions in yellow.

'What is this?' asked Gavin, scowling. 'I looked at all of this. There was nothing.' I felt bad that this was making him look bad, that he hadn't done a thorough job the first time.

That is, unless he was the mole. Then I didn't care how bad he looked.

'We did a little more digging. It turns out that Kresimir Skala has a secret account under a fake name.' I pulled up a fake passport photo that Linda had gotten her friends in tech to mock up. 'Bogdan Augustyn. He has an account in the Caymans.' I brought up another page from the fictional Bogdan Augustyn's transactions, also highlighted. 'He's been making weekly deposits, on the order of twenty thousand dollars. And regular withdrawals.'

Jacobs was looking intently at the documents in the folder I'd given her. Gavin was still scowling, and shaking his head.

'We also found a Bogdan Augustyn linked to real estate sales in Chicago. These three buildings, that we know of,' I said, changing the image on the monitor to another set of fake documents, showing the title reports for four buildings, all listing Bogdan Augustyn as the current owner.

'He's laundering the money under his fake name using real estate, and then putting it into this account. Then a portion of that money is moved out, presumably to an account that belongs to Brajen Krol, who's also presumably using a fake name.'

'Do we know Brajen Krol's fake account name?' asked Jacobs, looking up for the first time.

'Not yet, ma'am, but we're still looking,' I lied.

Linda and I knew that once Gavin took a close look at what we'd put together that he'd figure out that all of the documentation was false. But it would take a while, hopefully long enough to give our plan time to work.

As I was talking I tried to scan the room. One of the people in here was the mole. Whoever it was would have to be rocked by this information.

No one looked suspicious, or scared. Renfro and Nowak looked excited. Gavin was upset, for obvious reasons.

The machinations of forensic accounting were beyond Bowles' comprehension, but he took his cues from Jacobs, and she was obviously thrilled. He wasn't happy it was me making the break on the case, but he was doing his best to look pleased. Jeb was smiling at me.

No one looked like a mole that had just had his or her boss's secret identity discovered.

Maybe we were wrong.

'Great work, Ms Kaminski,' said Jacobs. 'Now we need to—'

'There's one more thing, ma'am,' I said, trying to keep my voice from quavering as I reached the critical part of the scam. 'We noticed that the amounts from the real estate sales don't match up to the amount transferred out of Bogdan Augustyn's account.'

'So?'

'So, we think Skala is skimming, taking money off of the top. A substantial amount. Basically, he's cheating Brajen Krol.'

'How do you know it's not what they agreed to?' said Bowles. This guy was nothing if not determined to put me down.

Gavin shook his head. 'This is a lot of skim,' he said, looking over the numbers.

'No,' said Jacobs, shaking her head. 'Brajen Krol would *never* allow this. Are you sure?' she asked, looking at me.

Tunnel Vision 213

'The numbers don't lie, ma'am,' a truism that we were in the process of debunking once and for all.

'How much?' she asked, handing the folder to Gavin.

His lips moved, as he flipped through the pages. 'Back of the envelope, I'd say at least fifty percent.'

Renfro let out a low whistle.

Jacobs raised her eyebrows as she exhaled a large whoosh of air. 'We've got him,' she said, finally smiling.

She nodded to Bowles. 'We'll put a BOLO out for Kresimir Skala,' he said.

I'd been worried we'd get more push-back on the new data, but I'd underestimated how badly Jacobs wanted to believe it. Gavin was the one who would eventually blow the whistle on us, given enough time, but he wasn't about to throw a wrench into the party before taking some time to do his research. A lot of time, I hoped.

Handshakes and hearty pats on the back followed me as I left the room. Normally I'd revel in it, but right now I just wanted to be alone. I demurred Jeb's offer for a drink, making an excuse about an appointment.

It didn't feel good, pulling one over on my team. It felt even less right to suspect one of them as working for the other side.

All I could do now was wait. If Linda and I were right, the mole would feed the information back to Brajen Krol, and he'd take matters into his own hands. Skala would likely be dead within hours of Krol finding out. And then the whole operation would collapse. And maybe Krol would leave.

If we were wrong, and the PD brought in Kresimir Skala alive, the case would fall apart. A closer look at the documentation would show we'd made the whole thing up. Everyone would know what Linda and I had done, and even though it had been sanctioned by Jefferson, I'd have a tough time recovering from this. Rats weren't tolerated, particularly when they were wrong.

I drove home, feeling sick. When I got there Sags and Michael were in the kitchen, cooking something. My mom and dad were there, too, sitting at our kitchen table.

Mom looked happier than I could ever remember. Dad was drinking water. I heard Michael laugh, a sound I hadn't heard in twenty years.

I couldn't even look at Sags. It was going to be hard enough, asking her to leave, before she'd integrated into my family.

'Good news,' I said to the group, forcing a smile. 'Michael gets to stay here for a while. They're not taking you into custody right now.'

'What do you mean, *right now*?' asked my mom. She didn't miss a thing.

'It's complicated, Mom. I've, uh, we've got some work things going. I'll be able to tell you more in a few days.'

THIRTY-FOUR

The daily task force meetings were put on hold. We were all waiting for the PD to track down and bring in Kresimir Skala. Everyone used the opportunity to catch up on paperwork, and sleep.

For me the wait was excruciating. Depending on what happened my life would take dramatically different turns. If the PD found Kresimir Skala before Brajen Krol did, they'd bring him in, and our financial fakery would be exposed. If they didn't find Skala, but Brajen Krol didn't believe that Skala had been cheating him, they would both continue their work. If that happened, enough time would pass that Gavin would figure out that all of the financial documents had been faked.

He was already looking everything over, obsessed at having missed something. And he wasn't stupid. I waited for the call to a task force meeting where he blew the whistle on us.

My biggest concern was that Brajen Krol knew where Michael was staying, and would come to the apartment and kill him, and maybe me. I asked Jeb to help out with security, and he installed a security system, and double locks on our door, neither of which would stop Krol if he were committed to killing Michael. We also made it a point to not share with anyone that he was staying with me. I knew that wouldn't last long, it wouldn't take a rocket scientist to figure out his sister was putting him up. But I held out hope that discovering that someone in his own gang was cheating him would cause Krol to let it go for the time being.

To pass the time I hung out with Michael. He was becoming a fixture in our apartment, as were my parents, who visited daily. All three of them would be on our couch, Michael sitting stiffly in between them, Mom resting her hand lightly on his shoulder. Whenever she was in his presence she found some way to touch him, however delicately.

Abby had said we should do our best to keep him from being overwhelmed, so we waited to tell Mark, Sophie and Lidia. Of course as soon as we did they came flooding over, Lidia taking the first flight out of LA.

I was amazed how quickly Michael transformed. He was still reticent to touch any of us, and frequently lapsed into silence during discussions, particularly when they related to the family. He had a lot to catch up on, and if not reveling in the proximity of his family, he seemed increasingly comfortable. The sound of his laughter was becoming more commonplace.

Had it been me, I'd have been mad. Resentful, at least, of the life that Sheila Johnson had stolen from me.

I'd asked him about it, one night when we were alone and Sags was at work. Or maybe she was out murdering a dealer. I still hadn't decided what to do about her. We were no longer talking.

I wasn't going to turn her in, or tell Jeb, but I'd decided I'd have to kick her out. It was one thing to know about the killing she'd done previously; it was a whole different thing when she was continuing to do it, and I knew about it while it was going on. Among other things, not reporting it made me an accessory to murder. I had no interest in going to jail.

'You don't seem angry at all at Sheila Johnson.'

Michael looked down at the beer in his hands. Now that he was getting regular showers and good food he looked completely different. He'd shaved his stubble, and my mom had cut his hair to above his shoulders, the curls that defined him as a child still evident in the wave. He was handsome, in my unbiased opinion.

'She took care of me. We always had enough to eat. And she read to me, got me shots, she even took me to the zoo.'

That was the ticket I'd found in her backpack, probably from their first trip together. It would have been shortly after she kidnapped him.

I was doing my best to balance the pleasure of getting to know my brother, and my parents' joy at his return, with the awful specter of the PD bringing Kresimir Skala in alive, and blowing up my whole scam with Linda.

Even with Jefferson's blessing, it would be the end of both of our careers. There was no way Bowles or any of the other commanders would stand for someone making up evidence. And Linda was already on thin ice; they'd been looking for a reason to get rid of her for years. This would be enough for them to jettison her. Maybe without her pension. She'd really gone out on a limb for me.

Jefferson might keep me around, but it was unlikely I could be effective, with everyone in the department hating me.

Tunnel Vision 217

I was also on edge because until Brajen Krol was brought in, Michael's life was in extreme danger.

Since we'd shut down their manufacturing site, bodies of Krol's gang members had been turning up dead. All of his men in the tunnels, with the exception of the chemist, were found bludgeoned to death, likely by Krol himself. Anyone for whom there was the slightest chance he'd leaked anything was put down.

Michael rarely left the building. When he did he was covered up, in hats, and bulky coats, even though it was still warm out. And he never went out in the daytime.

He didn't seem to mind staying in the apartment, and sleeping on our couch. He and Sags spent a lot of time cooking together, which he seemed to love. She was really good for him; watching them together reminded me of why we'd been such good friends.

Still, it was still only a matter of time before Brajen Krol found out where he was, if he didn't already. He had his mole in the PD, and by now everyone on the team knew that Michael was staying with me. I was surprised we hadn't heard from Krol yet, and supposed he was just waiting for an opportune moment that wouldn't get him or his people jailed.

How long would he wait, for Michael to leave the apartment? And would they go after me? Or my family?

The tension was becoming unbearable. I wasn't sleeping. And I was lonely. After Michael went to bed I'd sit up on the couch, sometimes just staring. Sags would come home, often after two or three in the morning, a time when we used to sit up and talk until sunrise.

Not any more. These days we talked as little as possible.

'Murder anyone today?' I'd said to her one night, after a few too many beers.

She'd ignored me, retreating to her room.

I was on the ragged edge. Barely making it to work in time, unable to focus. Jeb tried to get me out, take me for a drink a few times. I refused.

A week after we dropped the information about the fake Bogdan Augustyn I got a call from Jacobs that the task force was meeting, and that there was big news.

I drove to the station as fast as I could, barely able to breathe.

Everyone on the team was in the room. Jacobs was at the front, a small grin on her face. Had they brought in Skala, or found him dead?

'Kresimir Skala is dead,' she announced.

I tried to cover up an enormous sigh.

'He was found beaten to death, in Noble Square, two days ago.'

'Two days ago?' I couldn't keep the agitation out of my voice.

'We didn't want to release the news until we had a chance to find Brajen Krol. But he's disappeared.

'The ME believes the murder weapon might have been a nine iron,' she said. 'We're a little disappointed that we couldn't bring Skala in alive, but there is a very silver lining,' she added.

'I've asked Officer Renfro to keep track of what's happening with the Red supply. Any news on that front, detective?' she asked.

She'd clearly talked to him before the meeting. 'It's drying up. All the dealers have left is what they were given before Skala was killed.'

Jacobs was now smiling broadly. Even Bowles looked happy.

'What are our next steps, ma'am?' I asked.

'Next steps? There are none.'

'Don't we have to bring in Brajen Krol?'

She waved her hand dismissively. 'Our goal with this task force was to shut down the Greenpoint Crew's drug operations in Chicago. We've done that. Brajen Krol is in the wind, and the man behind the operation is dead. This is as good a result as we ever get.' Looking at my face, she added, 'Enjoy it, Ms Kaminski. And be proud of the fact that your efforts contributed strongly to this outcome.'

We were dismissed. Gavin, Nowak and Renfro stayed in their seats, laughing and making plans for drinks later. I made a beeline to Jefferson's office.

'Sir, Jacobs is shutting down the task force.'

'What did you expect her to do, Ms Kaminski? The task force did its job.' He looked happy, no doubt relieved that there would be a break in the enormous pressure he'd been getting from his superiors. 'And you were proved right. Your analysis showed there was a mid-level operator, and you found a way to flush him out. At some point, by the way, we'll need to share with the rest of the team what you and Sergeant Cohen did to get there. But for now everyone can enjoy it.'

'We still haven't identified the mole, sir,' I said.

'We're working on that. I've turned it over to internal affairs. They'll find out who it is. It's always about money, and I doubt it will take them more than a week or two to find the trail.'

Tunnel Vision

'Sir,' I said, sickened by the pleading tone in my voice, 'Brajen Krol is still out there. Everything we know about him suggests he's going to murder everyone he believes worked against him. My brother is one of those.'

Jefferson looked surprised. 'I talked to the DA and got your brother released, and he's not going to face any charges. His immunity deal stands.' He shook his head. 'I'm sorry, that's all we can do.'

Things changed quickly after Kresimir Skala's death. With him gone, the link between the gang's street soldiers and the drug source was broken. The thing that had made their operation so difficult to crack – a simple network of small cells run by one man – was also what made it vulnerable to dissolution.

Renfro's CIs confirmed that Red had practically disappeared from the streets. It wouldn't take long for the cartel to pick up the slack making and distributing their own tranq-laced fentanyl, but at least there'd be a halt to the chopped-up bodies dumped around the city.

I went into the conference room at ten for the daily briefing. The only one in the room was Renfro, taking down the pictures and notes on the wall, and cleaning the whiteboards.

'What's going on?' I asked.

'We're done,' said Renfro. 'There's going to be a final meeting to wrap up, but the task force is over.'

I'd held out hope that Jefferson might reconsider, and encourage Jacobs to continue to track down Brajen Krol, but he'd meant what he said. No one was going after him.

'We need to go after Krol,' I said. 'We can get him, for murdering Skala.'

'There's no murder weapon, and no witnesses. Not even a spec of circumstantial evidence.' Renfro shook his head. 'Let it go, Kaminski. Although it might be a good idea for your brother to leave town.'

Leave town? We just got him back. It would kill my parents, all over again.

I wandered numbly out of the conference room and to my desk. I didn't know how long I sat there before my phone chimed.

A text, from Linda. 'Meet me at our lunch spot.'

'I've been cataloguing the pictures from the festival,' she said as soon as I joined her on our bench in the park. She was holding a thick folder.

'I found something interesting.'

She opened the file and pulled images out, laying them between us on the bench. Most of them had been taken from the Taste of Polonia festival. Each one had markers next to Brajen Krol and his lieutenants, and of the men we'd identified as recruits.

'What are you showing me?'

'These photos were tagged, indicating Krol, his lieutenants, and his recruits.'

On top of the marked photos she laid down another set that looked the same, without tags.

'These photos weren't tagged. You can still see Krol with his lieutenants and recruits. Notice anything?'

I looked at the photos and shook my head.

She took her pen and pointed to the untagged photos. Each one contained a picture of Kresimir Skala.

I frowned. 'So we missed someone? It happens.' I wasn't sure why this was such a big deal.

'The first set of photos I showed you were submitted to the system. This other set,' she said, tapping the stack on top, 'were left out. I found them when I was cataloguing the case, and only noticed it because I'd worked on framing Skala with you.'

Realization dawned on me. 'Someone tried to keep Kresimir Skala out of the system.'

She nodded.

'Who had access to this file?'

'Everyone on the team.'

Damn.

'But that's not all I found.'

THIRTY-FIVE

The next day was officially the last meeting of the task force. It was more of a celebration than a meeting. 'I want to thank you all for your efforts,' Jacobs said, beaming. She'd brought in a case of champagne and was holding up her glass to us. 'This was not an easy operation, but we achieved an outstanding result. You are an outstanding team.'

She was moving on, back to Philly, as was Gavin. The PD was putting together a systematic sweep of the tunnels, talking to building owners, all part of a concerted effort by the city to fully seal them off.

I shuddered at the thought of anyone having to be in those tunnels.

'Enjoy yourselves, every one of you has earned some time off. The department is giving each of you a week of personal time, starting now.'

There were some 'whoops' and glasses clinked. Renfro and Nowak were already making plans to head to the local pub to continue the celebration when Deputy Chief Jefferson appeared at the door to the room. Two uniformed officers stood behind him. He nodded to me.

I took a big breath. 'I have something to add, ma'am,' I said to Jacobs.

She smiled. 'The floor is yours, Ms Kaminski.'

'No one ever investigated Officer Nowak's shooting,' I said, pulling open a folder I'd brought in with me.

'We didn't need to. She told us what happened. One of Brajen Krol's men shot her.'

I nodded. 'Right. Can you tell us again, what happened?' I said to Nowak.

She frowned. 'I've already submitted my report. You can read it. What's this about?'

'I did read it.' I put the paper up to my face, reading aloud. 'You said one of Krol's gang members shot you "from approximately ten feet away".' I looked up. 'You were really lucky. A through and through, the bullet didn't hit any organs, major arteries, not even a bone. I mean, from that distance, what are the odds of that?'

222 Wendy Church

'Where's this going, Kaminski,' asked Bowles.

'We have your clothes from that day.' I pulled out another page, this one with an image on it. 'This is your shirt, the one with the bullet hole.' I handed the picture to Nowak. 'Notice anything?'

'Yeah, it's my shirt, with a bullet hole in it.' She took the photo from me and tossed it on the table.

'Look at the bullet hole pattern. It's consistent with a shot fired from less than a foot away.'

'You can't know that, just from clothes,' she said.

'Maybe not. But we also had your clothes analyzed. It's interesting, what they can learn from the gunshot residue on clothes, particularly about how far away the shooter was from a victim. There was GSR on your shirt sleeve.'

Nowak scoffed. 'They find GSR on victims even when they've been shot through a window. It doesn't tell you anything.'

'No, but the *pattern* it makes does. The GSR pattern on your shirt indicated that the shooter was less than a foot away from you when you were shot.'

I tossed a stapled set of papers, *Gunshot Residue Techniques and Analysis* on the table in front of Renfro. 'Here's some bedtime reading, in case you're interested.'

'This is inappropriate, Kaminski,' snarled Bowles.

'It almost looks like whoever did the shooting was trying to get you off of the street, but cause the least amount of damage possible,' I continued, ignoring him. 'And with you out of commission, and the dearth of female undercover officers, it would be the kind of thing that could shut down the task force.

'But you're right, we can't be sure of anything, just from clothes. Do you mind, rolling up your sleeve?'

'I'm not going to sit hear and listen to this,' she said, standing up.

'Sit down, Officer Nowak,' said Jefferson. 'And please roll up your sleeve.'

She sat back down and rolled up her sleeve, revealing the bandage over her arm.

'Can you pull off the bandage?' I said.

She pulled off the bandage, exposing the wound.

It was healing, but still visible was the four-point star shape of the bullet hole.

'For those of you not up on your forensic pathology, this is what's known as a "stellate" pattern. It occurs with contact wounds. Whoever shot you wasn't ten feet away. For this pattern to occur, he would have had to put the muzzle of the gun against your arm when he took the shot. Do you have some kind of explanation for this?'

'Why does it matter? He shot me. It all happened very fast.'

Renfro shook his head. 'You'd have remembered, Valerie, if he was next to you, instead of ten feet away.'

She glowered at him. 'Have *you* ever been shot?'

'OK. It happened quickly, maybe you don't remember the exact details. And forensic science isn't perfect.' I opened up the folder with the two sets of photos that Linda had showed me, laying them on the table in two groups. 'You were responsible for taking the bulk of the pictures at the festival. Isn't it funny, that none of the pictures *you* took and submitted into the system had Kresimir Skala in them.' I pointed to the set of photos on the right. 'Even though he was there, all four days. The rest of us only took a few, and he managed to appear in several of them.' I pointed to the other set.

Jacobs had come from the front to the table next to us, and was looking over the photos.

Nowak was shaking her head. 'You have no idea what you're talking about, Kaminski. You've never done undercover work, and the one time you did you almost got killed. You think it's easy, being out there all the time? I didn't take perfect photos. So what.'

Watching and listening to her reminded me that she'd been a stellar undercover officer, remarkable, even, given her time on the force. It was a job that required the ability to lie, repeatedly, and convincingly.

'OK. You forgot about how you got shot, and you weren't perfect taking pictures,' I said, nodding. I pulled two more sheets of paper out of the folder, handing them to Jacobs.

Staring at Nowak, I said, 'The most interesting part of all of this is your sudden rise as a real estate mogul. Look at all the buildings you own,' I said, pointing to a map of a section of downtown. Next to several of the buildings was ownership information, the real ownership information, naming the owner as Valerie Zielinski.

'I thought the owner of these buildings was Skala?' said Gavin. 'You showed us the titles.'

'Those were fake.'

He frowned. Jacobs looked up quickly from the table at Jefferson.

'We'll talk about that later,' he said quietly. 'Please continue, Ms Kaminski.'

'Tracking the owner of these buildings was tough, until we had this name. Then it all fell into place. I'm sure we'd all like to know where you got the money to afford downtown real estate.'

'It says the owner is Valerie Zielinski,' said Jacobs.

'Want to hazard a guess, ma'am, what Officer Nowak's mother's maiden name is?' I said.

Jefferson nodded to the uniforms in the doorway and they moved to Nowak, each taking a place on either side of her. One of them was pulling out his handcuffs.

'I predict that the lab is going to find your prints on the envelope of drugs left in my desk, too,' I said. 'And, while I'm just guessing at this one, I'll bet that those two thugs that attacked me in the park after the retirement cruise were connected to you, too. You knew we were getting close to figuring things out, and you wanted to stop the task force. What better way to do that than take out one of the few remaining women who could work undercover?'

I didn't feel as triumphant as I sounded. It wasn't fun proving one of your coworkers was bent. Mostly I was just sad.

Jacobs had sat back down, and was slumped in a chair. 'You've been working with them the whole time, haven't you? They always seemed to be one step ahead of us. Because you told them.' Her voice was barely audible.

'I didn't hurt anyone.'

'The people they forced to work for them in the tunnels and murdered would beg to differ,' I said.

'They just wanted to run their business. What's the difference, between them and the cartels? The city's going to be flooded with drugs either way; there's nothing we can do to stop it. If it's not them, it will be someone else.'

She was pretty young to be this jaded. 'How much did they pay you?' I asked, as they stood her up and put on the handcuffs.

She stared at me, her eyes slitted. 'More than you'll make in your entire life.'

The uniforms escorted her up and out of her chair towards the door. As they passed by me Nowak leaned over, and hissed in my ear. '*Twój brat nie żyje.*' (Your brother is a dead man.)

EPILOGUE

The weather was starting to turn cold, the stifling humid summer moving rapidly into fall. It was a joke about Chicago, how quickly the seasons changed. One day you'd be sweating yourself silly, then overnight the leaves would drop, and the next morning it would be so cold that the mucous membranes in your nose would freeze the second you stepped outside.

I stood in my coat on a small hill in the Mount Olive Cemetery. Michael and my mother were next to me, looking at a modest headstone.

Sheila Johnson
Born February 28, 1973. Died 2024
Loving mother.

Michael hadn't been out in the daytime in weeks, Nowak's threat fresh in my mind. But Mom and Dad had paid to have Sheila Johnson buried, an act of grace I could scarcely imagine, and Michael had insisted on seeing her grave.

Jeb was standing by the car, waiting. We weren't back together yet, formally, but I realized I wanted him in my life. And it helped, with Michael, as I'd only agreed to let him leave the house if Jeb came with us.

Brajen Krol was still out there. We hadn't heard anything since they'd found Kresimir Skala dead, but I didn't think Krol had left the city. Everything we knew about him said he would stick around until every person who he thought betrayed him was dead.

Michael's friend Cam had died in the hospital, never making it out of the ICU. Michael was the only one left, as far as we knew.

Michael placed flowers on her grave. He'd been making a little money working for Sags at the restaurant, having discovered an affinity for the focused, repetitive nature of cooking. I'd been worried about him going there at first, but then realized he was no safer at my house than he'd be at the restaurant. As it was, he would sneak out before dawn and walk over, doing prep work and whatever else needed doing to get the restaurant ready each day. Sometimes he went over at night, too, helping with clean up.

Too bad it would have to end. I'd finally told Sags she needed to move out. She was my best friend, and Michael had grown close to her, but he had nowhere else to go, and had been sleeping on my couch. Mom wanted him living with her, but I'd vetoed that. It was too big a risk; if Brajen Krol found Michael he'd not only kill him, but whoever happened to be near him. I didn't want the rest of my family taking that risk.

I didn't think I could live with the fact that she was out killing people. Not to mention that it meant I'd have to continue to keep secrets from Jeb. He wasn't all that hard to deceive, but if he found out she was still at it he'd put her in prison. And me, too, possibly, if he learned I'd known about it, and hadn't told him.

It was all too stressful. And I couldn't imagine Sags continuing to employ Michael after I'd asked her to leave.

After a few minutes the three of us turned and walked away, Mom's arm around Michael's shoulders. Jeb drove Mom home, and then took Michael and I back to my place.

As he pulled up in front of my apartment we could see a group of people standing outside, staring at the front doors.

'Aren't those your neighbors?' Jeb asked.

'Yeah,' I said, getting out of the car.

We walked to the building and I pushed my way through the small crowd.

Across the double glass doors was '*Jesteś martwym człowiekiem*,' (You are a dead man), written in blood. Underneath was a rough outline of an eagle.

'Get inside,' I said to Michael, unlocking the door and shoving him in.

Jeb followed a minute later.

'Are you OK?' he said to Michael.

'Fine. I'm going to take a nap. I have a shift tonight.'

We watched him disappear into my bedroom and close the door.

'I called the station, they're sending someone to look into it.'

'What's to look into?' I said bitterly. 'Brajen Krol knows where he is. As long as he's alive, running free, it's just a matter of time.'

He couldn't argue with that. And he knew what I knew, that catching Krol at this point was at the bottom of the PD's priority list.

Tunnel Vision

'Want me to stick around?'

I mumbled a no and he let himself out. I walked into the kitchen and pulled a beer out of the refrigerator.

This was never going to end. Krol wouldn't stop until Michael was dead.

I looked over at the closed door to Sagarine's bedroom.

What wouldn't I do to protect my family?

I walked over and knocked on her door. She opened it, and stared at me without speaking.

'I want you to stay.'

She looked relieved, but said, 'I'm not going to tell you I'm stopping.'

I nodded. 'I know.'

'What's changed?'

'I need a favor.'

Acknowledgments

First of all, enormous, *enormous* thanks to Bruce G. Moffat, for his encyclopedic knowledge of all things underground in Chicago, and his willingness to share them. Bruce's book on Chicago's freight tunnels, *The Chicago Tunnel Story*, was invaluable in writing this novel, and I encourage anyone with an interest in underground Chicago to pick it up. There are a couple of editions; I recommend the latter one if you can find it, as it includes information about the 1992 Chicago Flood. Either edition will be comprehensive, interesting, and loaded with photos and maps. Of course any tunnel-related mistakes in this book are 100 percent my own.

At the time I started writing the *Shadows of Chicago* series, fentanyl hadn't yet become a household word. Since then, its use and abuse has skyrocketed; fentanyl accounted for over 70,000 overdose deaths in the US in 2023. That number has plateaued, for now, possibly due to the FDA's approval of Narcan for over-the-counter sales. If you or someone you know is using fentanyl, or one of the many drugs it augments, I encourage you to keep Narcan on hand. It's easy to use, and it works.

I'm extremely grateful for the ongoing support of Tina, Vic, and the team at Severn House, for your professionalism, your good humor, and for just being terrific to work with.

Thanks to Dr Karen Wolfe for your advice about medications, Tracey Padilla for helping me with the law enforcement elements, and Michele Grimes for your input on social services in Chicago. Laurie, thanks for putting me up and taking me around the city. I look forward to the next trip!

I would be remiss not to call out the inspirations for some of the food described in the book. The corn soup is taken directly from Jerry Traunfeld's *The Herbal Kitchen, Cooking with Fragrance and Flavor*. Like all of his recipes, which are tested in real homes prior to publishing his cookbooks, it's easy to make, and over the top delicious. I'd also like to give a shout out to Zac Reynolds, at *Cook Weaver* in Seattle. His smoked carrot corn dog is simply amazing, as are the rest of his innovative creations.

My beta readers are the *bomb*. Lynne Smith, Anna Hurwitz, Jennifer Shultz, Twila Church, Lesley Carmichael and Stuart Staple, every one of you made this better. *Thank you.*

Anyone who's ever written a book knows that after a while your eyes start to glaze over, and it's pointless to continue to edit it yourself. The inimitable Cindy Gaines, I can't thank you enough for your careful read-throughs and astounding ability to catch my many mistakes.

Thanks Kristen for being my friend, and to Anna. I still love cake.